ONE LOOK

THE SULLIVAN FAMILY
BOOK 1

LENA HENDRIX

LENA HENDRIX, LLC

Developmental Editing by Becca Mysoor, Fairy Plot Mother

Copy editing by James Gallagher, Evident Ink

Proofreading by Laetitia Treseng, Little Tweaks

Cover by Sarah Hansen, OkayCreations

For all of us who were ever forced to watch the "Big Game."

Who needs the quarterback when you can have the hot head coach instead?

LET'S CONNECT!

When you sign up for my newsletter, you'll stay up to date with new releases, book news, giveaways, and new book recommendations! I promise not to spam you and only email when I have something fun & exciting to share!

Also, When you sign up, you'll also get a FREE copy of Choosing You (a very steamy Chikalu Falls novella)!

Sign up at my website at www.lenahendrix.com

AUTHOR'S NOTE

As a big fan of hot sports coaches, I've done my best to portray aspects of college level football and the NFL as accurately as possible.

Midwest Michigan University and the town of St. Fowler are completely made up so as not to misrepresent the policies and values, curriculum, or facilities of real institutions. The views in this book are in no way a reflection of the NFL or NCAA, as it is a work of fiction.

This book also contains the death of a parent (off page/not detailed, but referenced) and a parent with early onset dementia.

ABOUT THIS BOOK

I'm a full-time single dad. A former NFL player turned coach, tasked with turning around a college team full of kids who either don't take it seriously or are determined to get injured. **I will absolutely not be falling for my new neighbor.**

Lark Butler is pure chaos wrapped in gorgeous, infuriating sunshine.

She showed up in my small town—getting paid to cry at a funeral, no less. Who does that? But somewhere between her offering condolences and crawling out of a literal grave site, we've found ourselves tangled in the drama of Outta-towner, Michigan—my coastal hometown with a decades-old feud and two aunties determined to end it.

I'm finally putting down roots so my daughter has a normal life, and I need to forget about Lark. Forget the way it felt the night we kissed or what it's like to finally take something just for me. But when those sparks ignited, it was more intense than either of us bargained for.

Trouble is, I can't trust her, and she never stays.

She's burning my carefully laid plans to the ground, and all it took was ***one look***.

"Do you think I'll get to see a dead body?"

I stared at my seven-year-old daughter, Penny, unsure about how to navigate this particularly morbid topic. I adjusted the sleeves on the white button-up I'd pulled on. "Get to or have to?"

Penny picked at the hem of her blue dress as she sat with the rest of the skirt rumpled beneath her. She didn't make eye contact, only shrugged.

I slipped a tie around my neck and worked to get the knot right. "It's a funeral, so there will be a memorial before we go to the cemetery. You won't have to go up there if you don't want to, but people will come to pay their respects to Mr. Bowlegs."

An unladylike snort came from her little body as her face scrunched up. "Bowlegs? That's his name?"

"Just a nickname."

"What's his real name?"

I paused and laughed a bit to myself. I had no fucking clue.

"I'm not sure. I only ever knew him as Mr. Bowlegs. Usually just Bowlegs for short."

Penny's lips twisted. "Why did people call him that?"

Her hearty giggle was infectious, and I tried to embrace the lightness of her mood. Maybe it would ease the dread pooling in my stomach. "Well, I guess because he was bowlegged."

Penny turned on the bed so she was lying on her back, her head dangling upside down off the edge. "Does everyone in your hometown have a nickname?"

I took a deep breath and shook my head. Ridiculous nicknames were only one of the utterly asinine aspects of Outtatowner, Michigan. Even the town name itself —Outtatowner.

What a joke.

I pulled the knot loose from my crooked tie and tried again. Penny waited for me to answer. Stubborn, that girl. She could outwait a monk if she put her mind to it.

"Not everyone," I conceded. "But a lot of people."

"Why?"

I shrugged. "Just something that started a long time ago. I think it's a small-town thing."

"Why?"

I quickly realized we were on the brink of playing the *why* game, and I'd walked right into it.

Not today, Daughter.

"I don't know. The town's just weird, okay?"

"You said it's not nice to call people weird."

It was annoying as fuck when your child threw your parenting back in your face. I looked over my reflection one last time and turned toward her. "You're right. They're just a little different. You ready to go, Pickle?"

She righted herself with a smile and bounced on the edge of the bed. "Is that why you call me Pickle?"

I stepped toward my precocious, pain-in-the-ass spawn. I tapped my knuckle on the end of her little upturned nose. "I call you Pickle because sometimes you're sweet and sometimes you're sour."

Penny pretended to chomp at my hand.

"My point exactly." I pulled her from the bed. "Let's go, kiddo. We have a drive ahead of us, and I don't want to be late."

Thankfully, Penny was feeling agreeable, and we left the cramped apartment without losing a shoe or misplacing her beloved Blue Teddy. Once she was securely buckled in the back, I laid my suit jacket across the passenger seat and got behind the wheel.

After embarking from the outskirts of downtown St. Fowler, Michigan, I drove through the college town. Penny kept her nose to the window, watching the buildings flicker past as we drove, Blue Teddy getting strangled by the crook of her arm.

Last Christmas she'd asked for a blue teddy bear—two days before Christmas. I had scoured the internet, and the best I could do was a baby-blue hippopotamus with a dark-blue ribbon around its neck. There was no fooling anyone, because it was definitely *not* a teddy bear, but Penny loved him, and though it was barely a win, I was taking it. Some days it felt like I needed all the wins I could get.

Her ponytail was lopsided, but despite the late-night YouTube tutorials between game-film playbacks, I still hadn't come close to mastering a french braid. That shit was pure witchcraft.

I swallowed a sigh. We had just gotten set up in St. Fowler, but it was our third city in three years. I didn't miss the sadness that crept into her eyes as I watched her from the rearview mirror. That look alone was why I needed to make this work.

"You'll like it here, I promise." A lump formed in my throat. I really hoped I wasn't lying to her.

"There's the church."

When I glanced up again, her index finger was pressed to the glass. I tracked her stare and, sure enough, in the distance was Wilson Stadium and the Athletic Center. It wasn't the biggest stadium I'd coached at—certainly not the biggest I'd played at, but for now it was home.

"Sure is, baby."

As the stadium whirred past us, Penny settled into her seat, squeezing Blue Teddy's neck a little tighter. "How long is the drive?"

I glanced at the clock. "Only about an hour."

The tiny sound of disgust told me I didn't have more than twenty minutes or so until she was bored out of her mind and the *why* game would start back up. Flipping through the radio stations, I found some toe-tapping garbage I knew she liked and turned it up a bit.

Then we headed west toward the coast. Toward the hometown I hadn't seen in years.

"WELL, holy shit. The prodigal son returns!" A grin split across my little brother Lee's face as he stomped across the parking lot of the funeral home. Even a few miles from the water, the fresh, coastal air stirred around us.

It had been a long time since I'd seen my little brother. He'd always been the reckless one, a bit of a wild card. A charmer. So it was no wonder that after his time in the service, Lee had found his groove as a local firefighter and had never left our hometown again.

His hand swooped to mine and gave it a hearty squeeze. Lee had bulked up too. His scrawny arms had filled out, and he'd gained a few inches in the years I'd gone without seeing him in person.

Before I could introduce him, Lee crouched down to Penny, who was tucked behind my leg. "Who's this rat? It's definitely not the Pickle I saw on FaceTime last month."

Penny rolled her eyes and stepped out from behind my frame. "Hi, Uncle Lee." Her voice was laced with boredom and annoyance, but it simmered with shy delight. Some days I swear she was seven going on seventeen.

Lee reached out and captured her around the waist, hoisting her high in the air. Her delighted squeals only egged him on as he bounced and jostled her.

"Who. Are. You. And. Where. Is. Penny?"

A hot lance of regret speared my side as she giggled and horsed around with my little brother. I'd denied her this simple joy.

That was on me.

After Dad got sick, our family was scattered, broken. I hadn't made it back to Outtatowner in years, and that meant Penny knew my family only through sporadic video chats and presents mailed at holidays and birthdays.

I cleared my throat to dislodge the hot coal that had taken up residence there. "Is Katie coming?"

Our youngest sister had found some random college in Montana, and with the encouragement of her idiot boyfriend, she'd left everything and never looked back.

Lee's smile didn't falter, but I heard a bit of sadness creep into his voice. "Nah. She couldn't make it in."

I pressed my lips together and nodded. "Duke?"

Lee set Penny on the ground, and she beamed up at him. "Getting Dad."

I nodded. Dad's early-onset dementia had deteriorated so rapidly that he lived in the local memory-care ward in town. It was difficult, but with the four of us as broken as we were and Aunt Tootie unable to care for her brother herself, we'd made the choice to provide him the nursing care he needed.

The thought of a fifty-eight-year-old man requiring full-time nursing care ate at me, especially when I thought about all the times he was lucid. Himself. Until I thought about how upsetting it was when he wasn't. Confused. Angry. Scared.

His sister loved him fiercely, but Aunt Tootie couldn't do it on her own, and we weren't equipped to help him. The thought of seeing him today, not knowing the kind of day he was having, stacked a slimy layer of unease on top of my already-churning stomach.

Let's get this over with.

I glanced around the nearly empty parking lot. "Figured the King boys would be here." My fingers clenched into a fist just speaking their name aloud.

"Aunt Tootie and Bug worked it out. Sullivans have the first hour, and then the Kings can pay their respects after."

I nodded. The long-standing feud between the Sullivan family and the Kings was a thing of legends, going back longer than I could remember. Though Outtatowner was a coastal tourist town, those who were from there, us townies, knew the line was drawn. You were either with us or with them, no two ways about it.

The only two who'd managed to find some peace were Aunt Tootie and the Kings' aunt Bug. Even though they didn't like each other, they took it upon themselves to make sure we didn't tear down the town around us when we got to arguing with each other. For the tourists' sake, we kept outward appearances, but it wasn't unheard of to have a throwdown at the pub on a Saturday night.

I reached out to Penny, and she tucked her little hand in mine. Together we walked with Lee toward the funeral home. The warm air inside whooshed out as I pulled the heavy door open. The familiar smell of roses and musk turned my stomach. I pushed down the flash of my mother's smiling face as I walked through the door.

The foyer was nearly empty. Hushed voices floated through the air, and small handfuls of people huddled in groups.

"Why is no one here?" Penny whispered.

My heart sank. I remembered Bowlegs as a kind and soft-spoken man. A little odd, even for a townie. Neither a Sullivan nor a King, he was a staple in our community. Every day he'd walk the town in his Moon Boots, collecting cans or feeding the wildlife.

My eyes swept through the sparse crowd and recognized every single person in the room.

Except her.

I hastily signed the guest book as Penny asked Lee a thousand questions about Bowlegs, my eyes tracking the unknown brunette quietly weeping in the corner.

Outfitted in a formfitting black dress that swept just past her knees, an air of elegance swirled around her. The short sleeves fluttered around her slim biceps. The woman dabbed a tissue under her pert nose, and a soft sob escaped her again. I watched her take a shuddering breath before fresh tears leaked out from thick, dark lashes.

I leaned into Lee. "Who the hell is that?"

His gaze fell onto the stranger, and he shrugged. "No clue."

"Daddy, I'm hungry." Penny pulled at my hand, and I looked down at her. Her eyes sliced toward the open casket.

Lee leaned down to her. "Are you starving . . . to *death*?" Mischief laced his tone as a cackle erupted from Penny. Heads turned in our direction.

I shot them each a warning glance as a hand clamped over her mouth, and Lee pulled his lips in to stifle his own laughter.

"I already paid my respects. I'll find Pickle a snack. You go ahead."

I looked at Penny to make sure she was okay with the plan, and when she laced her hand into Lee's, I knew she was relieved to not be going with me toward the casket. I nodded, and Lee brought Penny down the hallway toward the small room that would undoubtedly be filled with coffee and pastries.

As I made my way toward the front of the room, I couldn't help but watch the mysterious woman. I noticed others had started watching her too.

Deeply upset, the woman wept, silent sobs racking her body.

Did Bowlegs have a daughter?

Clearly a stunner like her wasn't some unidentified widow. Sure there were rumors he was secretly wealthy, but Bowlegs was an elderly man, and this woman was a knockout. Surely she had her pick of any man.

With a sad shake of her head, the woman looked longingly at the casket a final time before turning. As she swept past me, our eyes locked.

My breath seized.

My heart hammered.

What the hell?

Time moved in slow motion as her mossy hazel eyes swept down, her wet lashes nearly touching the apples of her cheeks.

The wind was knocked straight out of me. My head spun. My blood was thick, and all she'd done was walk past me.

I watched her leave, and despite the alarm bells clanging in my skull, I silently followed. Down the darkened hallway, the woman stood across from Tootie and Bug. The aunties nodded as the mystery woman smiled.

Just like that, the weeping probably-not-a-widow was clear eyed and smiling kindly at the women. I hung toward the wall, feeling like a creeping asshole watching the three women talking in the dark hallway, but then it happened.

Tootie reached into her purse and placed a stack of bills into the woman's hand.

What. The. Actual. Fuck.

2
___
LARK

THE WORST PART OF MY JOB WAS ALL THE DEAD BODIES.

A chilly breeze still clung to the air as spring made its creeping transition to summer. I sucked in the moist air, loving the fact that you could smell the water no matter where you were in town. I scanned the sea of faces standing around the grave site. My black mirrored sunglasses concealed my eyes as I looked from face to face, curious about those who'd come to pay their respects and imagining their lives like a movie playing out right in front of me.

Surprisingly, a few more people had shown up today than were at the wake yesterday. In my experience, the opposite was typically true. It was still a depressingly small number of people, and it was no wonder Tootie and Bug had needed my services.

I was alone, but that wasn't unusual nor uncomfortable for me. I simply held my head high, dabbed my nose at the appropriate times, and played the part. From my vantage point in the front, but nestled discreetly to the side, I could see two distinct groups of mourners forming.

The first consisted mostly of tall, imposing men wearing various styles of well-tailored suits. Even the one covered in tattoos, the ink peeking above his collar and out of his shirt-sleeves, wore a suit that looked to be made for him. Most resembled each other with broad shoulders, long straight noses, and an unmistakably dangerous glint in their eyes. More than one looked like he was ready for a fight. The woman who'd introduced herself to me as Bug stood in the center of them.

The Kings.

Among the imposing circle of suit-wearing beasts were two young women. Only one of the Kings was not shooting daggers toward the Sullivans. Rather, one of the women was sneaking glances in their direction. Specifically, toward the oldest Sullivan. Duke, if I recalled his name correctly, appeared completely oblivious.

Very interesting.

I schooled my face and looked down at the open hole in the earth. When one of my roommates in Chicago had told me about how her cousin had made a killing as an improv actor at funerals in New York, my wheels had started turning. One by one my roommates had moved on to New York or LA, some even giving up altogether and packing up to head for home. I couldn't give up the dream, not yet.

My big break was only a job or two away. I just knew it. The office temp work I'd been doing between acting jobs in Chicago was fine, but not enough to sustain my lofty city apartment rental. Or my thirst for adventure.

So one semiprofessional-looking website later, I was officially a mourner for hire in the Chicagoland and coastal Michigan area. After fifteen funerals, all the faces were starting to blend together, but observing and drawing conclusions about the strangers who moved in and out of my life was one of the best parts of this job. Improv acting kept life interesting, and the romance novels on my night-stand didn't hold a candle to the salacious stories I could come up with in my own mind.

Tootie and her group of mismatched, haphazard family members stood on the complete opposite side of the Kings. Her soft, round face smiled at those who walked up, and she offered enthusiastic hugs to everyone, whether they seemed to want one or not. The Sullivan men were also stupidly handsome.

They were dressed in jackets and ties, with some in freshly pressed denim, a bit more blue collar than the Kings appeared to be. They exuded confidence and charm. One look at the older man who stood beside Tootie and you could see where the men got their classic good looks. Though he looked a bit lost, the rugged lines of hard work outdoors made his face only handsomer.

I took in the distinctions between the two groups and how both shot angry, spiteful glares toward the other. As I continued to look on, my lips pressed together in a demure smile anytime someone's curious eyes lingered a moment too long.

Everyone except for *him*.

On the outskirts of the Sullivan clan was the man from yesterday. The one I couldn't seem to shake. He was tall and broad. His chin tipped up slightly, giving him an air of cockiness that would have been enticing if it weren't for the permanent scowl he wore with it.

When I had walked past him at the funeral home, I was so inundated with his rough and masculine smell and pointed stare, I nearly stumbled in my new heels. His haunting whiskey brown eyes had tracked my walk out of the room, and though I'd tried to ignore it, I could feel them all the way until I rounded the corner out of view.

The little girl was with him again today. She was too young to be his little sister, and the way she clung to his leg after coming back with a plate of cookies yesterday, and again today, revealed he was likely her dad. When he wrapped a strong hand around her shoulder and pulled her closer, my heart stuttered, just for a moment.

His masculine, protective vibe was sexy—there was no denying that—but I'd been given a job, and I doubted banging the brooding grump just to see if he'd crack a smile was part of the performance.

But seriously, who doesn't love a grumpy DILF?

Tootie and Bug had specifically requested actual tears after they found my website and hired me. I was also instructed to sprinkle in a few well-timed gasps and sudden shotgun sobs. Nothing too over the top, but enough to get people talking. My eyes flicked to the old women, who'd taken to completely ignoring each other in public.

I laughed to myself.

Those two are something else.

Then I felt it again, the intensity of his eyes, searing my skin from fifteen feet away. Family members like him could be dangerous and bad for business. They often singled you out over lukewarm tuna casserole and asked too many questions.

I took the opportunity to shake my head and release a ragged breath just in time for the preacher to begin his service.

~

ONCE THE CROWD HAD DISSIPATED, I stepped from the hiding place in my car and glanced around to be sure I was alone. Cursing myself for having to wear high heels at the funeral service when I knew flats were a better choice, I walked across the grass on my tiptoes, trying to prevent the heels from sinking into the soft earth. An impulse purchase of sexy new shoes with a delicate leather bow on the back meant the blister I was sporting was fresh and the flats I'd planned were totally out of the question.

Rookie move.

Steadying myself, I continued to trudge toward the area where they'd laid Mr. Bowlegs to rest while the preacher gave a truly moving service.

Bowlegs—well, that was a first.

Outtatowner had more quirks than I thought possible, but my favorite was the fact that many of the townies had special nicknames. Tootie informed me some were random, most were inappropriate, and once you'd been given one, it was damn near impossible to shake it.

I passed a groundskeeper who was working to stack and remove chairs. He scooped the hat from his head and nodded before slipping away to give me a bit of privacy.

I stood, peering down at the simple casket nestled in the earth. As it often did, a swell of emotion gathered in my chest as I cleared my throat.

I whispered down to him. "Thank you, Mr. Bowlegs, for the honor of attending your services. I hope that I provided your family with peace and comfort."

Reaching into the pocket of my skirt, I pulled out my phone. The music was queued up, and I glanced at it again.

God, I hope Bug wasn't playing a joke on me.

Shaking my head, I pushed play and closed my eyes.

The thumping chords of "Another One Bites the Dust" began flowing from the tiny speaker. An odd choice, but I pressed my lips together to keep the bubble of giggles that threatened to rise from bursting.

My finger pressed the volume louder as my left hand tapped my thigh to the beat. You couldn't deny that the song was a banger, and I smiled, hoping Bowlegs also had a sense of humor.

As I began to hum and mumble the words I knew, I sent my thoughts of love to Bowlegs.

"You gotta be fucking kidding me."

The sharp, deep rumble from behind startled me, and I flailed my arms as my heart leaped into my throat. In an instant, my heel was slipping, and the ground was no longer beneath me. With a crack, my feet hit something solid, one high heel snapping underneath me. My nails raked down freshly shoveled earth as realization dawned on me.

"Oh god. Oh no! Oh my god!"

"What the fuck?" The voice was above me now, sharp and angry.

Panic skittered under my skin as I took in my darkened surroundings.

In the hole. I am in the fucking hole.

"Help! Please help me!" Glancing around, I realized I was standing in the tight space beside the casket. My phone was in the dirt, Queen still wailing from the speaker, so I scooped it up and frantically pressed at the screen until Freddie Mercury shut the hell up.

I slipped the phone into my pocket and gently placed my hand on top of the casket. "I am so sorry. Shit! I'm sorry!"

I looked up again to see nothing but crisp blue sky

painted with streaks of pink from the afternoon sun. "Help! Anyone? Hello? Help me!"

There was no getting out, and it didn't seem like there was anyone up top willing to help me, so I placed my hand on top of Bowlegs's casket and apologized again before stepping on top. My knees stung from tiny scrapes, and my skirt was filthy from the fall. Using the leverage from standing on the casket, I wrestled myself to the surface.

As I was flat on my belly and wiggling myself out of the burial site, my eyes focused on a pair of shiny black leather shoes. I craned my neck up to see the scowl deepen and the gorgeous man from yesterday huff a breath as he crossed his arms.

"A little help here?" I grunted as I continued to pull myself out of the hole.

"What the hell do you think you're doing?" He offered zero assistance.

What a prick.

Finally, out of breath and streaked with mud, I sat back on my heels and smoothed my skirt over my knees. "Not getting any help from you, clearly."

"Who are you? What are you doing here?"

My face twisted at his demanding tone, despite the fact its rough timbre had the tiny hairs on my neck standing on end.

"Paying my respects. Though"—I glanced backward and down at the hole, where two muddy shoe prints were now stamped on the top—"typically it goes a little more smoothly than this."

I laughed at the pure ridiculousness of the situation I had gotten myself in. No doubt Aubergine and Eagle would laugh their asses off when they heard about it.

My laughter subsided, and I smiled up at him. I swear

his top lip curled as he said, "Do you have any idea how blatantly disrespectful, inappropriate, downright—"

I lifted my hand in the air as I maneuvered to stand. "I'm gonna stop you right there."

I'd had just about enough of his brash, arrogant tone. I swooped my hands in front of me. "Nothing about this was disrespectful. Well, except for the falling-in part, but that wasn't my fault. It was yours."

His rich, caramel eyes flared with anger. "My fault?"

I nodded once. "You startled me. I was having a moment with Terrance when—"

"Terrance? A moment?" The gorgeous man pinched his nose between his fingers, and I smothered a smile. "'Another One Bites the Dust'? That's your idea of respect?"

His hostile tone only fanned the flames of my fight-or-flight response. *Oh, game on, buddy.*

I smoothed my skirt once more and calmed my face, completely ignoring the fact that I was streaked with mud, one heel was broken, and my hair was rapidly coming out of its delicate chignon. "That song was his favorite. I felt compelled to play it one last time, in a *moment of privacy* between him and me." I pointed a finger at him. "You interrupted. You made me fall in, and *you* couldn't be bothered to help me out!"

"Who are you?"

He didn't even bother to pretend to be affected but let his eyes lazily lower down my body before quickly flicking back up to meet my gaze.

A haughty laugh shot out. "A friend of the family."

The man was stone. Unwavering in his assessment of me. Irritated, I rolled my eyes and stormed past him, hobbling as my uneven footwear stole any sliver of grace I still had. I turned to him. "You know what? Judge me all you want, but the only thing sadder than a funeral is a funeral no one shows up to."

At that, despite the fact I cursed myself for letting far too much slip, I stormed off toward my car, but not before I had the satisfaction of seeing realization spread across the sharp angles of his handsome face.

"Boogertown?" Penny's infectious giggles filled the back seat of the car.

My eyes rolled at the asinine name my grandparents had bestowed upon their own street.

Lee shifted so he could look at Pickle in the back seat. "You didn't know? Aunt Tootie and Uncle Tater live down Boogertown Road."

Penny laughed again. "Who would name it that?"

Lee's smile widened. "They did. When they built their house at the end of this lonely road, Tater needed a name for it. He was going to name it Pic—"

"That's enough." I cut Lee off and shot him a hard stare. He didn't need to tell my seven-year-old that our uncle almost named his road *Pickledick Holler* just to get a rise out of the mailman he hated so much.

Lee had the sense to look sheepish before crossing his eyes and making a funny face at Penny.

"Remind me again why you couldn't have driven your truck here?" I asked my little brother.

After I put my car in park, he climbed out and opened

Penny's door. "And miss a second with this rat?" Penny leaped into his arms and pretended to gnaw at him like an actual rodent. "Not a chance."

My chest pinched again.

Lee was cocky. Arrogant. He was a Sullivan, after all, but he was also good-natured. I often wondered if his happiness was a cover for the shit he'd seen when he was overseas, but he would never admit that. It was probably why he'd come back and immediately applied for a job with the fire department. That kid was always chasing the next adrenaline rush.

I huffed out a breath and felt old—really fucking grouchy and old—as I watched Lee bound up the steps of our aunt's expansive farmhouse-style home.

The afternoon sun was fading on the horizon, but there was a stream of cars making their way down the long, tree-lined driveway. Tootie would host whoever came to pay their respects. Though I figured people mostly wanted to eat her food and gossip.

The once-white paint on the home's exterior had faded to a dingy gray. The black shutters were faded and peeling too. As I climbed the steps, the wood groaned under my weight. I bounced once and was surprised when my foot didn't fall through the rotting wood. I knew the old home was in need of a few repairs, but the more I looked, the more it seemed like the years of neglect and emptiness were taking its toll. I'd have to talk with Kate and my brothers about what we were going to do. Tootie couldn't live in a house if it was unsafe.

"You coming in or just going to stand around looking lost?" Laughter was laced in Aunt Tootie's voice. That woman had a zest for life, and no matter how many blows she took, she'd dust herself off and keep plugging away. To be honest, there were plenty of times I wanted to give up, but knowing she'd twist my ear, I trudged forward.

"Get up here." Her arms spread wide, and I climbed the rest of the stairs to pull her into a hug. She was soft and warm. For a fraction of a second, I closed my eyes and tried to remember the last time I'd gotten a hug from anyone but Penny.

"Your father's inside. He can't wait to visit."

My jaw clenched. "Good day?"

When I released her, Tootie's eyes looked out over her yard and she smiled. "As good as any are these days, I suppose."

Without another word, she left me to greet and hug the stream of people walking toward the house.

Inside, the house was bustling with activity. Many people who hadn't bothered to attend the wake or funeral were filling Tootie's home, gossiping and catching up on Outtatowner news. Many conversations revolved around the Kings and how they continued to buy up businesses in town. Another fight between a King and a Sullivan. Rumors about how Outtatowner was changing and the many ways it was somehow the Kings' fault.

I cut through the crowd, purposely ignoring the eager smiles and wide-eyed recognition. Toward the back of the house, in the large living room, my father sat alone on the sofa. My stomach twisted. His arms were braced on his knees, and his unfocused gaze stretched out onto the carpet.

"Hi, Dad." I cleared the gravel from my throat.

His head moved up, locking eyes with me, but behind them, there was no spark. No recognition.

So much for a good day.

"Hi." Dad raked a hand down his face, his classic move

when he was trying to hide the fact that he didn't remember someone. "Good to see you."

"Wyatt," I provided.

"Wyatt. Yeah, I know. Good to see you, Wyatt. Damn shame about Bowlegs."

I nodded and looked around for Penny or my brothers. I stood awkwardly in front of my father.

When I caught the eye of Duke, my oldest brother, from across the room, he excused himself from the conversation and strode toward me. His beard was longer than I remembered, and he looked pissed. More than usual, even.

Duke was the only person I knew capable of being a bigger dick than I was.

When he closed the distance between us, I held out my hand, and we shook.

"Glad you could find the time."

"Been busy."

"Sure." Duke knew damn well I had obligations and a contract to fulfill. When I didn't take the bait to argue with him, he turned his attention to Dad and handed him the glass of dark liquid in his hand. "Got this for you, Pop."

Dad accepted the glass and took a sip. "I asked for Captain and Coke."

My eyes met Duke's. We all knew Dad couldn't have alcohol with his medication. Duke made a barely imperceptible twitch of his head in reassurance. "Tootie said no booze."

Dad grumbled and sipped his drink again. "Worse than a warden."

"How long are you staying?" Duke asked me, crossing his arms.

"We leave tonight."

"In and out, huh?"

I pressed my lips together. "That's the plan." I looked around the house again. People were milling about, eating finger sandwiches and laughing. If I didn't know better, it would seem more like a happy get-together than post-funeral mourning.

"Did you know with only twenty-eight seconds left in the fourth quarter, it was fourth and five on the ten-yard line. Couldn't find an opening, so he tucked that ball and ran his heart out to the end zone. We won the national title because of my boy. It was a thing of beauty."

Duke and I looked back at our dad, whose eyes were slightly unfocused, but a proud smile stretched across his face. He was talking about the game that helped launch my career.

I sat next to him. "Yeah, I remember. The defensive lineman was a monster."

Dad shot me a look of disgust. "Not for him. My boy is fearless."

"It was a great game," Duke added. We'd learned a long time ago that Dad's brain worked in mysterious ways, but he was calmer, more lucid, if you got him talking about topics he loved and, particularly, old memories.

It was those moments it felt like the dad we knew was actually still there. The dad who never missed a game and, even when we lost, called to pick me up and give me a pep talk. Red Sullivan was the strongest man I ever knew. When Mom died, he raised four young kids on his own. He made a point to speak her name every day. He said it was so that we would always remember our mother and the love we all had for her.

Lately it was considered a good day if he remembered his own name.

"Wyatt." Dad's voice pulled me from my thoughts as he

abruptly stood. "Damn good to see you! I didn't know you were coming."

He pulled me into a tight embrace, then held me at arm's length to look me over.

"Hey, Dad." I smiled at him.

His brows pinched together. "Don't you have a game this week?"

"No. The team is going into summer break. We'll prep for the upcoming fall season, but the players are busy with finals this week."

His wide palm slapped my back. "My boy doesn't need to stress about finals. The draft is coming up, and you'll be a top pick. I just know it. Maybe the Vikings? Or the Bears? The Bears. Wouldn't that be something?" He laughed and slapped my back again.

It was then I realized he thought I was still a college player, an NFL hopeful, and my stomach dropped.

Acid rose in my gut, and I took a step back. "I need to find Penny."

"You shouldn't be worrying about girls, Son." Dad's stern voice floated over my shoulder as I walked away.

Duke saved me and picked up the conversation with Dad as I left them behind and weaved through the gathering crowd, looking for my daughter.

"Couldn't hack it. You know that."

"Not a chance. He knocked up that girl, and now he's stuck."

"He got old, that's what happened. Damn shame."

As I wove through the crowd, my ears picked up the pieces of gossip that were undoubtedly about *me*.

So much for a little respect after a successful run in the NFL.

I'd learned a long time ago that in a small town

everyone was fair game when it came to the local rumor mill. It didn't matter if you were once a celebrated NFL quarterback or were part of one of Outtatowner's founding families. If there was gossip to be spread, it was out there.

I rounded a corner and heard Lee's deep laughter in the backyard. Penny was sitting on his shoulders as he ran down the length of the yard. Her arms were raised above her head, and her infectious laughter floated on the early summer wind. A hot poker burrowed under my ribs.

I wanted to get the hell out of there and head back to our quiet apartment in St. Fowler. I had shit to do and a team to check in on, but the happiness filling the backyard made me pause.

A soft laugh to my left had me turning.

"Cute kid." Outtatowner's local artist, and Lee's childhood best friend, balanced a plate of finger foods in her hand.

I smiled and tipped my chin in greeting. "Annette. Good to see you."

She smiled at my use of her real name. Everyone in town had called her Annie since she was a kid. With her unruly red hair, she had acquired the unfortunate nickname *Orphan Annie*, which was more insensitive given that she was a literal orphan. At some point, as it so often did in Outtatowner, it was the nickname that stuck.

"You too, Wyatt."

Annie smiled one last time at me before turning toward the house. Her gaze snagged a fraction of a second on Lee before she climbed the stairs into the house. It was obvious she had grown into a very pretty woman. Her coppery hair was pulled back, and she looked elegant in her simple black shirt and dress pants. Gone was the squirrely little redhead with unruly curls who'd followed Lee around and had chronically dirty knees.

Nowadays Annie was a stunner, and Lee's head was probably too far up his own ass to even see it.

Idiot.

"Hey, where'd Annette go?" Lee set Penny down, breathless.

My head swooped toward the door. "Inside, I think."

Lee only shrugged. I guess he didn't see or didn't care that a good woman was right under his nose.

I looked around the back porch while Penny sat in a chair and sipped a drink at the patio table. "Jesus, this place is in rough shape."

"Yeah, it's getting pretty bad," Lee agreed.

"Pretty bad? There's a box holding up that table. It's not okay." I pointed to the table leg, which was, in fact, a rickety stack of wooden boxes. "We need to call Katie."

A muscle ticced in Lee's jaw, and his fists clenched. He saw it too. Tootie was trying to make do, but the old house was rapidly crumbling around her. That stubborn woman would never listen to reason. But our sister, Kate, had a soothing way about her. She could scheme her way into convincing Tootie that calling a repairman was her idea, and maybe the worst of it could be fixed in a few weeks.

Worst-case scenario, if she didn't want to fix it up, I could just have it knocked down and build her something new. A fresh start.

"You heading out?" Lee didn't miss how my eyes flicked toward the exit more than once. The sad resignation in his voice made my gut feel heavy.

When I saw the crowd inside through the patio door, I tried to think of a good excuse to get us out of there. Work. Bedtimes. *Anything.*

My eyes moved to Penny, who had overheard Lee's question, and the sad resignation gnawed at me.

"I think one night might be okay, don't you think, Pickle?"

Penny's eyes shot to mine, and a huge smile spread over her sweet face. "Really, Daddy? Can we?"

She leaped from her chair and flung herself into my arms.

Lee laughed and clamped a hand down on my shoulder. "I'll let Tootie know you're staying."

As he climbed the steps to the patio door, Penny continued to hug my middle. "Thanks, Dad. Thank you. Thank you."

I rubbed a circle on her back. "One night." I was telling both her *and* Lee.

Lee laughed and shot a salute over his shoulder before he disappeared into the house.

LARK

You know, a girl could fall in love with Outtatowner, Michigan. I sat at a high-top seat along the huge picture window of the local bakery, the Sugar Bowl. My hot latte was steamed to perfection, and the ribbon design in the foam was almost too cute to drink.

Almost.

Happy faces moved in pairs down the sidewalks as I overlooked the quaint strip of downtown. Just as the main road entered the downtown area, there was a sign that read, Outtatowner, Michigan—where strangers become friends.

Tourists and townies alike were waving and smiling as the sun filtered through the trees that lined the middle of the main road, separating the two sides of town.

The chatter in the bakery was a soft din of noise, accompanied by the gentle clatter of coffee mugs on the wood-topped tables. I immediately recognized my server, Sylvie, as the sole King woman from the funeral services. She came more than once to check on me, and her welcoming smile convinced me to order another slice of lemon loaf and a second latte.

"It's pretty charming, isn't it?" The woman sitting a few chairs down from me looked up from her laptop and smiled. She had hair the color of burnt umber and deep green eyes, and she swiveled in her seat to face me. The woman leaned her elbows back on the long high-top behind her and looked into the little bakery.

I smiled at her and followed her gaze. People were milling in and out of the busy bakery. It smelled of cinnamon and sugar and warm, toasty coffee. A small group of old men gathered with newspapers in their laps, which they ignored, and chatted with each other. The line to the register was nearly out the door.

"It is," I agreed.

The woman leaned forward and offered her hand. "I'm Cass. In for the weekend?"

"Lark. I was, for work." I lifted the small folded newspaper in my lap. "It's cute here, so I'm just killing time now. You?"

Cass gestured toward her laptop. "I'm a reporter. For that very paper, actually."

"So you're a townie?"

Her smile widened. "Oh, okay. You already know the insider lingo in Outtatowner. So you've picked up a few things since Bowlegs's services."

I didn't recall seeing this woman at the services. When I just stared at her, she continued. "Small town. Not much gets past us. Although you, my dear, have become a bit of a mystery."

My back straightened, unsure of which angle to play to keep my employment a secret.

Cass lifted a hand. "A girl's gotta have her secrets. I'm

not going to pry. But to answer your question, I'm new to the townie life. Born and raised in Chicago. But . . ." Her eyes trailed behind the counter toward the kitchen, where a gigantic man entered with a tray of fresh pastries. Warm affection spread over her face, and her smile widened. "I fell for that guy, and the rest is history."

As if he could sense her, the burly baker looked out over the crowd and immediately locked eyes with her. His lips lifted in a smile, and I nearly swooned off my damn seat. His love for her was so painfully obvious I had to look away.

"Lucky girl."

She smiled and looked back at me. "Don't I know it. There's something in the water in Outtatowner. I'm telling you, the men here are something else."

My thoughts immediately flipped to the grump I'd run into at Bowlegs's funeral. A tiny sliver of me wanted to ask her about him. Probe, just a little, to see who he was and what the hell his deal could have been.

Before I had the chance, my eyes snagged on a ghost walking across the street. My mouth popped open to see Mr. Bowlegs, appearing very much alive and well, shuffling down the street. I slowly lifted a finger, and Cass's eyes followed.

"Oh!" She laughed. "That's Bowlegs's brother."

"Brother?" I was dumbstruck.

"Identical twins."

"Wow." My brain stumbled to find words to replace the shock to my system. "I didn't see him at any of the services."

"I'm not surprised. He is as much of a loner as Bowlegs. If you stay long enough, you'll find out all kinds of wild things about Outtatowner." Cass turned back to her laptop, shutting it and slipping it into a shoulder bag. "It was nice to meet you, Lark."

I said goodbye and watched her quietly slink her way through the crowd and toward the back of the bakery. Once she reached the baker behind the register, in one swift move, he wrapped an arm around her waist and pulled her through the swinging doors and out of view. Her laughter floated above the bakery noise, and I finally did let myself swoon with only the tiniest ping of envy.

Love was for the lucky, and *that* I was not. In fact, a fortune teller at a Renaissance festival had once told me that I was *cursed in love*. At the time I'd brushed it off as complete and total bullshit, but at twenty-nine and still woefully single, combined with my trail of disappointing breakups, I was starting to worry she might have been right.

"Daddy, pleeeeeease." My attention was pulled away from the cute couple and to the whiny grumbles of a familiar little girl pouting in line. My system jumped.

"Pickle, I said no." The little girl immediately crossed her arms and committed to a deep pout.

"Come on, Wyatt. You're only here for one night. I'll show her around the fire station." Tootie's nephew, Lee, pushed the shoulder of the grouchy man I couldn't seem to escape.

Damn small towns.

"Lee, you're not helping." Apparently I wasn't the only one this man was abrasive with. There was something about him that made me want to poke the bear—irritate him with positivity until he smiled *once*, for Christ's sake.

I scooped up my coffee and bounced out of my chair toward the trio. "Well, hey there, Sullivans!" I chirped. I leaned down toward the little girl. "It's a great day for a visit to the fire station, don't you think?"

A lopsided grin spread over Lee's face. "You're welcome anytime, Miss . . ."

Wyatt shot him a hard glare, and I laughed. My hand shot out. "Lark Butler. Nice to officially meet you. And that is so kind of you. I just might take you up on that." I headed toward the door and directed a smile at Wyatt. "See ya later, Oscar."

He straightened and frowned, and I stifled a little laugh. I knew damn well his name was Wyatt, but if he was going to be such a grouch, then Oscar it was.

Breezing past them, I stepped out onto the sidewalk and into the late-morning sunshine. I pulled a deep breath of coastal air into my lungs and let the warmth of the morning wash over me.

There was something special about this town and its quirky residents. I felt it in my bones. Outtatowner was definitely a place I would hope to come back to someday. After a little walk along the beach, I would check my website for messages and line up a new job and a new town.

"YOU COULD ALWAYS TRY CALIFORNIA AGAIN." My mother's voice was soothing as I cradled my phone to my ear and scanned the newspaper one more time.

California. *LA*. The city of broken dreams and hordes of hopeful actresses, like myself. I still couldn't believe I had sent out dozens of audition tapes and hadn't received even a single callback. Honestly, it was embarrassing.

No freaking way. "I don't know . . ."

"I'm sure you'll get that callback any day now!"

Her unwavering faith infused her words. If Mom could make things happen with tenacity alone, she would.

"It's been weeks and I haven't heard anything. I think that ship has sailed, Mom."

"Aubergine."

I rolled my eyes. Since moving to a commune, my mother and stepfather, Larry, had taken to being addressed only by their *spirit names*: Aubergine and Eagle. "Sorry, right. Aubergine."

"Goddess will provide."

In all sincerity, I came by my general positivity honestly. My mother was a literal ray of sunshine. Though what she lacked in firm parenting skills, she more than made up for in enthusiastic support.

"I'm just hoping Goddess will provide an interesting job and a decent place to stay." My website traffic was still surprisingly strong, but there hadn't been any new inquiries for my services yet. "There's not a lot in the small-town mourners market."

"You could come live here. We all provide for each other in blessed peace and harmony."

Live in the nudist commune with my mother and Larry? Hard pass.

I resorted to the story I told myself when doubt inevitably creeped in. "These immersion acting jobs are really good for me. I'm honing my improv skills, and it looks fantastic on a résumé, which I can't say of all the temp jobs I've been doing. Come fall, I'll go back to my rounds on the off-Broadway audition circuit again. This is only temporary. An adventure."

From the small bench on the sidewalk I had taken over, I scanned the long strip of downtown Outtatowner. The tourist season was picking up, and several storefronts had Now Hiring Seasonal Help or something like it posted on the front windows. Even the Sugar Bowl had a sign looking for a weekend barista.

The happy faces of tourists meandered past me.

I supposed it wouldn't be the worst thing in the world to hunker down in a cozy little town until the next job popped up. Granted, I would have to keep up the facade of Bowlegs's mysterious funeral attendee, but with so few people in attendance, that probably wouldn't be all that hard.

"Okay, Aubergine. I should get my day started and, you know, figure out the rest of my life. Love you."

"Many blessings," she replied, and I hung up with a sigh and a chuckle.

I closed my eyes, tipped my face to the sky, and let the warm sun soak into me. "Okay, Goddess," I whispered. "If I am supposed to stay here, then give me a sign."

I held on to my thought, willing some of my mother's faith in *Goddess* to spread to me. I took a few deep breaths, cracked one eye open, then the other. The town continued to bustle around me.

Absolutely nothing had changed.

I sighed and stood. With determined steps toward my car, I flipped the local newspaper into the trash. Something would come up; it always did. For now I could head up the coast to find a new beachy town before making my way back to the hustle of the city.

My white Converse high-tops walked a determined line up the sidewalk and around the crowds of shoppers and families heading toward the beach.

I tried to ignore the tug, something deep inside me telling me driving away so soon might be a mistake.

"Yoo-hoo!"

I turned my head, scanning the crowd to follow the voice.

"Hello, dear!"

My heart swelled at the sight of the kind, elderly

woman's warm smile, and I felt myself grinning at Tootie waving wildly at me from across the street.

I lifted my hand and waved back, then checked the roadway before crossing.

"What were you doing on that side of the street?" Tootie smiled but held me in place with her stare.

I looked around. In reality I was wandering around aimlessly. "Um, I . . ."

Tootie leaned closer and pulled me in by the elbow. "That's the Kings' side." She waved a hand between us. "No matter. I suppose Bug and I did come to some sort of agreement over you."

Still unsure what to say, my brows furrowed, and I offered her a confused sort of smile.

Tootie winked. "You're a Sullivan. I just know it."

Warmth spread through me, and I fought the urge to let her nephew's ruggedly handsome face pop into my mind.

"Are you leaving so soon?" Tootie looped her arm in mine, and we walked down the sidewalk.

"I think so. I'm lining up my next job and a place to stay." I leaned down to whisper. "And we can't let our little secret get out."

Tootie's laughter was infectious. "Nonsense! Let them wonder. This town needs a little fun. A job and a place to stay?" Tootie patted my hand and squeezed. The motherly gesture was unfamiliar and sweet. I hugged her closer. "You let me take care of that."

Oh yeah. This is definitely *my sign.*

WHEN TOOTIE SET HER MIND TO SOMETHING, SHE WAS a powerhouse. Within three hours, I was set up with a place to stay and several prospects for seasonal summer work. I stepped over the threshold and looked over my new temporary home. The apartment was small, simply arranged with a living space and kitchen in the middle. It had two tiny bedrooms and one bathroom. The apartment itself was on top of a large barn that was more like a giant storage shed, and the property itself was massive.

It shared a large parcel with an old farmhouse that looked to be well maintained, but empty. The apartment was perfect.

Definitely better than some unknown motel or sleeping in my car.

From the back bedroom window, I could look out over rows and rows of blueberry bushes, and in the distance, just over the trees, I could barely make out the coastline.

She tried to fuss, but I assured Tootie that it was more than adequate, and part of the fun would be opening it up to let the breeze in while I got settled. I glanced at the list of phone numbers that she'd handwritten. I had been assured that all I had to do was mention her name and a job would be mine.

Just like that. *That's how small towns work,* she assured me.

It was up to me to decide whether I wanted to brew coffee or wait tables or sell tchotchkes to tourists.

After opening all the windows to let in a cross breeze, I rifled through my duffel bag and pulled out a pair of gym shoes. Across the expansive yard, at the edge where the blueberry field met a tree line, was a walking path.

Filled with a sense of adventure, I tossed my hair in a ponytail and bounded down the stairs and across the yard toward the path. When I reached the trailhead, my toe brushed across the limestone. A sign indicated the path was part of a thirty-four-mile former railway that had been converted to a path for walkers, bikers, and horses. While thirty-four miles was definitely out of the question, an afternoon exploring and clearing my head sounded perfect.

I pulled out my phone and dropped a pin at the trail-head so, knowing me, when I got lost or turned around, I could at least manage to find my way back. Impressed with my own forethought, I let the path lead the way.

The path was empty, but along the trail scattered signs taught about local wildlife, the old railway, and other random facts about Western Michigan. A slight breeze shook the leaves of the towering trees, and I was transported.

Late-afternoon sun filtered through the canopy, and the heat of the day had yet to burn off. I peeled off my hoodie, comfortable that I was alone, and tied it around my waist. I wore only shorts and a sports bra, but in the time I'd been on the path, I hadn't seen a single walker, let alone a bicycle or a horse.

As I trudged farther ahead, the path took long, winding curves. I thought back to dropping a location pin at the start and mentally patted myself on the back for being so responsible. On and on I walked down the path, sucking fresh air deep into my lungs.

Then something in the distance caught my attention, and my ears pricked. I stopped in the center of the path and listened.

The breeze. Birds chirping. The wind through the trees, but . . . something *else*.

My mind immediately went to the true-crime documentaries my mother used to watch on late-night TV. *This is why we should live somewhere away from people,* she used to say. I looked around and didn't see anyone ahead of me or down the path from where I came. When I heard the rustling noise again, my panic spiked.

There was a small dirt offshoot of the trail and quickly darted down the narrow path. It was a much smaller trail, and through the trees it looked as though it led to a round body of water. I followed it down and breathed a sigh of relief when the trees opened up.

A lake.

It was picturesque and had a charm about it, with its rickety dock and large boulders dotted around the edge. Rocks jutted into the water, and during the hottest days, I imagined this would make the perfect spot for high schoolers ditching class to hang out, leap off the rocks, and impress their friends.

The warm sun beat down on me as a bead of sweat rolled down my back. I listened again and heard nothing but the quiet sounds of the forest. A smirk tugged at my lips as I impulsively untied my sweatshirt. I looked around again, comforted by the seclusion of the forest as I toed off my shoes and stripped down to nothing.

Content and naked, I reached my arms up and felt a cool breeze dance along my skin.

A twig snapped closely behind me, and my hands flew to cover my chest. Suddenly, the sheer solitude of the lake had my heart hammering. This could be the perfect place for a high school ditch day *or* a gruesome, unsolved murder.

Hell no.

My eyes flew to the rocks jutting into the water. If I moved quickly, I could hide behind them and let whoever or *whatever* was stomping through the forest pass by. I assessed my clothing, realizing that I had no time to cover myself. When another twig snapped, all rational thought flew away as I kicked my shoes and clothing behind a large pile of rocks.

I ran toward the water, holding my boobs and trying to get to safety behind the rock face as quickly as possible, cursing myself for being so skittish. Dirt and leaves clung to my bare feet. The cool water hit my toes, and I inelegantly flung myself forward, desperately trying to get behind the rocks before someone saw me.

I huddled behind the rocky outcropping. My breaths sawed in and out as my heart beat wildly. My ears strained to hear anything over my panting, so I willed myself to calm the hell down. And there it was. The rustling was louder and most certainly getting closer.

A deer? A bear? Cold-blooded killer?

Rhythmic pounding rattled through the still forest. I listened harder but didn't dare peek out from behind the safety of the rocks. Finally the steps came to a halt, and I could hear labored breathing that wasn't my own.

As smoothly as I could manage, I gently lifted my head to peer over the rocks.

No. Freaking. Way.

At the edge of the water, not far from where I stashed every scrap of my clothing, was Wyatt Sullivan.

Hands on his trim hips, he was panting and sweaty from a run. In one swift, utterly masculine movement, he reached behind him and tore his shirt from his back. Sweat dappled across his chiseled chest and down. Lower and lower still.

My mouth went dry. I couldn't tear my eyes away.

Wyatt plucked headphones from his ears and tucked them into a pocket of his shorts. He twisted left, then right, stretching the muscles of his back and arms.

I squeezed my eyes closed. "Go away. Please just go away." My breath bounced back against the rocks as I let free my barely audible whisper.

My eyes opened to see that Wyatt had not, in fact, gone away. Instead, he hooked his fingers into the elastic of his shorts and in one move, stripped away his shorts and underwear. He toed off his shoes and socks and kicked the pile of clothing.

There he stood. Gloriously naked as the day he was born and without a care in the world. As he moved toward the water, I inched to my left to get a better view. I watched him push back the long strands of his brown hair off his sweaty forehead. My eyes burned a path across his thick biceps and over his flat stomach. I stifled a giddy *holy shit!* scream when I saw the size of his dick. It wasn't even hard, and it was already one of the biggest I'd seen. Definitely in the top three.

I rolled my lips together and didn't bother to fight the tingles that prickled over my skin. A hundred dirty thoughts flooded my brain.

I want to trace that line of sweat with my tongue. I want to feel him get hard in my hands. I want my mouth on him. Goddamn, he's huge. What would it feel like to be stretched open by a cock like that? Maybe he'd let me find out. I bet he could stalk over here and rail me against these rocks and I'd never be the same. He could tear me apart and I'd fucking love it.

I realized my hand had dipped below the waterline, and I snatched it up. What the hell was wrong with me? Wyatt was practically a stranger, and I was spying on him like a total creep.

Still, when he waded into the water and his gorgeous body dipped below the surface, I couldn't help but feel disappointed for losing the view. Wyatt dove under the water, disappearing completely and heaving me back into reality. If he swam any closer, he would *definitely* find me spying on him.

Shit!

As he splashed to the surface, I looked around. I could exit out the other side of the rocks, but my clothes were still hidden in a pile near his. There was no way I could slip away without him catching me.

I just had to wait him out.

I bit my lip and sneaked another peek. My foot inched forward. The soggy lake bottom gave way, and something slimy wriggled beneath my feet.

A very loud, very unladylike shriek burst from my chest, rattling the peaceful forest.

6

WYATT

When you're bare-ass naked and you hear a shriek that sounds like it came from the depths of hell, I dare you to not piss yourself. I scanned the area and almost immediately saw the source of the scream.

From behind a rocky outcropping, Lark thrashed around, splashing water in every direction. "It touched me! Something touched me!"

My hands flew to my junk before I realized I was hidden below the water. Lark moved toward the center of the lake, her bare shoulders peeking just above the surface.

My heart rate slowed as I realized there was nothing dangerous, only Lark Butler, the woman my aunt had *paid* to cry at Bowlegs's funeral.

After seeing her at the bakery, had I pried every ounce of information from Lee? You're damn right I did. He was reluctant to tell me, but once he started talking, he spilled everything. Tootie felt bad that the feud between the Sullivans and the Kings meant the attendance at the services was likely to be scarce, so she and Bug had conspired to hire someone to mourn him.

My mind still couldn't wrap itself around the type of person who would choose *lying at funerals* as a profession.

Clearly, someone who isn't one with nature, if Lark was any indication.

When I'd decided to take a dip in old Wabash Lake after my run, I hadn't planned on an audience. A cocky part of me wondered how much she had seen and whether or not she liked the view.

I trudged bare-assed toward Lark.

"Calm the hell down. What happened?"

She turned toward me, pink flaming her cheeks. "Something in the water. It . . . touched me."

I stifled a laugh. "Probably a fish or a turtle. This time of year they nest near the rocks. What are you doing here anyway?"

The pink in her cheeks deepened to crimson.

Oh yeah. She definitely got an eyeful.

"Well, um . . . I was going for a walk and I heard something and kind of freaked out." Lark brushed a wet strand of hair behind her ear and lifted her chin.

I gestured toward the shoreline. "Well, by all means. Since you're out of danger."

She rolled her eyes and expelled her breath in a huff. "Just get out."

"I'm not getting out." I was just starting to enjoy this. I knew she was trying to get under my skin at the bakery, so I could do the same to her. Her small nostrils flared once.

Lark crossed her arms, pushing the tops of her breasts to the surface of the water.

Oh shit. Is she naked?

She clearly recognized a challenge as I stared her down. "You get out."

I crossed my arms. "Oh, I'm not getting out."

"Well, I . . . I can't. I'm . . . nude."

My jaw shifted. *I knew it.*

The water droplets rolled lazily down the slope of her shoulder, and I could only imagine the tight little body that was just below the surface. I reined in the flash of desire after my dick started perking up.

"So you got scared and your immediate reaction was to get *naked* and get into the water?"

Her mouth popped open, and she quickly snapped it shut. "I was already naked, all right?" She grunted in frustration. "It's hot outside. I didn't think *you* would be here. Plus, you had the same idea!" When she gestured toward me, a small wall of water splashed my way, but I sidestepped to dodge it.

I lifted my chin, but Lark only held my stare in defiance. "Fine. I won't look. But don't forget, you creeped on me. I think it's only fair." I moved my head toward the shoreline. "Ladies first."

Her jaw flexed, but then a wicked grin spread slowly across her face. I didn't actually think she'd take the dare, and I wasn't so much of a prick that I would force her to get out of the water when she was naked. I was just messing around.

Mostly.

When she tipped up one eyebrow, I knew I was done for.

Oh man. I think I fucked up.

Moving through the water, Lark shouldered her way past me despite having the entire lake to move around. Rivulets of water sluiced down her smooth back as she made her way toward the edge. My eyes followed as the flowing water lines nipped in at her waist and flared out as her bare bottom came into view. It was muscular and round.

Fucking perfect.

If my dick wasn't paying attention before, it was at full salute and hailing the world's most perfect ass.

Lark shot me a look over her shoulder, and my eyes whipped up to meet hers, then darted to the side. Too late. She'd caught me checking her out, just as she'd intended.

Without shame, she walked slowly toward the edge of the lake, gently rising out of the water like some sea goddess, and I stared like the lowly peasant I was. My chest squeezed at the sight of her. I wondered if she felt as soft as she looked.

Fuck. I hadn't slept with someone in nearly a year, and the way my body was reacting to the mere sight of Lark told me I was well out of practice.

Once on the shoreline, I respectfully looked away as she moved behind a low rock and bent. Apparently she'd stashed her clothes, and it explained why I hadn't seen them before I'd decided on my post-run cooldown.

From my peripheral, I tracked every movement as she turned away from me to dress herself. I scanned the tree line. A protective surge built in my chest as I looked out for anyone who might see her naked.

Anyone but me, I guess.

This woman was a nuisance—disrupting my plans and causing rumors to fly around my hometown, but damn.

She was intriguing.

Once she pulled on her shorts, sports bra, and shoes, she tied the arms of a hoodie around her hips. I turned to face her again. Before leaving me alone in the woods, Lark turned, her defiant little chin still high in the air. With her arms spread wide, she lowered herself into a curtsy before taking off up the path and out of view.

I fought the playful laughter that threatened to rumble in my chest.

~

"WE CAN'T STAY HERE." I pressed my fingertips into my eye sockets and reached as deeply as I could for an ounce of fucking patience.

"Why?" Penny had her arms crossed and wore a familiar look of mild annoyance.

"Because I have to get back to campus."

"Why?"

"Because I'm the head coach. I have a season to prepare for—game tape to review, plays to develop. The players and other coaches need me."

"Why?"

"Even in the off-season there's work to do."

"Why?"

Damn it. I'd walked right into the why *game again.*

"Enough. We aren't staying." My clipped tone caused Penny's lower lip to jut out even further. I felt like a jerk, but the truth of the matter was we did need to get back. I was already fielding calls about next season, summer break, and what I was going to do about the players who were on academic probation.

When I transitioned from successful quarterback to coaching, I thought it'd be as simple as mentoring college players, passing down my tips for mental strength and agility on the field.

Yeah fucking right.

The majority of it was politics, strategy meetings, and keeping the star players from getting themselves booted from the team.

My phone buzzed and the name of Gary Whitman, the university athletic director, flashed across the screen.

Case in point.

I raised a finger to Penny, who only rolled her eyes and flopped herself onto Tootie's well-worn couch.

When I answered, the athletic director wasted no time on greetings but barreled ahead. "Sullivan. I have your list of ineligibles."

"Ineligibles?" I glanced at my watch to check the date. "Already?"

"One for sure, but another on the brink."

I let go of a deep sigh and felt a headache start to form. "All right. Let's hear it."

"Kevin Williams is on academic probation. Didn't pass his finals."

"Yeah." My heart went out to Kevin. He was a good, smart kid. Hell of a ball player, but he lacked the discipline for college. Namely, showing up for goddamn class.

"Also, Michael Thompson."

That one surprised me. Michael was a straightlaced hard worker. He could run like the wind, and I'd never heard of any issues with him so far.

"He's got nowhere to go. We're still waiting on campus housing to come through, but he says he doesn't have a place back in Oklahoma."

My gut turned. I didn't know my players well enough yet to have much insight into their home situations, but I couldn't just send a kid packing without knowing he had a home to go back to. "I'll take care of it."

"You better." Whitman laughed, but it lacked any semblance of actual humor. "We were all excited to have you sign on, but when it comes down to it, you need a winning season just as bad as we do. Get these boys under control, and hopefully we can talk long term."

I didn't need to be reminded of the stipulations of my contract. For a Division I football coach, satisfying the university's media and sponsorship contracts was only a small part of the gig. If at the end of it all I didn't produce a winning season, my contract wouldn't be extended. With the team I had agreed to coach, I was on shaky ground at best. My eyes flicked to Penny, who was still pouting on the couch and likely ruminating over the *Worst Dad Ever*.

"Got it." I hung up the phone and tossed it aside. I sighed and felt the tension creep into my neck and shoulders. "How about we go visit Uncle Lee at the fire station, Pickle?"

Penny immediately perked up. "Really? Right now?"

I smiled, knowing making her happy was the easiest win of them all, and I needed a win today. "Right now. Let's load up."

AFTER A FULL TOUR of the fire station, if Penny hadn't already been over the moon for her uncle, she sure as hell was now. They were two peas in a pod, and she smiled up at him as her head wobbled under the weight of a firefighter's helmet.

She ran a hand across the red fire engine.

"Hop up there." Lee gave her a boost, and Penny enthusiastically disappeared into the darkness of the truck.

"Just don't touch anything," I warned.

Her head popped back into the doorway and she frowned.

Lee laughed and lifted a hand. "Hit all the buttons you

want. Just don't mess with the tools. Especially the ax. I don't want you getting blood on my clean truck."

Penny giggled and disappeared again as Lee handed me a can of Coke.

"It's good to have you back, man."

I shook my head and lifted my brows. "I'm not back."

A smirk tugged at Lee's lips, but he let it go. "At least you're in the same state. It's a start. But you know as well as I do that an hour commute is nothing, really."

"Says the guy who sleeps at work and then has two days off." Busting Lee's balls about his life at the fire station was easier than letting the doubts of my recent decisions creep in. I needed to focus on my job. I couldn't lose sight of that if I wanted any kind of stability for Penny.

"You can't do it all. Look at Dad. After Mom died, he tried to be everything to everyone, and you know where that got him." Lee's usually upbeat attitude waned. We both knew Dad's illness was shitty luck, but knowing that didn't sting any less. "Maybe you need some help."

"I don't need help." I also didn't need my little brother riding my ass and telling me things I already knew. He didn't need to worry about me either. I downed my drink and stood.

I had no desire to talk about work anymore. For some reason I wanted to tell him about my interaction with Lark. Maybe tell him to back off a little if he also had a thing for her. Fighting over women had never been an issue before, but after he'd eagerly offered to show her around the fire station, I felt a strange need to stake my claim.

"So, uh. That Lark woman is still in town."

Lee's eyebrows crept up as he sipped his own drink. "That so?"

"Yeah, I, uh, ran into her on my run yesterday. Down at Wabash Lake."

"You get her to flash you before jumping off the rocks like Mindy McAllister in high school?"

I laughed and shoved his shoulder. I listened for Penny, but she was still occupied in the truck.

"No, but I did see something else." A sly grin spread across my face. "She was skinny-dipping and I got an eyeful."

"You saw her ass?" Penny's head popped between us, and Coke nearly flew out of Lee's nose as he choked out a laugh.

I turned to her, schooling my features and willing the laugh to stay buried in my chest. "Don't say *ass*. It's impolite."

"But you say it." She crossed her little arms over her chest. "And you saw, like, the whole thing."

"It was an accident." *Sort of.* "We don't need to talk about it. And why can't you call it, like, a heinie or something cute?"

Penny shrugged. "Butts are funny." She looked at Lee, and they both erupted into a fresh fit of laughter.

I shook my head and turned to face her, setting my can on the edge of the truck. I pulled Penny forward at the waist and hiked her over my shoulder to move her away from the doorway. She squealed with delight and kicked her legs out behind me.

"Say bye to Uncle Lee. We've got to get on the road." I'd have to find another way to figure out if Lee had a thing for Lark and decide whether or not I should do something about that.

Penny went limp on my shoulder. "Bye, Uncle Lee." Her little voice was morose and dramatic.

"See ya later, Rat." Lee tickled her sides, and she wiggled and laughed.

"It's PICKLE!" she giggle-shouted.

I smiled and mouthed, *Thank you,* to my little brother. He was a good kid and an even better uncle. That gnawing ache came back with a vengeance. That same one that said maybe I was making a mistake by taking Penny away from Outtatowner and my family so soon.

7

LARK

For the second time in three days, I was spying on Wyatt Sullivan. This time, instead of it happening behind some rocks while we were both butt naked, it was from the comfort of my own rented kitchen. And he was fully clothed, unfortunately.

I cracked open the gauzy, white kitchen curtains and looked out over the large lawn toward the old house. Wyatt stared up at the empty house with his arms crossed and his signature scowl across his face.

What is he doing? Why is he here?

As if he could sense me staring, his head swiveled in my direction. I stifled a yelp and ducked down below the countertop. I didn't understand that man. I'd googled him, of course. Every picture of him was either on the field looking like a god or grinning at the camera, and holy shit, did I wish I had watched more football.

Where the hell was that guy, and why do I get Mr. Stick-in-the-Mud instead?

The Wyatt I met was grumpy and short tempered. Maybe it was because he wasn't in the NFL anymore, though, based on the articles I had scoured well past midnight, it seemed like he left while he was still at the top of his game.

Some articles hinted that the change in career paths had to do with his daughter, but he was famously tight lipped about his little girl. For the most part, reporters seemed to respect his protectiveness for her and focused more on his stats and the fact he was ridiculously wealthy than on his family situation.

Still, I couldn't help but wonder.

He didn't wear a ring, and so far no one had mentioned a wife. Was he a widower with some super-tragic sob story? Maybe that was why he had a stick up his ass. Though Penny seemed pretty content, at least outwardly, for not having her mom around.

After a few minutes, I heard the sound of tires receding down the long driveway. I slowly stood and peeked out the window again.

Wyatt was gone.

It was for the best. I didn't have time to fantasize about former NFL players who shot me heated looks one minute only to scowl at me the next. If anything, men like Wyatt meant one thing.

Heartache.

It didn't matter that the way his brow furrowed or eyes turned a deeper shade of caramel when he was annoyed turned me on. I had a date tonight.

A date with Wyatt's own aunt Tootie, sure, but it was a date nonetheless.

I walked to the small bathroom to check myself out and fluff my hair before flipping off the light and carefully navigating the rickety steps on the outside of the barn. They were steep and a little treacherous, but it was better than having to go *inside* the barn to get to the apartment. It was dark and creepy, and I wanted nothing to do with it.

I started my car, rolled all the windows down, and cranked the radio to full blast. In my travels, I had discovered that cruising down long stretches of country roads with music up and the wind in my hair was good for my soul.

I was invigorated by the time I rolled into downtown Outtatowner. It was a busy Thursday night. I smiled at a family headed away from the beach. Their cheeks were red from the sun, and the two little boys' eyelids were already heavy from a day on the water. I checked my text messages again to be sure I had the right address when I pulled up to Bluebird Books, Outtatowner's local bookstore.

After she handed me the keys to the apartment, Tootie had invited me to her weekly book club. I loved reading, though I doubted my secret love for faerie Why Choose romance was up her alley. It didn't matter. I had zero plans, and she was too sweet to decline her offer. Tootie assured me it didn't matter that I hadn't read the book, and I figured I could suffer through a few hours of polite book talk and maybe meet a friend or two.

Beats a lonely night in the apartment, wondering about the noises coming up from the creepy old barn.

When I walked up to Bluebird Books, a wooden sign read CLOSED FOR THE BLUEBIRDS. I peered through the window to see a few women milling around, so instead of going in, I knocked. Their heads turned in my direction, and when Tootie saw me, her face lit up. She motioned enthusiastically with her hands and mouthed, *Come in, come in.* I smiled and pushed through the door.

To my surprise, the Bluebird Club was a hell of a lot more fun than I had imagined. It was in the back of the quaint bookstore, and the women who gathered all had drinks in their hands. In a cozy corner were mismatched chairs, a comfy love seat, and large tufted ottoman seats spread haphazardly. Candles were lit and soft music played in the background. It was like walking into a chic, secret club.

A large side table had an array of drinks—both alcoholic and not—and it seemed everyone had brought some kind of appetizer to share. Everyone but me.

I leaned into Tootie. "I'm so sorry. I didn't bring anything."

She smiled and patted my hand. "Nonsense! You're my guest. Now let's meet the ladies."

Tootie shuffled me past each woman, carefully introducing me. It seemed the age range of the women spanned from Tootie's early sixties to a few in their mid twenties. The age gap didn't seem to faze anyone as they milled around and laughed with each other.

"And of course," Tootie said with a smile, "you know Bug."

"It's nice to see you again." I smiled and tried to ignore the wary glance Bug whipped in Tootie's direction.

She caught it too. "Oh stop, you old sourpuss. She's one of us now."

Bug looked down her long, straight nose at me. "*Us* as in a Sullivan or a King?"

Slowly the chatter around me died down as the book club's attention was squarely on me and the two women in a strangely possessive standoff beside me.

Tootie's happy laugh broke through the uncomfortable silence. "You know as well as I do there's no place for that at book club." With a wave of her hand, she guided me around Bug's assessing eyes and toward the small table with drinks.

"Don't mind her," she whispered. "There's a good heart

under all that bluster. But don't you dare tell her I said that."

With her low hum, I felt like I was being let in on some very important town secret—a society of women who, despite the decades-old feud in town, had come together for their love of books.

Only . . . besides the books on the shelves, there were no actual books present at book club.

After only a few minutes, it became apparent that the Bluebird Book Club was a facade for the women of Outta-towner to come together in secret to gossip, solve problems, and maybe even just be themselves.

I immediately fell in love.

The bell on the door jingled, and our attention was brought to a young woman juggling a tray of something that looked like brownies and a canvas bag hanging from the crook of her elbow.

I didn't recognize her, but she smiled widely and slid the tray of dessert onto the table and flopped into an empty chair with a huff.

"Long day?" someone named Mabel asked.

"Long week," she replied.

"And Red?" Tootie's eyes were wistful.

The woman pressed her lips into a flat line and shook her head. "Not a great day."

A hand went to Tootie's back in comfort. The woman's eyes slid to me, and she sat up. "Oh, hi."

I smiled and stretched out my hand. "Hi. I'm Lark."

"MJ." She shook my hand and smoothed her hair back before sneaking a glance at Bug.

Bug tipped her head toward Tootie, who was lost in another conversation. "Lark's a Sullivan."

MJ's lip twisted, and her shoulders slumped a bit, almost in . . . disappointment, maybe?

"To be fair, I'm neither a King nor a Sullivan. Just the new girl." I offered another smile, and she returned it before relaxing into her chair.

MJ leaned closer, her smile warm and friendly. "If Tootie's claimed you, it means you're definitely a Sullivan." She held out her hand. "Julep King, but most people call me MJ."

I took her hand in mine. "MJ?"

Her eyes crinkled and she shrugged. "Mint Julep."

Before I could protest, Tootie lifted a small bell and rang it. Side conversations died down as Bug also stepped forward.

"Ladies. As you can see, we have a new guest. Lark, meet everyone. Everyone, Lark."

Murmured greetings floated through the group, and I smiled and awkwardly lifted my hand.

"Now that that's settled"—Bug clapped her hands together—"let's have a drink."

A woman to my left leaned closer. "Is it true you and Bowlegs were having a secret affair?"

Another woman butted in before I could even laugh at the suggestion. "I heard you were his long-lost daughter." Her eyes were wide and hopeful.

I looked around, and my mouth dropped open.

Do I lie?

Tootie swiftly came to my rescue. "Bug and I arranged for her to attend the services. Lord knows the men in this town cause enough drama, and we couldn't stand the thought of no one being there to mourn him. We hired Lark. She's a friend of the family, and that's the end of it." Her tone was sweet, but her words were final.

The two women sat back, but as I was stuck between them, they both eyed me. I'm sure *secret lover* and *long-lost daughter* were only the tip of the iceberg when it came to the rumors swirling around town about me.

"I swear I'm not a spy!" I laughed uncomfortably as the group took me in with wide eyes. Conversation wilted around me, and I wanted to crawl into a hole and die.

The pretty redhead next to me popped a bite of food in her mouth and looked as though she was about to burst out laughing. "I'm Annie. Technically a Sullivan. The whole spy thing is kind of a sore subject."

I leaned closer. "Are you serious?"

She smiled and lifted a shoulder. "It's one of the many legends of the Sullivan–King rivalry. Military spies on opposite sides. Lines drawn in the sand." She rolled her eyes and swatted her hand in the air. "Small-town lore, really."

It was utterly ridiculous but also a little fascinating and a whole lot charming. "And no one seems to think that's a little silly to still be mad about?"

Annie laughed. "Not when the idiot men in this town keep it alive and well with their pranks and insecurities."

MJ piped up, pointing a fruit kebab in Annie's direction. "Speaking of, I have it on good authority that a little payback's coming to Lee. They know it was him who helped let loose those pigs with the numbers one and three on them at the high school reunion."

Annie lifted her chin. "I have no idea what you're talking about." She winked, and they dissolved into a fit of laughter.

"They looked all night for pig number two."

Laughing with the women was easy, natural. The tension between the Kings and Sullivans seemed to sit squarely on the men's shoulders and had no place for the Bluebirds.

"Lee. The firefighter, right?" I affectionately remembered the youngest Sullivan brother who'd invited me to the fire station, though I was pretty sure it was just to get a rise out of Wyatt.

"He is now that he's home. He was overseas with the military for a long time. We're all relieved he's back." There was something there, in Annie's voice. A sad history that hinted at something deeper, but she changed the subject before revealing any more. "MJ here is a nurse up at Haven Pines, the assisted-living facility where Red stays in the memory care ward. Keeps an eye on him for us."

MJ offered another shy smile. "Doesn't matter if he's a Sullivan or a King. No one should have to suffer through what he has." Annie nodded and hummed in agreement, though I wondered if everyone felt the same way.

My brow furrowed. Red Sullivan didn't seem all that old, especially for him to be living in an assisted-living facility. If he was staying in the memory-care ward, he likely suffered from dementia or another kind of brain injury. It explained the little lost looks I picked up on at the services.

Annie leaned across and placed her hand on MJ's. "He's lucky to have you. We all know it."

MJ smiled but looked away, and my heart squeezed in my chest at the women's soft and comforting exchange. My lifestyle didn't lend itself to forming lifelong bonds or close friendships. While I had some girlfriends from high school, most of those had faded away with time and distance. I loved meeting new people and exploring new places, but there was something to be said about being tied to a place. Having a history and people who understood it with only a look.

"So you're staying at the Highfield House? Kind of big for just one person." MJ promptly changed the subject.

"Sort of. The barn apartment?" Both women nodded. "Though I did see Wyatt checking out the main house today." I tried to keep my voice indifferent, but inside I was dying to know if they would share any other information about the broody middle Sullivan brother.

"That's weird." Annie took another bite of food and scrunched her face. "I saw him and Penny leaving town on my way in, and I assumed he was headed back to St. Fowler."

Oddly, my heart sank, just a little.

"THIS PLACE SUCKS."

I frowned at Penny's words, not because she was seven and shouldn't be saying shit like that, but because I couldn't really argue her point. "Language, Pickle."

Her eyes widened. "What? I could have said 'this place freaking sucks,' but I didn't!"

I shook my head to stifle my laughter and bundled the covers under her chin. "You're making me old and gray."

"Daddy, it *does* suck." Her pout deepened. "I miss Uncle Lee and Aunt Tootie. Even Uncle Duke said that next time we went home, he'd take me out on the tractor."

Home.

A few days in Outtatowner and Penny already considered it more of a home than this place.

I smoothed my hands down her arms. "I know it's hard, but we're still new here. We just have to make it our own. We've got this. Two against the world, right?" I touched the tip of my nose to hers.

Her freshly minty breath whooshed over me as she grumbled. "Two against the world."

I lifted my head and smoothed back her hair. Penny had become everything. More important than a big cushy NFL paycheck. More than a Super Bowl ring I'd never get to wear. More than anything I could think of. There was nothing I wouldn't do for her.

"Can I call Mom tomorrow?"

"'Course, baby. First thing, if you want to." My thoughts flicked to my ex, Bethany. We'd burned hot and bright, but flamed out fast. I wish I could say that we tried to make things work, but the truth was, when she ended up pregnant after our third date and needed a paternity test from me *and two other teammates*, things fizzled fast. While we'd never discussed anything long term, I had wrongly assumed exclusivity was a part of the deal. I'd learned a lot since then.

I did what I could to support Bethany throughout the pregnancy, but she didn't seem to want much. We'd talked about options, including adoption, but in the end I just couldn't agree to it. Bethany said she'd never really considered children and didn't want the responsibility, which I could respect. She'd signed over her parental rights, and I became a single dad to the greatest kid on the planet.

And I'd make that choice again in a heartbeat.

Penny talked to her mom often, and I paid for regular visits and flights whenever either asked. Once I wrapped my head around the fact that we were having a kid, I vowed to never talk shit about Penny's mother, and I was proud I'd kept up my end of the bargain.

There was nothing more important than Penny.

"Do we have to stay here?" Her soft whisper was so sad in the dim lighting of her bedroom.

My voice felt rusty. How do you break the heart of a

seven-year-old? "I don't know, Pickle, but I'll figure something out."

I kissed my daughter good night, flicked on her nightlight, and walked toward the door before stopping. She was already looking at me expectantly.

My smile widened and my chest pinched. "One more. One more." I never left without just one more hug, and she knew it.

I bent and Penny's arms wrapped around my neck. "Thank you, Daddy."

I wasn't sure what she was thanking me for just yet. Leaving St. Fowler and staying in my hometown would cost me nearly everything in terms of focus and how that could impact my career, but being her dad was everything.

As her bedroom door clicked behind me, I pulled my phone from my pocket and started making calls.

"IS THE QUEEN SATISFIED?" I swooped into a dramatic bow as I pushed open another bedroom door.

"It's perfect!" Penny's squeal could break glass. She was full of shit; the house itself was grimy and needed serious cleaning, but she was in love.

"Ours forever?" Penny twirled, and her little feet created a semicircle of dust on the floorboards.

"Definitely not. It's temporary. Let's see how the summer goes." I didn't want to make any promises to her if I couldn't keep them, but after her sullen, heartsick words a few days ago, I immediately started making arrangements to spend the summer in Outtatowner. Being only forty miles from the university, I'd managed to convince myself, and the board I reported to, that I could be the perfect dad *and* a successful head coach.

My phone buzzed with another voice mail from Gary Whitman, and anxiety crept up my back.

What the hell did I do?

"Hello?" My aunt Tootie's singsong voice echoed down the hallway.

"Back here," I called, slipping my phone into my pocket.

Penny ran down the hall and into my aunt's arms. They hugged and swayed in a circle. Tootie smiled at me. "It'll do?"

I nodded. The house was one of the few properties the Kings hadn't yet scooped up, as it was a part of the Sullivan family farm. They'd have the fight of their lives on their hands if they ever tried to move in on the old farmhouse Tootie and Dad had grown up in. Though it wasn't the main farm parcel, Tootie refused to sell even after Dad's health declined, and I loved her for it.

While I figured out how to juggle my career while not emotionally scarring my daughter for life, we could stay.

"Oh, one small thing I forgot to mention. The apartment above the barn is being rented for a bit."

My brows pitched down. "You forgot to mention that?" I didn't need some stranger lurking around when Penny was playing outside or bugging us for a cup of sugar or something equally annoying.

Tootie waved her hand in the air in dismissal. "It's nothing. Lark is a friend. You won't even know she's there." Tootie booped Penny on the nose. "Just don't go bothering her without permission."

Lark.

The woman whose perfect heart-shaped ass was permanently implanted in my memory. The mysterious woman who'd breezed into town and had everyone talking. The woman I couldn't stop thinking about. As if I didn't have enough on my plate.

This is a problem.

When I said as much, Tootie only laughed and bustled Penny into her car, giving me time to deep clean the house before we officially moved in.

A *girls' day* she called it.

As the car disappeared down the driveway, my eyes moved to the small window above the aging barn. It was cramped and dark and the insulation was thin, so you could often hear the barn cats lurking around after dark. In high school it made the perfect place to sneak a few friends and throw a party, but that was a long, long time ago.

I needed to get to work cleaning the house up if Penny and I were going to make it our home for the summer. Cleaning the layers of grime and dust that time had placed on the home was surprisingly satisfying. I didn't hate the mind-numbing break from the stress of my everyday life. Unfortunately, when my phone rang and it was Gary Whitman *again*, the tension that lived between my shoulders came back with a vengeance.

"Hey, Gary."

"You in town?" He sounded annoyed. Pissed off. This was not good.

I looked around the dusty living room, cradled the phone between my shoulder and ear, and lifted the window open. "I'm not. I won't be staying locally for the summer." He started to protest, but I'd been backed by the board, so I plowed on. "My schedule won't change. I have a plan to be available and take care of what needs to be done."

"Well, I hope you included three unruly college students in that grand plan."

"Three?" I was still working through figuring out what to do with Michael and Kevin.

"Joey Lupo. Fractured his pinkie."

I sank down on the open windowsill and released a frustrated sigh. "He did what now?"

"Ultimate Frisbee."

"Jesus." Joey was a wild card. A showboat. Reckless. He was naturally talented, but that also meant he wasn't hungry. He expected everything to come easily and—fortunately or unfortunately, depending on how you looked at it —it usually did.

"Between him, Kevin, and Michael, you've got your hands full. We need those boys at full capacity for the season. Keep a close eye on them. Help them stay out of trouble. I expect them to be fresh and eligible if we're going to have a winning season."

A winning season. Everything came down to a winning fucking season.

"I'll take care of it." I ended the call abruptly and tossed my phone beside me on the couch.

I stared at the black mirrored screen, contemplating what the hell I was going to do next. My entire life was imploding. On a sigh, I reached for my phone and dialed one of my best friends, Mitch, a long snapper from the last team I played for.

Thankfully, he picked up on the second ring. "Ready to come back already?"

I scoffed. "Fuck no. I'm living the easy life." I swallowed past the guilt at how easily the lie slipped out. "Just making sure you're not getting into trouble in the off-season."

"You know me; there's always trouble, baby!"

I laughed at his arrogance, and we fell into a comfortable rhythm of catching up. He asked about Penny and shared his concerns about signing with the Steelers.

"I don't know, man. Sometimes I think you got out right in time. First time I'm starting to feel old, you know?"

I hummed in agreement. Every year we played together we'd commiserate that the new players felt younger and hungrier. If you were lucky enough to keep playing beyond your late twenties, you were practically ancient.

"It's been an adjustment," I admitted. "Sometimes I think it was easier to show up, throw the ball, and go home. Now I've got an entire program riding on my shoulders."

"If anyone can handle it, it's you."

"Thanks, man. Listen, I should go. I just wanted to touch base before I called up my ineligibles and let them know I'd be riding their asses all summer."

Mitch chuckled. "Give 'em hell, Coach."

I ended the call and looked around the dirty old farmhouse and considered how the hell I was going to keep three more kids out of trouble for the summer and ready to play ball.

Tiny particles of dust floated up when I sighed again.

Looks like I just found my cleaning crew.

I COULD SEE LARK PLAIN AS DAY, CREEPING ON US FROM the apartment's kitchen window that overlooked the driveway and main house. She may have thought she was stealthy, but my eye flicked to the upper level with every flutter of the thin, ruffled curtains.

I made quick work of unloading the car. Penny hauled her light-blue suitcase with flowers on it up the front porch steps and chatted away at Kevin, who stayed quiet and nodded at whatever she was rambling on about.

As we unloaded, I gestured the boys toward the house and silently hoped this summer wasn't the shit show it was lined up to be. Kevin, Michael, and Joey filed inside, and I couldn't help but notice when Lark bounded happily down the rickety steps of the old barn apartment. A flash of her stumbling on the steep, nearly rotted wood made my shoulders bunch. I'd have to find a way to fix the worst spots without her noticing.

Don't want her suing Tootie and all.

She was dressed for another run, and a prickle of awareness crept down my forearms. Her tight black leggings left zero room for imagination, and they hugged every one of her dangerous curves. My jaw flexed. Even her top rode high on her rib cage. It was hot enough today that she didn't bother with another hoodie. When Joey stopped dead in his tracks to take his own look, I clamped a hand on his shoulder and helped him forward with a light shove.

"Go on in."

Joey nodded and I followed behind him, though my eyes stayed glued to Lark the entire time she made her way to the small opening of the trailhead at the back of the property. My eyes scanned above the trees. We were headed into summer, but it was getting late, and the evening sun was already dipping over the tree line. I pushed down the small wave of worry and shook my head as I followed my unlikely foursome into the house.

Hopefully, the woman would keep her clothes on this time.

IT WAS TOO dark for Lark to still be out on her run.

Pickle and the boys had settled into their rooms by dumping their duffel bags in the middle of the floor. Penny would have the room closest to mine, and the boys had opted for sharing the finished loft on the top floor of the old farmhouse.

Little did they know, that damn loft squeaked and groaned with the lightest footsteps. There'd be no sneaking out and finding trouble if the thought dared to cross their minds. It was my job to keep them healthy and out of trouble for a few months so they wouldn't have the opportunity to throw away their careers before they even started, and I was taking it seriously—whether they liked it or not.

I wasn't such a hard-ass that I was keeping them under lock and key, but unfortunately for them it also meant check-ins and curfews. Earlier tonight they had piled into Michael's beat-up car and headed into town. Knowing the tourist season hadn't ramped up quite yet, and without the influx of people keeping the businesses open, there was very little to do in Outtatowner. I was betting they'd be back in an hour. Two, tops.

When I stepped onto the porch, my eyes darted to the dark window of Lark's apartment, and worry settled in my neck. With Penny tucked in bed, I snagged a beer from the fridge and sat on the top step. My back leaned against the post, and I looked out across the yard toward the small opening in the trees that served as the trailhead.

If she wasn't home by the time the boys got back, I was going looking for her. The crushed limestone path was easy to follow during the day, but I had no clue what her navigational skills were, and the last thing I needed was for her to get lost or break her neck. The moon was full, but the canopy of the trees allowed very little light to shine through onto the trail.

I took a sip of my beer and tried to quell the overprotective, intrusive thoughts that crept up. Normally those nagged me only when Penny was away or she was going somewhere new without me.

I'll just drown them out with a beer.

When it wasn't doing the trick, I set the bottle aside. As I was about to stand, the sound of an off-key rendition of "Neon Moon" floated across the yard. I squinted and tried to see through the thick darkness.

The song coursed through me, and a hazy, distant memory of bouncing in the front seat of my father's beat-up old truck flooded my brain. I'd loved riding shotgun in

Dad's old Ford. He'd pop in a cassette of George Strait or Tim McGraw or Brooks & Dunn while I hung out the window and made an airplane of my arms.

The memory was like a bruise, and I swept it aside as soon as the chartreuse yellow of Lark's tennis shoes contrasted against the dark grass. She was hauling ass across the yard, still singing.

Loudly.

I settled back into my darkened spot, watching her as she crossed the grass and stopped on the gravel between the barn and the house.

She huffed out a deep sigh and bent at the waist to catch her breath.

I grunted in frustration. "Kind of dark for a walk." I internally flinched at my own words, sounding like more of a prick than I'd meant to.

Lark's startled scream rang through the night air, and she jumped back and clutched her chest.

"Whoa. Sorry." I lifted my hand. "It's me. Wyatt."

Real smooth.

"Shit. Hey." Lark was breathless, and I forced myself to stay focused on her face and not the way her shirt stretched across her chest with every breath.

"What are you doing out here?"

Lark exhaled an audible huff. "I could ask you the same thing. Isn't it past your bedtime?"

My jaw ticced at her ribbing. "Just wanted to be alone."

She looked at me but stayed silent. I hated that with her my default mode seemed to be permanently stuck on *dickbag*, and I couldn't quite figure out why. Especially considering I was spending far too much time thinking about how the fading light turned her hazel eyes a rich shade of moss and cedar.

I cleared my throat and tried again. "I was enjoying a peaceful country night until Brooks & Dunn crashed the party."

Even in the dim lighting I could see her shy smile as she brushed a piece of rich brown hair away from her face. I wanted to reach out and feel the softness of the strands through my fingertips. I flexed my fingers instead.

"Oh. Yeah." She laughed. "I sort of misjudged the sunset and spent the last twenty minutes walking in the dark. To keep myself from totally freaking out, I cranked my headphones up as loud as they could go and sang at the top of my lungs. I thought it might scare away any creatures that might mess with me."

"Well, what you're doing is scaring away the neighbors."

"We have neighbors?" Lark looked around as if she'd missed a house or something. We were coated in darkness.

I huffed a laugh and took the last swig of my beer. "Just you."

The barn also loomed in the shadows, and Lark looked at the darkened stairs.

I need to change that light bulb too.

I was about to go back to my solitude when she surprised the hell out of me.

"Got any more of those?"

I gestured with my empty bottle. "A beer?"

"Yeah. It's hot. I worked up a thirst."

Her words hung in the air. I was sure she didn't mean anything by them, but my body had all kinds of devious thoughts about how we might work up a thirst together. In my younger, wilder days, I could've had her in my lap in less than half a beer.

"I've got an extra." I unfolded myself and went inside as Lark waited. I slipped through the front door and

tossed my empty bottle in the recycling with a loud clank
—*Shit*.

I went stiff as I listened for Penny. The house was silent,
so I pulled open the refrigerator door. On our way back
from getting the boys, we'd stopped at the small local
grocery store and picked up a few supplies. The six-pack
was an impulse buy, but now that Lark was waiting just
outside my doorway, I was half-glad I'd snagged it.

Before heading back outside, I held both bottles in one
hand and paused at the end of the hallway and listened
again. No stirring from the back of the house. I ran a hand
through my hair, hoping it wasn't a total mess before
scolding myself.

Who gives a shit what your hair looks like?

I reminded myself that Lark wasn't a woman I was chasing. She was a friend of Tootie's—no, not even that. An
employee. She was also bold and unpredictable. Too cheer-
ful. A nuisance.

Nodding at myself for thinking clearly and not making
decisions with my dick, I headed toward the front door. The
last thing I needed was drama with a woman when I was
barely keeping this ship upright as it was.

Even if in the short time I'd known her, Lark had
somehow come to occupy every waking thought—and that
was a problem.

Even if she was the most gorgeous woman I'd ever laid
eyes on and even considering the fact I knew firsthand she
was just as gorgeous underneath her clothing, which nearly
killed me.

The image of Lark rising up out of Wabash Lake, water
running down her back, had made for an interesting
shower when I'd jerked off to the thought of her and tried
to finish as quickly—and quietly—as possible. Staying here

with Penny and the boys made me feel like a teenager again.

When I stepped onto the porch, Lark was sitting on the top step, opposite of where I'd been posted up.

"Man, it is *dark* around here."

"Yep." I handed a bottle of beer to her, and when she used the hem of her shirt to pop open the top and take a healthy swig, I almost smiled.

"Mmm." Her throaty moan wasn't doing me any favors. "Thank you." She turned the label around and laughed as she read it. "Beer Thirty—*Any time is the right time.*"

"It was all they had."

"Is that a mountain with an arm sticking out of it . . . holding a beer?"

"Yep."

Her laughter floated over me, and in the safety of near darkness, I let it soak into me. She looked out into the yard and then over the old front porch of the farmhouse with a small, satisfied smile. "Looks like you're running a full house over here. I'm sure it's a comfort to have family around all the time."

I grunted in response. "You'd be surprised. I have no idea what I'm doing with these kids. This is the first quiet moment I've had all day."

Lark's eyes crinkled as she smiled at me. "Well then, cheers—to quiet."

I only shrugged in response, but she happily clanked her bottle to mine as I sat across from her on the porch steps. For a long stretch, neither of us spoke, but instead listened to the sounds of a dark country night.

"Do you feel it?" Lark whispered. When I only looked at her, she continued. "Alone? Sometimes I think I have a knack for that . . . feeling alone even in a crowded room, right next to someone." She hid the sad words with a bright smile, but it was her eyes that gave her away.

I shifted and draped my arms on my knees. Sitting with her, I didn't feel alone. In fact, I liked that even a few feet from Lark, my situation with the boys or juggling work and caring for Penny didn't seem quite so insurmountable. I felt eerily calm in her presence, and it made my throat itch.

Maybe it was the Beer Thirty.

"With a family like mine, in a town like this? I'm never alone."

She hummed in response, closed her eyes, and tipped her face toward the starry sky.

I ignored the hunger that gnawed my gut at the glorious sight of her, carefree and completely content.

It struck me that I wasn't alone, but there were times I did feel *lonely*. I was used to loneliness. Lived with it and came to peace with the fact that solitude was meant for me.

My garbled throat clearing caught her attention, and she peeked open one eye at me.

"Also," I started, unsure of how to say this to her. "If you're going to be around, I should let you know that Penny knows we—I, um. That I saw you naked."

She sputtered and both eyes flew open. "You told her?"

"No. Sort of. Not really." I sighed in defeat. It was best to just get it all out there. "Listen. I was relaying the story to Lee, and she overheard."

"So you told your brother?" She didn't seem mad. More . . . interested, maybe.

I tried to hide my smile and shrugged. "I left out the good parts. But Penny has no filter, so I wouldn't be surprised if it came up."

"Noted." Lark's bubbling laugh had heat coiling beneath my ribs.

I liked it. *A lot.*

"She seems like a good kid."

"The best," I agreed, and Lark smiled at me. When she shivered, my eyes flew to the cropped shirt she was wearing. Her nipples still strained against the thin fabric, and I nearly groaned. I took another swallow of beer instead and looked out over the lawn.

I shrugged out of the flannel I'd been wearing and tossed it over her knees.

She didn't protest, but a small smile played on her lips. Her eyes caught mine as she slipped her arms into my shirt.

I cleared my throat and changed the subject. We spent the next few minutes talking about everything and nothing. Lark was sunny. Carefree and a wanderer. She told me the roundabout way she'd stumbled into becoming a professional mourner, and it was so simple it seemed almost logical.

Almost.

For a moment, the stress of single parenthood, coaching, my players, the team, my family . . . it all just melted away. Lark laughed, a lot. She found humor and delight in almost everything. I couldn't remember a time when I didn't feel the pressure of my family or my team counting on me. Being a leader and the responsibility that came with it landed squarely on my shoulders, and I had been proud to bear the burden. It was only lately that it had started to feel like the weight was more and more unmanageable.

But Lark was wholly unburdened. Effervescent, if not a little bit flighty.

She talked openly and answered my questions, unfazed when I skated over thinly veiled questions about Penny and her mom. That was too close. Too personal. Besides, I liked listening to her talk and to the musical quality of her voice when she told a story she thought was funny.

She was also touchy. Sometimes, when she'd lean forward and laugh, her fingertips would graze over my knee, or she would gesture wildly with her hands, and I imagined capturing one midair and hauling her onto my lap just to hear her surprised little squeak.

Sitting this close to her was a mistake. I was a wreck. Two sides of me at war with each other—one that knew, bone deep, the only way to maintain control was to never be vulnerable. And the other . . . the tiny, hidden side that wanted to lean in, open up to her in a way that was completely foreign and uncomfortable for me.

Lark took a drink from her beer, and I watched, in slow motion, as the condensation from the bottle dripped down and landed on her knee. When her throat worked up and down, all I could think about was planting my mouth there, feeling her heartbeat hammer under my lips for long, delicious moments.

I wanted to feel, not just hear, the moans I could drag out of her.

Our conversation faded away, and the night sounds blanketed us as we sat. Staring.

"It's getting late." My voice was gravelly and hard. Under different circumstances those words might have been an invitation, but not tonight. I had responsibilities. I flexed my jaw to try to work out some of the tension.

Lark leaned back against the post, peering around it at the starry night sky again. I took the opportunity to let my gaze wander over the tops of her breasts. Lower still to her rib cage and to where her small waist nipped in before flaring out to her hips. Her leggings did nothing to hide the fact that she was all woman under there.

Jesus Christ, is she not wearing underwear?

The singular thought ran on a loop in my head as I tried to ignore the faintest outline of her pussy beneath the thin material between her toned thighs.

Her eyes moved back to me, dancing with mischief, as always. She shrugged. "It's not that late."

My skin tingled. I recognized the sultry, low dip of a woman's voice when she was not quite ready to call it a night. Hell, if she was offering, I'd happily toss her around and show her just how worn out we could make each other.

But I wasn't that man anymore, was I? Life wasn't as easy as a quick fuck to get it out of your system, and something about Lark told me that she was sticky. The kind of woman who stayed with you long after you left, like a cattle brand.

I didn't need that kind of complication messing with my head. I had a daughter and a team to focus on. I could handle it on my own. But I also couldn't halt dark thoughts of Lark pinned under me. I rose and peered down at her.

Fuck it.

"Inside." I tipped my head toward the front door. An invitation that sounded much more like a demand.

She didn't wither under my frown but rather drained the last of her beer, stood, and held the bottle out for me, just out of my reach.

The amber glass dangled at the end of her fingertips. When I reached forward to take it, I let my fingertips drag along the backs of her fingers. Long and smooth. I ached for more.

Lark sucked her full bottom lip into her mouth, her teeth pressing into that supple flesh, and her eyes raked over the door. If she stepped through it, it was game over. She was *mine*.

Her tongue slicked over her bottom lip as she stood. One step forward and she was in my space, her scent of soft cinnamon and citrus moving over me and filling my lungs.

Lark rose on her tiptoes as my face tipped down to hers, ready to capture her lips in mine. My hands gripped her hips.

"Good night." She let out a soft breath through her nose and smiled. Our breaths mingled. The smallest sliver of space separated our mouths, and if she closed that distance, I'd be all over her in a heartbeat.

Instead, Lark turned and bounced down the porch steps. When she reached the bottom, she twirled before smiling up at me.

Her arms wrapped around the flannel I'd given her as she hugged herself against the cool summer breeze.

A grin spread across her gorgeous face. "I'm keeping the shirt, Oscar."

I watched her walk away. *She turned me down.*

I should have been disappointed. Instead, I let my laughter erupt from my gut and watched in fascination as my sunny, alluring neighbor disappeared into the apartment above the rickety old barn.

I rubbed the achy little spot that bloomed in the center of my chest, protesting her absence, before I scooped up the bottles and headed inside.

Goddamn, something in me wanted Lark Butler to be mine.

THAT NIGHT I HAD A FITFUL NIGHT'S SLEEP WHERE I imagined how differently things would have gone had I accepted Wyatt's invitation. The dangerous rumble of his voice when he ground out *"Inside"* still sent a shiver through me.

Stupid. Stupid, Lark.

I stepped out of Bluebird Books and into the afternoon sunlight. Of all the places I'd traveled, none had been quite as picturesque as Outtatowner. I breathed in the warm, humid air and tipped my face to the sun.

Who would have thought?

After stopping at my car, I slung the small bag with my bikini, a cover-up, and a towel over my shoulder. I ditched my shoes and socks. A lazy afternoon on the beach was calling me.

In the short time I'd been there, more and more tourists had descended on the small town every day. Happy families and groups of teenagers walked along the sidewalk that passed the marina, cafés, and other little shops that led down to the water. I dipped into the small building that served as a restroom and concession stand, the Sand Dollar, to peel off my jean shorts and tank top.

My bikini was cute, with a bright-yellow top that wrapped around my boobs and made them look bigger than they actually were. It dipped low in the back, and the ties crisscrossed into a big loopy bow. The bottoms were my favorite part—a navy background with lemons and leaves gave off the perfect, happy summer vibes. The high sides and ties at my hips, combined with the peekaboo cut in back, was sexy without revealing my *whole* ass. It also packed well, and I could dig it out of a suitcase and throw it on whenever I pulled up to a beach town.

Over the top, I threw on a knitted cover-up that was more like a giant long-sleeved shirt. The large boho knit allowed a breeze to float through and also didn't give me weird tan lines. I'd forgotten flip-flops, so when I cut across the full parking lot, I had to run on tiptoe to keep the bottoms of my feet from burning.

It was no surprise that on such a gorgeous day the beach was packed with people, even though it was only midweek. I wove between coolers and large umbrellas and little kids building sand castles and digging moats. When I smiled at a little blond-haired boy, he gave me a sandy, gap-toothed grin, and I felt lighter than I had in days.

My toes dipped into the cool Lake Michigan water, and I exhaled. My stress melted away, and I let the waves lap over my feet. For a moment, it felt like summer and its endless possibilities were just beginning. To the right was a long concrete pier with a lighthouse on the end. On the other side, as far as I could see, the beach stretched on and on. Rocky outcroppings jutted into the water where the land refused to be taken by the vast Great Lake. Behind me, massive sand dunes loomed overhead. Hundreds of feet above the water, it was like nothing I had ever seen. I walked around one of the fallen trees that dotted the shoreline. Its massive roots jutted into the air, water and time having stripped it of bark and leaves and life. The waves from the lake had cut into the earth in places, and with a brush of my hand, sand trickled down and fell to become a part of the beach.

I could come back in a year and I bet nothing would be the same.

It was amazing how much time changed things—even those things, like earth itself, that seemed so constant.

On top of the dunes people walked through the tall grasses, exploring and looking out over the beach from above. Older kids were running, arms and legs flailing, down the huge sand piles and splashing into the water below with roaring laughter.

I made my way up toward the dunes and found a small worn-down footpath that climbed up, up, up, to the top of one of the dunes. My calves burned, and my toes dug into the soft, shifting sand.

Holy crap. I need to work out more.

I bent at the waist to catch my breath and calm my overexerted heart. The roots of the wispy beach grass stuck up in places, poking my feet, and the sun heated the sand. It was a wonder anything could grow where there seemed to be so little nutrients in the arid sand itself. Finally, at the top of the dune, I looked out onto Lake Michigan.

It was breathtaking.

The water stretched out forever, disappearing into the horizon. People below me were nothing more than little ants, dancing and moving around the beach. From that vantage point, I could see that the main strip of beach was packed tightly with families and umbrellas and volleyball games, but farther down, it was far less crowded. In the distance, large buildings that looked to be condos or *really* expensive vacation homes dotted the shoreline. Between the two, there were quiet stretches of beachfront that seemed cocooned from the chaos of the public beach area.

Intrigued, I headed in that direction, searching for a way to return to the shoreline. I smiled at a couple hiking and stopped to watch more kids hurl themselves down the dunes. They laughed and jeered at each other as one by one they raced down the steep slope.

No. Freaking. Way.

When I'd gotten to the quieter section of beach, there wasn't a clear way to make it down to the water. Much farther along a set of wooden stairs zigzagged down the dune, but it appeared to be private property, and the last thing I needed was to get into trouble when I was so new in town.

I peered over the edge of what felt like a gigantic cliff. I tested my footing with a little bounce. If I could just get down to the water, I could explore a little and then walk my way back up the beach toward town. I searched a little more until I found where the sand dune wasn't quite so steep. It seemed stable enough, so with a final deep breath, I carefully stepped down.

The sand was dryer and more like quicksand than I anticipated.

"Shit!" I plopped to my butt and inelegantly slid part of the way down the dune. My bag bounced behind me as I tried my best to not face-plant. It slipped from my shoulder and careened off the dune, landing below me with a plop. Finally, my heels dug into the moving sand and slowed me to a stop about two-thirds of the way down the dune.

Embarrassed, I looked around to see if anyone had seen

me make a fool of myself, and—thankfully—no one was nearby. I caught my breath and looked for a safer way to get to the beach. Preferably one that didn't include breaking my neck. I could always walk up the beach and retrieve my bag.

I tried to stand, but the earth shifted below me.

Well, shit.

Going back up wasn't an option, and straight below me was a harsh drop-off that would certainly end in a broken leg or two.

I hugged my knees and clutched the grass, trying to figure out how to get myself out of yet another mess I'd thrown myself into. From around a fallen tree, voices floated up. I ducked behind the tall grasses.

Clambering over the trunk of the tree, little Penny came into view. My heartbeat ticked faster as I looked for her dad.

Then I heard his deep, commanding voice before I saw him. "Just be careful, Pickle."

I hid lower, praying they would just walk by and I wouldn't have to admit that I'd gotten myself stranded on the side of a sand dune that was determined to kill me.

Wyatt had on dark sunglasses and a pair of swim trunks that did nothing to hide his ridiculous body. His languid movements came into view, and my breath hitched. His hair was tousled and lifted in the breeze. He was so much more than *cute*—he was absolutely, ridiculously gorgeous. His brother Lee walked beside him, and the pretty redhead from the book club—Annie, I remembered—bent to look at something Penny had found in the sand.

My thighs burned from crouching, and the heat from the sand was starting to become unbearable.

"Please keep walking. Just leave," I whispered to myself. It was a quiet stretch of beach, but I hoped none of them would spot my bag or look up and see my helpless and stupid self, clinging to dear life on the grass.

I'd rather die.

The group moved closer and I closed my eyes. Maybe if I pretended to be invisible, they'd just keep walking and I could succumb to my death in peace.

"Planning to stay up there all day?"

My eyes opened to see Wyatt directly below me, his hands on his hips and a frown across his stupid face. He looked like a cranky dad—Penny's incredibly hot, cranky dad, actually.

"I'm fine." The fake cheeriness I tried to infuse in my voice sounded crazed in my ears.

"Looks to me like you're fucked."

I adjusted my feet, and more sand trickled over the cliff. Wyatt sidestepped the curtain of debris that fell and let loose a heavy, annoyed sigh.

He held up his arms. "Come on."

"What?" I stared down at him as I clutched the grasses that were the only things keeping me from falling off the dune.

Wyatt flicked his wrist. "I said come on. I'll catch you."

I shook my head. "No way."

He lifted a shoulder. "Fine. Break a leg. Just don't come hobbling over for help or you'll scare my kid." He turned away.

"Stop!" More sand shifted below me, and panic started to set in. "Okay, fine. Please."

He turned, and a ghost of a smirk crossed his face. "Come on then."

I stared down at him. If I continued forward, Wyatt could reach up and pull me down, but my boobs would be right in his face. If I turned around, he would get a face full of my ass. Indecision gnawed at me.

"What are you waiting for?"

I looked around and noticed we'd caught the attention of Lee, Annie, and Penny, who were now watching the whole scene play out.

Of fucking course we did.

"Give me a minute!" I tried to adjust my grip on the grass, and a small squeak escaped me.

"What are you doing? Just come down."

I swallowed hard. The firm line of his lips was making my insides all gooey, and I couldn't get the image of his large hands wrapping around me out of my stupid head. "Boobs or butt?"

"What?"

"You're about to get a face full of something. There is no graceful way to maneuver this so . . . boobs or butt?"

This time he was grinning right at me. "Well, I am kind of an ass man."

I rolled my eyes. Wyatt was definitely enjoying my discomfort and the fact that I had, yet again, made a fool of myself.

Still gripping the sand and grass, I inelegantly rolled onto my belly. "You are the worst."

He chuckled softly. "I know. Just shimmy down here."

I shot him a glare over my shoulder and faced the sand. My eyes squeezed shut. "Please don't drop me."

"I got you, Lark. I promise." The confidence in his voice was comforting. I believed Wyatt wouldn't let me fall.

I wiggled my hips and started to lower myself. My cover-up rode high as I moved down, and my legs began to dangle over the cliff.

"Where are you? I don't feel you!" I wiggled my foot

and it connected with the side of his face and nose. "Shit! Sorry!"

Wyatt spit, unaffected. "You're fine. Keep going. You're almost there." His hands connected with my calves, and warmth spread through me.

Higher and higher his hands smoothed over my legs. In any other circumstance it would have been delightfully sinful. When his palms reached my hips, he gripped me tightly, fingers digging into me. Sure enough, my butt was inches from his face. His strong arms took over, and when I let go of the grass and sand, he lifted me effortlessly until I was planted on the ground.

I closed my eyes and steadied my breath, thankful to be on solid ground again. Wyatt's large frame hadn't moved and was still enclosing me between him and the dune.

A hand ran down my back. "See? You're fine."

I could barely breathe. I turned and had to practically tip backward to look him in the eyes. In the reflection of his sunglasses, I could see how owl eyed and breathless I looked.

"Thank you." My hands rested on his forearms.

I stared up at him, and everything around us fell away. The air stuck in my lungs. For a moment I forgot where we were, what day it was, and that we had an audience. Somehow his hands were back on my hips.

Wyatt's chin tipped down. I glanced at his lips as they tipped up in a smile.

"Dad, you're a hero!"

My toes curled into the solid ground.

I stepped away as Penny ran up and hugged her dad from the back, shoving him a step forward.

"Yeah, a knight in Coppertone armor." Lee smirked in our direction and crossed his arms.

Annie joined us, and I took two more steps away from the group of Sullivans, who were looking at me like I'd lost my mind.

"Okay. Thanks. Sorry about that." I ran my hands through my hair and brushed the thick layer of sand off my stomach and thighs.

What an epic disaster.

"Hey, Lark," Annie called out. "Let's do lunch sometime, okay?"

I raised my hand and nodded as I hurried away. "Yep, lunch sounds great. Bye!"

Wyatt was still staring at me as Penny kicked at the waves with laughter and Lee and Annie talked and meandered along the beach.

I knew he was still staring even as I made my inelegant exit—I felt his heated gaze on my back the entire walk up the beach.

Why did I like that so much?

I REALLY SHOULD HAVE KISSED WYATT.

I *wanted* to kiss him that night on the porch. Something about his rough, grumpy exterior was working for me. *Really working*, and in that moment I had wanted nothing more than to wrap my legs around him and let him *devour me*. Maybe it was the way he always seemed a little lighter around his adorable daughter. Or the way he was looking after three unruly college football players. Or the fact that despite being back in his hometown, he seemed really, *really* lonely. His broad shoulders and chiseled jaw certainly didn't put any marks in the *This Is a Terrible Idea* column.

I groaned inwardly. I definitely should have kissed him.

"Hey, can you clear that table over there?"

Torn from my thoughts, I gave Sylvie a shy smile. "On it."

Tootie had called in a favor and gotten me a summer job at the Sugar Bowl, and so far it was . . . not great. They didn't really need me. It was a pity hire. I knew it, and they knew it.

Sylvie worked behind the register and seemed to run

the bakery as kind of a general manager, while Huck Benton, the burly owner and baker, mostly kept to himself in the back. Huck had nodded a brusque greeting and disappeared into the kitchen.

I smiled, remembering how I'd met his fiancée my first day in Outtatowner. The way they'd looked at each other was the sweetest thing, and a little pang of envy pinched beneath my ribs. Sylvie had already started rambling on about the bakery's daily specials and attempted a quick rundown on how to use the commercial coffee maker.

A barista, I was not.

I quickly learned that the machine wasn't nearly as simple as a Keurig, and between pumps of mocha, shots of espresso, and steamed milk flying everywhere, I was quickly relegated to table-busing duty.

Sylvie was kind and patient but also annoyed, so I quietly slipped the barista apron from around my neck and picked up a rag.

I piled up small plates, cups, and saucers as I maneuvered through the crowded bakery.

The Sugar Bowl was a gathering place for many Outtatowner locals. Overhearing conversations about the rapidly approaching "busy season" and plans for the influx of tourists was fascinating. Several times I got caught up in the conversations, pausing to listen in with a smile on my face until scrunched noses and curious looks broke me from my wandering ears. I offered a polite smile but kept moving.

But I couldn't help it. The town was intriguing. Many people had wacky nicknames, and it made my head spin trying to keep everyone straight.

Bowlegs's twin brother came in, and someone bought him a black coffee and a chocolate chip muffin. He joined the small group of old men, and despite the fact he wore a trapper hat and was missing several teeth, no one batted an eye or made it seem at all uncommon.

From the few conversations I could catch in passing, Bowlegs and his brother were neither Sullivans nor Kings— among the few people who managed to straddle the line. The local bar, the Grudge Holder, was open to everyone. Huck's bakery was also one of only three businesses that also refused to pick sides. Sylvie was a King, and I didn't miss how she'd subtly slip into the back whenever too many Sullivans came around. With the patrons inside, there was also a visible divide between Kings, Sullivans, and tourists, if you knew to look for it.

The tinkling of the bell on the door was constant, and I was already sweating before 10:00 a.m. I had placed the last pile of dishes from a high-top table into my arms and swiveled to carry them to the back when I crashed into the back of an older woman waiting in line.

"My goodness!" the woman shouted.

Startled, the dishes slipped from my arms and crashed to the floor. The commotion drew every eye in the bakery as I sank to my knees and frantically tried to clean the broken plates and spilled coffee.

Heat burned my cheeks. "Crap! I am so sorry. I'm sorry."

Sylvie knelt beside me with a large plastic tub and a rag to help gather the mess.

"I'm sorry, Sylvie. I didn't see her."

"It's okay." Her kind smile eased the sharp edge of my nerves, and Sylvie glanced up at the woman. "Your order is on the house today, Ms. Tiny."

"Thank you." Her nose tipped up at Sylvie, but then she added, "I suppose accidents do happen." The woman named Tiny smiled at me, and I finally exhaled.

I leaned closer to Sylvie. "Thank you. Really, I am sorry."

Sylvie winked at me as she discarded the last shards of a broken cup. She leaned in closer to whisper. "Just be glad it wasn't me who knocked into her. Ms. Tiny can be a bit of a bear, but since you're a Sullivan, she's willing to overlook it."

My cheeks flamed again at being lumped in with the Sullivans. Part of me really liked that. Being claimed by a tribe of fiercely loyal family members.

"I'm not really anyone's, I guess."

Sylvie's shoulder pushed against mine. "Well, don't tell her that."

We both got to our feet and moved toward the kitchen. I grabbed the square bucket from her. "I'll take care of this. Thanks for your help."

"Hey—not that side!"

Just as I pushed through the swinging doors to the back kitchen, I crashed into Huck and the tray of pastries he was carrying.

Muffins went tumbling.

Scones flying.

My eyes were huge as I looked into his deep frown, and a thick well of emotions clogged in my throat.

Weren't out-of-work actresses supposed to be good servers? How am I so bad at this?

I pouted, defeated, and as I lifted my face to the ceiling, I shouted, "I just want to be a cliché!"

Huck's deep, rumbling laughter was unexpected but broke me from feeling completely sorry for myself. His gentle hand landed on my shoulder.

"Trust me, I wish you were too. How does dishwashing sound?"

I couldn't help but laugh—at his kind response along with how epically tragic and short lived my first day was. I was fired for sure.

"Just lock me up back here. Maybe people will be safer."

He shook his head. "At the very least, the scones will be."

Surprisingly, Huck didn't fire me.

Instead, he offered to let me stay on and do the work no one else liked to do—dishwashing, general cleanup, and organizing in the back. After years of temp work I could slide in to organize, clean, and thoughtfully do whatever tasks were handed to me, apart from waitressing, obviously.

As it turned out, Huck was a *very* messy baker, and he and Sylvie went round and round about the disasters he left in the back kitchen. The thought of returning to the Sugar Bowl for another humiliating day of *Let's See What Else Lark Is Bad At* felt daunting, but Huck assured me that my tenacity for tackling his disastrous pantry was enough to keep me around.

I had spent the afternoon organizing every shelf and ingredient by expiration and how often it was used. I'd even started a spreadsheet to track what ingredients would need to be ordered. I had plans for labels. So many labels. By the time my shift ended, I was tired and covered in flour, not to mention that there was something sticky under my shoe.

As I crossed the street and headed to my car, I maneuvered past a set of very long legs, which a man had stretched from a bench onto the sidewalk.

As I wound around him, I heard him call out, "Staying a while, then?"

His words stopped me, and I looked up. *A King.*

I recognized the man from Bowlegs's funeral—the

intense one with all the tattoos. I looked around, making sure he was speaking with me, and when no one else seemed to pause at his words, I nodded.

Am I supposed to be talking to him? Is a Sullivan spy going to be around the corner and sic Ms. Tiny on me?

It was odd, feeling as though my loyalties were squarely in Sullivan territory, and talking on the open sidewalk with a King felt brazen, wrong almost. When I looked up, he was sitting just outside of a shop, King Tattoo. His tattoos covered both arms and trailed from his biceps down to the tops of his hands. His sharp features were fierce, and a shot of worry danced through me as my thoughts immediately flew to Wyatt.

"Um," I attempted an answer with a smile pasted in place. "I'm new in town, I guess. Enjoying a coastal summer."

His eyes roamed over me in a lazy, confident way. I was sure women fell *hard* for that all-encompassing, attentive stare.

"Friday nights are a good time 'round here. Maybe I'll see you out and you can save me a dance."

I laughed politely. "Yeah, maybe." *Maybe not.*

I scooted around his legs and picked up my pace toward my car. Something in my gut told me that messing with a King, even for a newcomer, was a very bad idea.

~

"HI, MS. LARK!"

I squinted against the sun as I looked across the driveway at Wyatt's farmhouse. Penny's face was squished against the mesh on the screen door.

I called back to her from my open kitchen window. "Hey, Penny! What are you up to?"

"Dying of boredom."

I chuckled at her sullen, squished-up face.

"Pickle, stop bothering the neighbor." The deep rumble of Wyatt's voice floated up to me.

With a smile, I left the apartment and took the stairs down. "It's no bother," I called out.

Penny burst through the door. "See! She's not busy! Do you want to play? Dad told me you were busy, but you're not." She gestured toward me.

I laughed and spread my hands. "Nope. Not busy."

"Perfect! We can do cartwheels or draw or go for a walk. We can't watch a movie, because Dad has to look at *boring* football videos."

"Pickle." Wyatt pushed through the screen door and stepped onto the covered porch as I stifled a smile. "Leave her be."

My tongue felt thick as I took in Wyatt, barefoot in jeans and a T-shirt.

Penny's shoulders fell. "I thought you said we were going to have fun."

My heart went out to her, and I scrunched my nose. "Football videos don't sound like much fun."

Wyatt's lips pressed together in a firm line as he nodded in defeat. "It's work."

"How about a walk? I can take her around the trail and give you a little time to work. Would that be okay?"

Penny lit up at my suggestion as Wyatt looked me over. Under his assessing gaze, I held my chin high and hoped my smile didn't falter. I loved kids, and Penny was hilarious.

"Please, Daddy! Please please please please."

"You're sure it's not interrupting anything?"

Penny's fist shot in the air when she knew she'd worn her poor dad down.

"I have all the time in the world. We'll have a great time." I held out my hand to Penny as she leaped off the porch stairs to stand at my side.

I had turned to walk away when Wyatt's grumpy voice rang out. "Be back before dark."

A shot of laughter erupted from me as I turned to salute him before leaning down and giggling with Penny. "Yes, boss."

～

BY FRIDAY NIGHT, curiosity got the best of me, and I decided to explore the nightlife in Outtatowner. During my first few days, I'd managed to keep my head down at the bakery, stay in the back, and try not to break any more dishes.

I was mostly successful.

As the days lurched on, more and more tourists had filtered into town, and I could see the shift from lazy days to the controlled chaos of the full-blown tourist season.

The Grudge Holder turned out to be the local Outta-towner bar and dance hall on the far edge of the main strip of roadway. Music pumped from the speakers, and signs outside boasted SUMMER SPECIALS and bands that were scheduled all summer long.

In my travels, I found that random townie bars were ripe for people watching and picking up quirky mannerisms I could use on my next gig. It also gave me something to do other than not-so-casually stalk my kitchen window to see if I could catch a glimpse of Wyatt across the driveway.

By 8:00 p.m., the band was playing, the dance floor was

full, and happy cheers of encouragement filled the neon-drenched space. I sat back, enjoying the view from a stool at the main bar. The band played a mix of rock-and-roll classics along with a few country songs. I laughed aloud at a twangy version of Harry Styles, and it was good enough to almost get me to my feet.

I spotted Sylvie, and she offered a friendly wave but was deep in her conversation, so I settled on a high stool near the bar. When the bartender leaned over, I shouted above the music, "Do you have any Beer Thirty?"

The man shot me a confused look, so I just smiled and waved a hand in the air. "Whatever you have on draft is fine."

He nodded and stepped away.

"May I have this dance?" I turned toward the deep voice to my left.

My mouth popped open to find the guy from the sidewalk, dressed in jeans and a formfitting black shirt, extending his heavily tattooed arm. He smiled, and the edges of his eyes crinkled, making him much friendlier than he appeared. "I'm Royal."

My brain stuttered. "Royal? Royal . . . King. Your parents named you *Royal King*?"

He laughed and pulled his hand back, straightening to his full height.

"No, ma'am. They actually like me."

I couldn't help but laugh. He was charming in a direct, slightly aggressive kind of way.

"In a place like this, nicknames have a way of sticking."

"Ah." I smiled and took a sip of the beer that had appeared in front of me, but I didn't make the move of stepping down from my stool. "That's good news, then."

"If you stick around a while, maybe I'll let you in on my

real name." He winked and a weird sensation passed over my clammy skin. "So what do you say? One dance?"

I looked around the crowded dance floor, trying to find some excuse to politely refuse him, when from across the bar, I saw Wyatt Sullivan stomping across the beat-up hardwood with murder in his eyes.

Zero. Fucking. Chance.

My pulse hammered as I stalked across the dance floor toward Lark and Royal fucking King.

From the second she walked into the Grudge, I couldn't keep my eyes off her. She wore cutoff jean shorts that showed off her smooth, toned legs and casual high-top sneakers, but that wasn't what drew me in. It was *my* shirt. She wore my flannel, cropped short and tied in a knot. My blood ran hot for her, and a flash of her grin as she shot me down that night on the porch ran through my mind. I'd also jerked off a shameful number of times to the image of her perfect ass as it slid in front of my face when I'd rescued her from the dune.

Lark had come to the bar alone and seemed content to be a happy observer. She probably didn't realize it, but she'd positioned herself squarely on the east side of the bar—King territory.

I pictured her smiling down at my kid as they walked away together, and every cell in my body protested.

It wasn't until Royal sauntered up to her with his lazy

smirk that my blood began to boil. Lark was new in town. She didn't know that by being friends with us, she'd been claimed as a Sullivan.

Being a Sullivan meant that the generations-long feud drew distinct lines in the sand. It was more than the stupid pranks. Years of backhanded deals and a muddy history meant the Kings couldn't be trusted and Lark was ours.

I wasn't a caveman. I didn't intend to stomp over to them, pound my chest, and haul her over my shoulder. Though the thought of her perfect ass right next to my face again made my palm itch to smack it.

I dragged my hand down my face, and my feet started moving. *Jesus. What the hell am I doing?*

Before I could even come up with a plan, I'd inserted myself right in front of Royal and Lark. Lee and Duke were posted up right behind me, their arms crossed and legs planted wide. I smirked, knowing they'd have my back if this thing went south and we ended up brawling—*again*—in the middle of the Grudge.

"She's not interested."

Royal only tipped one eyebrow in my direction and dismissed me with a laugh. Lark slipped from her seat, but her small frame barely came to our shoulders. She was squarely in the middle of two grown men having a pissing contest.

"Hey, Wyatt. What's up?"

The muscles in my jaw worked, and I flexed my fist. I lifted my chin. "Oh, he knows what's up."

Lark sidestepped between us, and some of the fire in my gut died down. She couldn't be this close if things got physical. It wouldn't be safe. The Sullivans and the Kings had had hundreds of scuffles in the past, most ending with black eyes and sometimes a broken bone or two. I flexed my fist.

"Yeah, GB. What's up?" Royal tossed around my high school nickname like I gave a shit the town wasn't creative enough to come up with something other than *Golden Boy* after my football career took off.

I rolled my eyes and then squared my shoulders to him. "Lark is with us."

He only nodded his smug fucking face. "Is she? Seems she sat on our side. Maybe she's with us."

"You know I'm right here, right?" Lark was clearly annoyed that we were talking over the top of her head, acting like she wasn't standing right between us. The scowl on her face was almost cute, had I not been containing my simmering rage at Royal trying to claim Lark as a King.

The tension boiled up around us, crackling in the air as someone stood behind Royal to back him up. More eyes were drawn our way, and murmurs began to float through the bar crowd.

This was not going to end pretty.

Lark threw her hands in the air. "You know what? I'm out."

Shoving the both of us in the chest to push past, she sailed toward the front entrance. Watching her walk away let the wind out of my sails.

I lifted my chin at Royal. "Stay the fuck away from her."

Royal only scoffed and leaned against the bar, then signaled to the bartender for another drink. "She'll come running once she realizes she's caught the eye of a King."

Goddamn, I wanted to land my fist at his jaw. Just once.

Duke's hand clamped on my shoulder. "It's over. Let's go."

Duke and Lee steered me back toward the table where we'd been sitting. They both sat back down, but I remained standing, my eyes trained on the entrance to see if Lark would come back inside.

I owed her an apology for acting like a child fighting over a toy. She deserved better than that.

"That's a fucking shame." Lee shook his head before swiping his beer bottle off the table and taking a deep pull. "Would have been a fun little tussle."

Duke shook his head at our grinning little brother. "You're an idiot."

Lee's grin only widened. He was always ready and willing to back up a fight or end one—especially one with the Kings.

"So what was that about?" Duke asked, motioning toward the door.

I swiped my hand across my face. I glanced toward the entrance. Lark was long gone. "I gotta run. I need to check in on the guys, and Tootie'll be back early with Pickle in the morning."

Duke let his question hang in the air. He already knew the answer. Together we eyed the Kings from across the bar. They didn't seem to be watching us, so the likelihood of me getting jumped on my way out was slim.

Duke only nodded as I said my goodbyes and pushed out the front door of the bar.

The summer air had become stickier as the June temperatures climbed higher and higher. Even the lake breeze was still. I looked down both ways of the sidewalk, hoping to catch a glimpse of Lark before she disappeared into the night.

She was gone, but I knew where to find her.

I needed to explain myself. Apologize for being a dick and ruining her night out.

The drive home was quick, and the light was still on in

her apartment. I climbed the rickety stairs and made a mental note to get to work on fixing those before she broke an ankle.

I had raised my fist to knock when the door flew open.

Lark stood, hands on her hips and her eyebrows raised. "Can I help you?"

Jesus, she was stunning when she was pissed. I wasn't expecting that. My mouth was dry at the sight of her flushed cheeks and the wild look in her eyes.

I scrubbed my hand at the back of my neck. "I owe you an apology."

Lark's eyebrows pinched down, and she dropped her hands and sighed in defeat. "Oh. Well, that's no fun."

Confused, I just looked at her.

"I was ready for a good fight, but then you showed up"— Lark's hand flicked between us—"looking all sad and sorry. I can't fight with you now."

Lark crossed her arms and pouted. I couldn't help but laugh. That woman was ridiculous.

Charming.

Dangerous.

"Look, I don't know what got into me."

Sure I do. Royal was moving in on something that was mine, *and I didn't fucking like it.*

I cleared my throat and my errant, utterly ridiculous thoughts. "Royal can be a pain in the ass. He didn't need to bother you, but I didn't think about the fact that maybe you didn't mind him . . . you know, talking to you."

A slow smile played on her lips. "You were jealous."

I shot her a blank stare, hoping like hell she couldn't see right through me.

"Well." She sighed. "Come inside before someone drives by, accidentally looks my way, and throws you into a jealous rage." She liked to tease, and while I wasn't completely unhinged, the thought of Royal driving up to her apartment was enough to further sour my mood.

Shoulda hit him.

Lark moved from the doorway, and I glanced back at the house across the driveway. Through the living room windows, the dull glow from the television meant the guys were still up, probably watching some late-night show. After tonight, I didn't want to leave things awkward with Lark, so instead of doing the right thing—saying good night and walking away—I walked inside her little apartment.

It was like stepping back in time. Nothing had changed in the small space. There was even the old hunter-green recliner that Lee had lost his virginity in. I pointed to it. "Hey, Lark?"

She turned to look at me.

"Don't . . . sit in that chair."

Her eyebrows crept up her forehead before she laughed. "Ooo . . . kay."

Shaking her head, Lark walked to the fridge, and her face disappeared as she leaned inside. I had another perfect view of her ass as she bent over to reach for something. When she straightened, my eyes flew to the ceiling.

"No Beer Thirty, but I do have some day-old peanut butter cookies."

"Alice?" Alice made the best peanut butter cookies in Remington County.

"Big Barb, I think?" Lark shook her head. "I swear I can't keep up in this town."

I laughed. "It gets easier with time. But I'll warn you. Big Barb likes to smoke while she bakes, so sometimes you get a nice little ashy flavor baked right in."

Without breaking eye contact, Lark took two steps

toward the trash bin and tilted the plate, dropping the entire contents into the garbage. "Noted."

My laughter came free and easy. It was uncomfortable in my chest and sounded a little rusty, but it also had a strangely freeing feeling right behind it.

"You look far less grumpy when you laugh." She took one step forward. "The little crinkly lines around your eyes come out, and I find that *very* handsome."

Lark was in my space, breathing the same air, and my hands found her hips.

"That's called being old."

Her smile widened. "Debonair. Dapper. Weathered." She gave a little nod of approval with each word.

As her breath moved over me, I stopped thinking. I reached up, wrapped one hand around the back of her neck, and pulled her into me, crushing my lips to hers.

I swallowed the little shocked moan that pushed through her lips as I devoured her. Her mouth opened for me, and her back arched as I leaned into the kiss. Lark's arms wound around my neck, and one leg hitched up.

God, she tasted bright and amazing and altogether irresistible.

My hand found her bare thigh at my hip, and I squeezed. I ran my hand up the back, feeling the smooth skin of her curves as I poured myself into that kiss. I reached down, grabbed the back of both thighs, and pulled her into me as she wound her legs around my hips. My hands found her ass, grinding her against my cock as the denim of her jean shorts stretched. I stepped forward, pressing her against the countertop as my mouth moved over hers.

When her hand went back to steady herself, a glass toppled over, spreading water across the counter and soaking her shorts before rolling to a crash on the floor.

It broke apart, and I took a step back. "Fuck. I'm sorry."

Lark swiped a hand across her swollen lips before she hopped down. "No, it's fine." She pulled a kitchen towel from where it hung near the sink and dropped it on the water.

She looked around, a little shell-shocked. Then she swiped her hands at the back of her jeans while I bent down to scoop up the broken glass with the towel and soak up some of the water.

I shook out the glass into the garbage can as she quickly picked up the rest of the mess.

"I'm sorry," I said again.

She shook her head with a slightly dazed smile. "No, it's all right. Just a broken glass and a wet ass."

My chest rose and fell, and I couldn't seem to catch my breath. I needed to leave. If I didn't, I would be dangerously near to closing the space between us and putting my mouth on her again.

All over her.

"Good night, Lark." I quickly retreated from the shrinking apartment and barreled down the stairs.

I didn't have the balls to look back up at her before I stormed across the driveway and into the house. I only lifted a hand in greeting at the three boys playing a video game in the living room and closed myself behind my bedroom door.

What the hell was that? What was I thinking? As if I don't have enough on my plate.

I had no business acting like a jealous idiot at the Grudge and then making the situation a million times more awkward by mauling Lark in her own kitchen. To me, it had been clear that she wasn't interested in sex when I'd invited her inside my house and she turned me down.

I was pissed at myself for the total lapse in judgment.

What if I'd taken it too far? Was my plan just to rail her against the countertop with three college kids within shouting distance?

I ran my hand over my face. I needed to pull my shit together. I needed to focus. Get my head in the game.

Lark was only passing through, and I was doing everything in my power to plant some roots for Penny. That all hinged on a winning season for MMU, which meant the three kids currently vying for the FIFA World Cup in my living room were also my responsibility.

The cold shower did nothing to cool the blood coursing through my veins. So what if I convinced myself that jerking off to the way her trim little body fit against mine was better than the alternative. Lark Butler meant chaos and complications.

Trouble was, even after I came to the image of her body pressed beneath mine, I still couldn't shake her.

Something had to be done.

13

LARK

"That's Pammie and Buck." Annie sat across from me at the diner, discreetly pointing out patrons around the room. "And over there is Lefty, but we call her Aunt Sissy."

I smiled wide and shook my head. "And everyone just . . . calls them by their nicknames? Like it's their government name?"

Annie shrugged. "Of course. Honestly, I don't know the birth-given names of half the people in here." She laughed as if she only then realized how ridiculous that sounded.

"Unreal." I popped a french fry into my mouth and continued looking around the small café. "What about them?"

Annie followed my line of sight after I gestured toward a small booth in the back. "PawPaw Rabbit and Soapy." Annie's eyes lit up. "I *think* he sold soap at one time? Maybe? Oh! And on the left is Brother, but his real name is Terry."

"And once you get a nickname . . . ?"

Annie's face went serious. "Stuck with it. For better or worse." She smiled again and leaned in. "Do you know

Aunt Tootie was once married to a man named Bumper? Bumper. I found out a month ago his name is Jim. The whole time I'd run around as a kid asking, 'Where's Uncle Bumper?' No one even questioned it." She was on a roll now, and her eyes danced with amusement. "Oh! During county elections? We had to put people's nicknames on campaign signs"—she leaned forward to emphasize—"*but also on the ballots* because no one knows Itchy's real name."

Together we laughed, and it felt so easy, so natural, to share lunch and laughter with Annie.

How long has it been since I've had a friend? That I've spent long enough in one place to form a genuine friendship?

"Stick around long enough and you'll see." Annie winked in my direction.

A strange emotion was thick in my throat. *Would I be here long enough to see?*

"There's a book at the library if you really want to study up," she offered with a slight shrug as she went back to her lunch.

"A book?"

"Yep. Bug's worked there since the 1970s, and she keeps it up."

I considered it for a moment. "So what about you? How'd you get lucky and not have an unfortunate nickname?"

She pinned me with knowing eyes and leaned forward again. "My real name isn't Annie."

My grin widened. "Seriously?"

She raised one hand. "Honest truth. My name is Annette, but everyone took to calling me"—her nose scrunched—"Orphan Annie."

I made a face as we conspired and leaned in together over our sandwiches.

She gestured to her tumbling red curls. "They're not always the most creative nicknames. Once when we were kids, Lee started calling me Annette as an act of defiance, but only *Annie* stuck."

"So no one calls you Annette? But you're a successful, professional grown woman . . ." I couldn't believe it.

She shrugged, but her eyes stayed glued to her plate. "Mostly just Lee."

Her blue eyes then flicked to mine but then quickly darted away. There was *definitely* something there, but I didn't know how to ask without seeming nosy.

"I'm used to it now. But Kate? The boys' little sister? People call her Catfish Kate. Now *that* is unfortunate. It's no wonder she packed up and moved to Montana."

"Wow." I had no words.

We continued to chat about life in a coastal Michigan town, different acting jobs that led me here, and my mom's new life as a naked hippie. Becoming friends with Annie was simple. Easy and refreshing.

Annie popped a french fry into her mouth. "How're things with the new neighbor?"

I could feel color popping up on my cheeks. I rolled my eyes to try to downplay my attraction to Wyatt, but the way Annie smiled, I doubted I was fooling her. "He's fine. Moody."

She scoffed. "Yeah, that's Wyatt."

I leaned closer. "Seriously. Half the time I think he hates me; the other half of the time I think he wants to tear my clothes off, and the rest of the time I don't know what to think."

"That math doesn't add up," she quipped.

"Exactly! This morning I waved to him, and he made a face and *ignored me.*"

I shook my head, and when I looked at the clock, I was sad to see it was almost time for my shift at the Sugar Bowl. I let out an aggravated groan. "I need to get going. Huck will be pissed if I'm late *and* a disaster."

Annie nodded. "You gonna eat that?" She pointed at my last few fries. I smiled and pushed the plate toward her.

Maybe sticking around Outtatowner wouldn't be so bad after all.

~

"PLEASE GO DOWN. Please. *Please* go down . . ." I watched in horror as the water level in one of the steel kitchen sinks rose higher. Dangerously higher.

"No, no, no, no." I frantically looked around, trying to figure out what to do. Huck was going to murder me if I clogged his sink again *and* got water all over the floor.

I kicked the support leg of the sink. A sad, burbling groan moved up to the surface as a lone bubble popped.

Fuck!

I looked at the swinging doors that separated the kitchen, Huck's haven, from the busy bakery service area. It was only a matter of time before he came back from stocking the display case and I was busted.

The water level steadily rose. "No, no. Where are you even coming from?" I looked around but couldn't see how or why the water level in the sink was rising higher and higher.

I dashed away, if I didn't do something, I was bound to make a bigger mess, and then I'd really be in deep shit. I moved quickly toward the swinging saloon-style doors. I knew to *always* use the right side after crashing into Huck. I peeked through the small opening.

The bakery was busy, as always. I looked back at the

sink and, of course, the water level was still going up and up.

I cleared my throat. Sylvie looked up and sucked in a deep breath. She was really getting tired of my shit.

"Sylvie, Huck. I need some help back here. Quickly."

The muscles in Huck's jaw moved, and he looked at Sylvie. "I got it."

He followed me through the doors, and I led him to the sink.

"Damn it! What the—hit that switch. On the wall." He pointed to a small switch nearby, and I immediately flipped it up.

A motorized whir rose from beneath the sink as the water churned, and it finally started to recede. After the water started to go down, the gurgling was replaced with an angry chewing noise that did not sound good.

"Kill it."

I obeyed, flicking off the switch and then standing there with my hands behind my back.

Huck sighed and rubbed his hands on a dish towel before pressing the heel of one hand into his eye. "The dish-washer's water line is tied to this sink. You can't shove shit down the sink and not turn on the disposal. It'll get clogged, and the dishwater has nowhere to go. Also"—he reached down into the depths of the sink and pulled out a mangled plastic spatula—"this is the food-prep sink, and this is the dish sink. They have to be separate." He gestured to each sink in the kitchen.

"Got it. I'm sorry, Huck."

His lips pressed into a thin line. "It's fine." He really was a nice guy, and I was just fucking it all up.

Feeling low, I quietly finished my cleaning in the back before slipping to the front of the bakery to see if I could help Sylvie with busing tables or anything else to stay out of Huck's way.

Wiping tables was something I could manage without incident, so I made sure those white tops shined. Bowlegs's twin was sitting on one of the stools along the large front window, wearing a red T-shirt and worn-in Moon Boots. "Good afternoon."

He looked at me, confusion clouding his vision.

"I'm Lark." I used my apron to dry my hand, then held it out.

His wrinkled hand fit into mine. "You the girl who cried for Bowlegs?"

I stifled a grin at the fact even his twin brother called him Bowlegs. Looking at the puffy ski boots he wore in June told me how he likely got his own nickname, Bootsy. "I did."

"Much appreciated." He grinned at me and I smiled back.

"Can I get you anything?"

He shook his head. "I'm just resting my legs. Enjoying watching GB have a meltdown."

My eyes tracked where he was looking, and I spotted Wyatt just outside the bakery. He was pacing along the sidewalk. His hair was a mess and looked like he'd raked his hands through it a thousand times. Penny sat on a cement flower planter, looking annoyed as she picked rocks from the planter and tried to toss them at her dad without him noticing.

Wyatt turned to her and said something that made her scowl even harder. Bootsy and I looked on, fascinated by the chaos of the scene playing out in front of us.

"What do you think is happening?" I whispered to the old man.

"Trouble with the law." He said it so certainly. "Or

maybe the NFL wants him back. A real comeback number where he finally gets that Super Bowl ring." Bootsy nodded as we continued to watch Wyatt pace and gesture wildly. "Think I saw a movie like that once."

I hummed in agreement. I think I saw that one too.

Just then Wyatt turned and caught us staring. I quickly shifted, giving him my back and pretending to be in deep conversation with Bootsy.

The door whooshed open, causing the bell to clank against the glass. I froze.

"Don't send anyone. I'll handle it." Wyatt's rumbly, grumpy voice sent tingles racing down my spine as I moved deeper into the bakery to avoid him. "Lark."

His voice thundered over my name in one deliciously crabby syllable.

I slowly turned and smiled, praying it didn't falter, as every eye in the bakery was on us.

"I'm hiring you."

"You're what?"

"Hiring you. Let's go." He gestured toward the exit, expecting me to follow.

"Wait—I can't just—where are we going?"

He let loose an annoyed sigh. "Look. Everyone knows you're a terrible server. Huck can't afford to lose any more dishes, and I need your help. Trust me, if I could ask anyone else, I would."

Ouch. Okay, well, that stung.

I crossed my arms over my chest. "Who said I would even want to work for you?" I spread my arms wide. "I have a perfectly good job here."

"Huck!" Wyatt shouted across the crowded bakery at my boss, who was stacking fresh pastries into the display case. "Will you please fire her?"

A sly grin spread across Huck's stupid face. "Lark, you're fired."

I rolled my eyes.

"See?" Wyatt said smugly. "You need a job. I have a job for you. You're hired."

Huck sauntered over, not even bothering to hide his amusement. "Sorry, kiddo. You're kind of terrible at this."

I scrunched my nose at him. "Not cool."

Wyatt grabbed my shoulders and gently steered me toward the exit.

"If it makes you feel any better," Huck called out, "I'll throw in one complimentary latte a day for all the work you did organizing the pantry. That spreadsheet is a lifesaver. Consider it a severance package."

I scowled at him. "One latte"—I raised a finger to point in his direction—"plus a lemon blueberry scone when you make them."

Huck nodded, satisfied that his karma was still intact as Wyatt wound me through the crowd and out into the midday sunshine.

As soon as we got outside, I turned on him. "What the hell, Wyatt?"

"Hey, Lark!" Penny called out as she walked on the top of the cement planter.

"Pickle, get down." Wyatt held out a hand, and Penny hopped off the planter and sat cross-legged on the sidewalk.

I glared up at him. "You kiss me and then ignore me and then I'm—"

"Keep your voice down." Wyatt encroached on my space, and the fight died from my lungs as he guided me away from the sidewalk to press up against the brick of the Sugar Bowl.

"Look. Kissing you was . . . it was . . ."

Don't say a mistake. Please *don't say it was a mistake.*

"It happened, all right?" He dropped his hands, defeated. "I know. I'm sorry, but I'm desperate. I've got the board of directors breathing down my neck, these kids are going to kill me, Penny is going feral . . . I think I need help."

"Why me?"

His jaw clenched. "Fuck if I know. Why not you?"

I narrowed my eyes at him. I was pretty sure he was dodging my question, but a sick part of me wanted to peel back his layers and get a glimpse of the man hiding underneath.

I may be punctual, a damn good actress, and amazing at poker, but I really was a *terrible* server. Like so, so bad.

Wyatt pinched the bridge of his nose and sighed in defeat. "I don't know why, but I think I trust you. And I do need you."

His unfiltered desperation did me in. "Fine. I want two hundred and fifty dollars a week."

"You don't even know what the job is."

"Five hundred." I raised my chin, hoping he wouldn't call my bluff.

"A thousand. All I need is for you to handle my calendar, hang out with Penny if I can't find someone to be with her, and check in with the guys to make sure they're not going off the rails. Can you do that?"

One thousand dollars a week? For that kind of cash I'd throw in laundry, cooking, and a blow job.

I swallowed hard at the thought of Wyatt and his big dick. I'd felt it plain as day when I was rubbing up against him while he devoured me in the kitchen. I felt hot all over, and it definitely wasn't the June sun.

Damn it.

I thrust a hand in his direction. "Deal."

"The board feels you pulling away. They're getting nervous, so they want to sweeten the deal. They're willing to hire an assistant for you. Someone to manage your calendar, the responsibilities with the players, your child." I could feel my neck on the chopping block as the athletic director spoke to me like I was an inconvenience. I ground my teeth to keep quiet.

The fact that Penny was last on that list of priorities showed me how much less the board cared about me as a human than as a successful coach. They were looking to solve the problem. Namely, *me*.

Whitman continued. "There are several administrative assistants that have open hours during the summer," he rambled on. "We will assign one to you—"

"That won't be necessary."

"You need a personal assistant so you can handle your obligations."

"I'm aware. I spoke with a few members of the board yesterday and got approval to hire my own assistant. It's taken care of."

Slightly miffed at my dismissal but pacified, Whitman ended the call, and I pressed my fingertips into my eye sockets. In a moment of utter panic, I'd hired Lark to be my assistant.

I'd nearly laughed in her face when she'd suggested such a low salary for herself. The board would cover a few hundred a week, and I was more than happy to throw in the rest if it meant this problem would go away.

She was the last person I needed complicating my life, but when I saw her sweet face next to Bootsy, staring out of the bakery window with a look of pure amusement, I just did it.

Plus, hiring Lark as my employee meant I definitely couldn't fuck her. That was a good thing.

Isn't it?

A gentle knock at the door had me straightening. It had to be Lark.

Game time.

"Morning!" Lark was fresh faced and sunny for so early in the day. Pickle was just getting up, and the boys would probably sleep a few more hours.

I took in the way her chestnut hair was bouncy and smooth. My fingers itched to run through it and feel its softness. I clenched my hands into fists and stepped aside, welcoming her into the house.

Lark followed me back to the kitchen. I reached up and grabbed a mug, filling it with coffee from the fresh pot I'd brewed. I lifted it. "Cream and sugar?"

Lark looked surprised that I'd made her coffee and blinked. "Oh, um . . . both, please. Thanks."

I nodded and set the cup on the table between us. I plopped down the sugar bowl and box of creamer and pushed it toward her.

After she doctored up her coffee, she blew over the top and took a tentative sip. My eyes tracked the shape of her lips and the dart of her tongue as she tasted. A part of me wished I could lean into her and brush my fingers down the length of her arm.

"So what are my marching orders, boss?"

My jaw locked tight. "I have a few meetings at the university this week. One in person today and the rest I can take remotely from here. Michael and Joey can pretty much do whatever they want—but I gave them your number, and they need to check in at least once." I pinched the bridge of my nose. "Just . . . keep them out of trouble, if you can."

Lark nodded, taking in my instructions.

"Kevin should spend some time at the library studying. He's retaking a class online and has a test coming up. I have your email, so I also shared my calendar with you last night."

Lark laughed. "Oh, I saw. That thing is a mess."

I just stared at her while her eyes danced with teasing amusement.

"If you need me, call or text. I'll leave whatever meeting I'm in. Penny and I will be in and out of the office, so it's best to just call my phone."

From the living room, Penny flopped herself lengthwise on the couch. "No, Daddy, no. I don't want to go to St. Fowler. That car ride sucks, and your office is *so* boring. I want to stay home and go to the beach with Lark."

"Pickle," I warned. We weren't having this conversation for the twelfth time this morning.

Lark shrugged. "She can hang with me today. I don't mind."

I immediately shook my head. "You're not a nanny."

Oh god. Now all I could think about was fucking the nanny. Awesome.

Penny immediately perked up, and hope filled her big brown eyes. "Please, Daddy. Please. I'll be good. I promise." She held up her hand, her two fingers crossed. Pickle still didn't realize that crossing your fingers while you promised meant you'd break it, and it hit me just how damn cute she was sometimes.

Lark's eyebrows raised up, and she smiled, like it wasn't a thing in the world for her to look after my kid. I considered it. So far, Lark seemed completely normal and had settled comfortably into Outtatowner. Tootie adored her, and I trusted her enough to be my assistant. I had to go with my gut on it and was comforted knowing, deep down, that Lark would care for Penny. Plus, I had an entire town that would look out for her too.

Lark smiled down at Penny as I weighed my decision. "I think we can find some trouble today."

I grumbled.

"Fun," she corrected with a laugh. "We'll find some *fun*." Lark winked at Penny as she moved to take over the couch.

"Fine. We'll use today as a test run. Just be safe and have a good time." I looked at Lark again. "I'll add extra for today."

She rolled her eyes and batted a hand in the air. "It's really no big deal. Penny mentioned on our walk that she's starting to read small chapter books but doesn't really have any. We could head into town and get her first library card. Would that be okay?"

I paused to take her in. *Penny's first library card.* Fuck, I hadn't even thought of that. Part of me felt terrible that I ever thought Lark wouldn't take this seriously.

I cleared my throat. "Yeah, that would be great. Thanks."

Lark smiled and lifted a shoulder like it wasn't a thing in the world to step up for my kid. When my phone buzzed again, I slid my keys into my pocket, strode toward Penny to kiss the side of her face, and headed toward the door.

I didn't look back when Lark stood in the doorway, waving, as I walked to my car. "Have a good day, dear!"

And her playful words stayed with me all damn day.

THE HECTIC DAY had gotten away from me. There was really no other way to describe it. I took calls, reviewed game footage, started on practice drill outlines, and spoke with Kevin's academic counselor about his requirements to be eligible to play in the fall.

I also had to prep for an upcoming press conference.

My plan to head back to Outtatowner by midafternoon was shot to hell after the portly athletic director shouldered his way into my office and filled the chair across from me. By the time the afternoon hours melted into early evening, I had to call it. My last meeting of the day could be taken from my car as I drove back home.

When I pulled across the gravel driveway, the farmhouse was lit up. Soft music wafted out of the open windows. The front door was open, and I could see movement just inside.

Trying to leave the stress of work behind me, I checked my calendar app one last time. I looked at it, closed the app, and opened it again. Curiously, it was now color coded.

Huh. Hadn't thought of that.

There were clear distinctions—virtual meetings, in-person meetings, press conferences, practices, and team meetings—all neatly arranged, time stamped, and simple to find. Noting there was nothing pressing for the next day or so, I let a tiny bit of stress melt away.

I climbed the stairs, ready to see what new disasters awaited me at home. I figured we could grab a pizza or something in town because there was no way in hell I had the mental energy to cook something after today. When I pushed through the door, my players looked as if they were getting ready to leave.

"Hey, Coach," Michael called.

"Guys." I dropped my keys by the table at the entrance. "What's up?"

"We're headed out. There's a thing down by the beach."

The boys filed out of the house, and I watched them bound down the porch stairs.

"See ya later, Lark!" Joey called out before he let the screen door slam behind him.

I looked at Lark and popped a thumb over my shoulder. "The beach?"

Lark stood in the kitchen by the stove, stirring something that made my stomach growl. She shrugged. "While we were at the library, I saw on the bulletin board that there's a hangout at the beach where people pick trash and then have free pizza in the pavilion afterward. The librarian there said it's a lot of kids the boys' age. Michael needs service hours *and* they were getting stir-crazy so . . ." She shrugged. "Win-win."

Well I'll be damned.

"Hey, Dad!" Penny skipped down the hallway from her room.

I ran a hand down the twin braids at the back of her head. "You're looking cute."

She beamed up at me. "Lark can do *dutch* braids!" Penny spun in a circle. "They're not even all wonky." She left off the *like yours always are*, and I smiled in appreciation. "Can I watch a show?"

"Sure thing, Pickle." I turned toward Lark, whose attention was back on the stove. "Busy day?"

Lark smiled, but I saw the fatigue in her eyes. "A good day. When you texted that you'd be a little late, I threw this together." She smiled. "It's edible."

We stood silently assessing each other as the bouncy music from Penny's show chirped in the background.

Subtle tension grew thick around us. I felt a pull toward Lark, like it would be the most natural thing in the world to draw her in close and hold her against my chest.

Eventually Lark cleared her throat. "Okay, well, I'm going to go. Same time tomorrow?"

I frowned. Part of me hoped she'd sit and eat whatever delicious-smelling dinner she'd made for us. It looked like spaghetti, and my stomach turned on itself again as I realized I hadn't eaten much all day.

It felt easy. Comfortable. Coming home after a long day to Penny's smiling face, a warm meal, and Lark in my home? It felt *too easy*.

Instead of doing what I wanted to—asking her to stay and have dinner with us, I only nodded. "Same time works."

A pinch twisted under my ribs when her eyes lowered and she moved toward the door.

I fucked that up.

"'Night, Pen!" she called into the living room, and Penny leaped from the couch to wrap Lark in a hug. "See you tomorrow." When Penny released her, Lark's eyes met mine. "Good night."

Every part of me wanted to step forward and offer to

walk her up to her apartment so I might steal another kiss. My eyes shifted down to her lips. She didn't move. A lump formed in my throat, but the music from Penny's show pulled me out of the moment, reminding me of my ever-accumulating responsibilities.

"'Night. Thanks again for today."

Lark only smiled and gently closed the screen door behind her.

15

LARK

"I'm not going to lie. Organic chemistry is not my strong suit." I flipped the thick textbook over in my hands and aimlessly thumbed through the pages. It seemed like . . . a lot.

Kevin held out his hand, and I dropped the heavy textbook into his palm. He looked down at it. "It's not that. I actually think this stuff is really interesting. The content isn't really hard."

He looked defeated. Embarrassed. I was sure it wasn't easy admitting he had to retake the course and that it was putting his football season at risk. We needed a different approach.

"Okay, so what is it then? If the coursework isn't hard, what's the issue?"

Kevin considered my question. "It's the projects, I think. The reading and the written work I have to do . . . it's always due at the same time, and I never feel like I have enough time to do it all. Before I know it, it's late and I get zeros or half credit."

I hummed in acknowledgment. "I see. So then what's

the point if you've dug a hole so deep you can't even get out of it."

His eyes met mine. "Exactly. Last semester I could have aced every test and still ended up with a D."

I glanced at the open computer screen and then down at the pile of books beside him. Then it hit me.

"Chunking," I said with a satisfied smile.

"What?"

"Chunking. I think that's what you need." I spun his open computer toward me. "It's something I learned when prepping for an audition and you have zero time to learn a whole script or monologue or whatever. Okay, here. Look." I pointed at the long, overwhelming list of tasks Kevin needed to get done. "This is everything for the whole summer session, right?"

He nodded, his shoulders slumped in defeat.

"Well, it's not *all* due tomorrow or even this week. We need to prioritize. If I can help you figure out which things to do when, do you think you can handle the rest?"

He eyeballed the syllabus again. All I got was a shrug.

I bumped his shoulder. "That's the spirit! Give it a try. If that doesn't work, we'll figure something else out!"

I pulled out the seat and plopped next to him, then tore a fresh sheet of notebook paper out of his spiral. I glanced over the syllabus, making notes on due dates, identifying longer projects that needed to be broken into manageable pieces, and separating everything into neat little rows I could put into one central place for him.

Kevin looked on quietly. His voice barely above a whisper, he said, "Thanks, Lark."

Affection for this sweet, lost young man swelled in my chest. I stifled a goofy grin and nodded.

~

"NOW THIS I could get used to." My face tipped up to the summer sun. The sand was warm beneath my towel, and the waves crashed only a few feet from where Penny, the boys, and I had plopped down on the beach.

Tourist season was in full swing, and in the three weeks I'd been Wyatt's assistant and all-around go-to gal, we had all settled into a happy routine. It was far and away less stressful and more fun than the Sugar Bowl had been. Most days were filled with keeping Penny occupied and checking in on the others.

Michael and Joey had gotten part-time summer jobs working the snack shack on the beach—they claimed it was to make a few extra dollars, but I knew it was because working at the Sand Dollar allowed them to meet *a lot* of girls who were spending time at the beach with friends or family. They were good kids, but they were also nineteen- and twenty-year-old boys.

Penny was next to me, building a sand castle while Michael and Kevin were down the beach playing sand volleyball with another rowdy group of kids. I glanced at the Sand Dollar, and when Joey saw me, he flashed a grin and an awkward thumbs-up. His pinkie was still bandaged, though I suspected it was fine . . . he just liked when girls asked about his *devastating injury*.

I rolled my eyes and laughed to myself; then a shadow fell across my lap. I peered up into the frowning face of my boss.

"Hey, Oscar. What's up?"

"I saw my calendar had blocked off this afternoon as *Beach Meeting*."

I grinned. "I'm glad you saw that it was also marked *Important* and took that note seriously."

He only grunted in response, but when Penny noticed him and flung herself into his arms, he softened. Sand flew everywhere, including in my face, and I sputtered and wiped at my thighs.

"Easy, Pickle. You're getting sand all over Lark."

"Daddy . . . it's the *beach*." After she released him, she turned to me. "Lark, can I go back to the playset?"

I glanced at Wyatt, a little uneasy that she was asking me instead of her dad. "As long as it's okay with your dad."

He looked out over the sand to the playground crawling with children. "Stay where we can see you."

Without another word, she was off like a shot. I continued to brush at the sand that had piled up on my towel.

Wyatt untucked a towel he had stuffed under his arm and laid it beside me. He was in a T-shirt and swim trunks, along with flip-flops. While he didn't dress up every day, this was much more casual than the Dockers and football polos he usually wore when he traveled into work. He was casually undone in the sexiest way, and my insides went melty at the sight of him. But even his dark sunglasses couldn't hide his frown.

"You don't have to stay . . . if you don't want to."

I looked out over the water and watched as kids and families played in the waves of Lake Michigan. "Kicking me out already?"

"No, I . . . I just don't want you to think that you're *required* to be here. You're off the clock."

"Ah," I said, easing back on my elbows. "Don't worry." I looked over the top of my sunglasses and winked at him—then had to swallow my smile when I noticed how his jaw worked in response to my playfulness. "I won't charge you."

Truth was, I felt guilty taking his money. Penny was a riot to hang out with and really easy. The boys were, well, overgrown children, really, but nothing I couldn't handle. They respected me and checked in when I asked them to. I think it also helped that I didn't always let Wyatt in on *everything* they were doing. We were operating strictly under the "you can get into a little trouble, just don't get caught" kind of parameters.

Within minutes Penny got bored of the playground equipment and found her way back to the beach toys a few feet away.

I reached into my overstuffed beach bag, around rogue Cheetos and a racy paperback. "It's getting hot, Pen, we should probably reapply your sunscreen."

When I lifted the bottle up, Wyatt plucked it from my hands. "I got it."

Penny trudged through the sand and plopped in front of him. "I hate sunscreen."

I laughed. "Me too, but when you're my age, I promise, you'll be glad you used it."

"Why?"

"It keeps your skin safe and helps prevent wrinkles."

"Why?"

I shrugged. "I guess it helps you not become a shriveled-up prune."

"Why?"

"Penny." Wyatt's tone was terse, and she sulked at him, cutting short her favorite game of *Why*.

Penny looked at me. "Well, if I have to, so do you."

I smiled at Penny, loving her tenacity. "You're right. I need some too."

I picked up the lotion and squirted a blob on my palm, then worked it into my shoulders and arms. From behind my sunglasses, I sneaked a peek at Wyatt, whose jaw flexed, but he stared straight ahead as he finished Penny's back, and she scrambled to get up and play.

"Don't forget her back, Daddy."

I lowered my lashes, trying to hide the flood of color I could feel rising in my cheeks.

Penny stubbornly crossed her arms. "You always say I have to even though I hate when it feels sticky."

Wyatt swallowed hard and nodded.

"Would you mind?" I looked over my shoulder at him.

He looked around, searching for the discarded bottle of sunscreen. "Yeah." He cleared his throat, and I hid a smile. "Of course."

Satisfied that she wasn't the only one being tortured with sunscreen, Penny walked back toward the hole she'd been digging in the sand.

Wyatt squirted a dollop of sunscreen on his hands and rubbed them together. I wiggled on the towel, mostly to inch a little closer to him but also to help ease the ache that pooled between my legs.

Jesus, he smells good—like sun and sand and spicy man cologne.

Nothing more had happened between Wyatt and me, but the memory of that one kiss was seared into my mind. His hands hovered over my shoulders for a fraction of a second before his wide palms smoothed over me. Warm and rough, his hands made slow work of moving down the slopes of my shoulders, up the back of my neck, and across my shoulder blades.

Despite the summer sun, goose bumps erupted on my skin. When I thought he was done, he squirted another blob of sunscreen on his hands and moved lower, smoothing lotion over the rest of my back.

I looked at him over my shoulder. "Very thorough," I teased.

His hands moved slowly up my back. His fingers toyed with the slim strap forming an X across my shoulder blades, dipping beneath them and tracing over every inch of exposed skin.

"I like to be thorough."

Oh, hell. I'm sure you do.

I pressed my knees together and hugged them. We were surrounded by families, and his kid was only feet away, but all I could think about was him hovering over me and pressing me into the warm sand as he covered my mouth with his. My nipples hardened to needy little points.

I wanted to see just how thorough he could be.

I had opened my mouth to speak when a volleyball inelegantly plopped beside me, sending little grains of sand flying up. The rowdy laughter of Kevin and Michael broke the spell, and Wyatt hopped to his feet.

I also stood and shook out my towel before stuffing it into my beach bag. I had to go. There was no way I could sit with him, with my *boss*, on the beach and not think about naughty, delicious things I wish he would do to me. It was better to keep my distance.

Flustered, I threw my bag over my shoulder. "Okay, well, I think I am going to go after all."

Wyatt frowned again, and I turned from him to power walk toward the car.

"Hey, Lark."

I stopped and turned toward him.

"Tootie is having everyone over for dinner tonight. She asked me to see if you're free."

I glanced at my watch.

As if I have anything else to do.

"Yeah, sure. I can make that work."

"I'll drive." Wyatt flashed a rare grin, and I nearly melted in a gooey puddle right there.

I checked my hair for the seventeenth time and cursed myself for feeling nervous.

It's just dinner.

"I'm ready!" Penny shouted from her room, so I exhaled and headed her way.

She met me in the hallway and my smile widened. She wore high-top sneakers, a silver tutu, and a T-shirt from Halloween with Frankenstein's monster below the words *Let Me Be Frank.*

"Bloomers?"

Penny inelegantly lifted her skirt to reveal the bike shorts she wore under dresses and skirts. "Yup."

I laughed and ruffled her hair before calling up the stairs. "We're out of here. Stay out of trouble!"

Footsteps pounded down the stairs as three of my top athletes practically fell over themselves to get to us.

Kevin made it down first. "We're coming with."

I looked at their eager faces.

Joey shrugged. "Free food."

I shook my head at them. "You always have free food. I feed you."

"Will Lee be there? I was going to talk to him about the service." Michael had lowered his voice, and I clamped a hand on his shoulder and nodded. Michael was smart. He was a great athlete, but he also knew pro football wasn't always something that panned out—even for the best players. He was hedging his bets. My chest pinched for him. Of all my players, he had the most raw talent, and I wanted his football dreams to come true as badly as he did.

"Yeah, he'll be there. Load up, guys."

I watched as they razzed each other and messed around, Penny tucked between them and looking up as if they'd collectively hung the moon and stars. I didn't know how it happened, but somehow our quirky little family was growing.

After closing the front door, I looked up the barn steps to watch Lark's hand glide down the banister to join us. On the last step, she made a little bounce and looked up. "They're fixed."

The muscles in my cheek flickered, happy she had noticed. "Yep."

A part of me wanted to point out that the light was also working now, but I kept my mouth shut and opened the back car door for Penny.

"Can I ride with them? Please, Daddy?"

Penny's hands were folded under her chin, her big brown eyes full of hope.

"Fine with me." Michael shrugged.

I reached into my car and grabbed the small booster seat she still needed. When Michael reached for it, I paused. "No hotdogging. *Under* the speed limit."

He smiled. "You bet."

I sighed. "You know what? Just follow me."

They piled into the car, Penny nestled safely in the back, her little sneakers kicking with excitement. I rounded my car and opened the passenger door for Lark.

"Thank you." Her voice was soft, and her perfume's notes of cinnamon and citrus floated over me. My entire body ached. I still wasn't used to how good she always smelled. Suddenly the thought of being alone in the car with her on the drive to Tootie's house, even though it was short, was unbearable.

Lark smiled as I got behind the wheel. Her fingertips toyed with the hem of her dress. It was a soft, fluttery thing. Deep, navy blue with large wooden buttons that went from the hem all the way up to the scooping neckline. Her arms were bare, and a bright-green belt was tied at her waist.

Lark was gorgeous, and I knew the short drive was about to kill me.

I focused on the road, my eyes constantly flicking from the smooth skin of her thighs to the rearview mirror, ensuring Penny and the boys were safe. Lark was unfazed, and she made the conversation easy and light as we drove the few miles to where Aunt Tootie lived.

As we pulled in, both Lee and Duke were already there, which likely meant my dad would be joining us too. It would be a full house, which normally would make me itchy, but it also meant lots of opportunities to avoid looking at Lark.

Since the moment I hired her, she had ingrained herself more and more into our everyday lives. It felt effortless. I started looking forward to her smiles, the tiny adjustments to my calendar, notes she'd leave on the counter about Penny's day. I craved even the smallest moments where our shoulders would brush or I was close enough to see the golden light dance in her hazel eyes.

I had never wanted anyone as bone deep as I wanted Lark.

And it was a real problem.

~

ROLLING to a stop in front of my aunt's house brought with it a flood of memories. Happy ones. The house was down a quiet country road, hidden by a long driveway and careful landscape that provided cozy privacy.

When we turned down the drive and bumped over the railroad tracks that ran alongside the property, my grip tightened, and I tried to ignore the way Lark's mouthwatering curves bounced along with it.

A bark caught my attention as Duke's three-legged dog ran alongside the vehicles. Lark looked on with concern.

"That's just Ed."

She looked at me. "Ed?"

"Duke's dog."

"In a town with grown men named Itchy and Bumper and Bowlegs, the dog's name is Ed?"

I shrugged and offered a small smile. "Technically, he became Three-Legged Ed."

"What happened to him?" she asked as I pulled the car to a stop alongside Lee's truck.

"He stopped, but the car didn't."

Horrified, Lark got out of the car and bent to pet the shaggy, overly friendly dog. "I'm so glad you're okay, Ed."

I walked up beside her as the boys and Pickle hopped out of Michael's car, and the dog took off to sniff the Goldfish crumbs off Penny's skirt.

We walked up the steps to Tootie's home, and I frowned, remembering the rotting wood. I noted that one of the shutters on the top floor was missing. Lark looked out across the yard toward the acres and acres of blueberry bushes.

"It's beautiful."

I nodded. "It's really pretty in the spring when they're flowering. Do you see that opening there?" I leaned in dangerously close, motioning over her shoulder to point at a small break in the tree line. "If you follow it long enough, it winds around and you run right into Highfield House."

Lark turned her head, and our faces were inches apart, eyes locked on each other. "Like a secret passageway. That's very cool."

I could lean in. Indulge myself and brush a kiss against her lips. Feel her moan as I kiss her.

I cleared my throat and stepped away. At the front door, I knocked once and walked right in.

My aunt was bustling in the kitchen, stirring something with one hand and bending to check something else in the oven. Lee and Duke were out in the back, so we said hi to Tootie, but when she shooed us out of the kitchen, we joined my dad where he sat on a recliner in the living room. The boys opted to walk around the expansive property before dinner. I suspected Michael went in search of Lee.

"Papa!" Penny pulled him into a hug, and Dad smiled widely. He stood to shake hands with me.

A pretty good day, then.

"Dad, this is Lark."

Dad held out his hand. "Red. Pleased to meet you."

Lark smiled brightly and didn't remind him that they'd already met at Bowlegs's funeral. Instead, she took a seat on the couch closest to Dad as we all settled in.

"He dropped back but couldn't find anyone downfield." Dad leaned forward across the arm of his recliner, lost in the memory of one of my games.

Lark leaned in, unfazed by the abrupt drop into the middle of a conversation. She listened intently to a story I'd heard him tell a thousand times.

"He dropped back but saw an opening—pew!" Dad clapped his hands and made a whistle with his mouth. "Straight up the middle for thirty-seven yards. No one was even close to touching him."

Dad smiled at me, pride evident on his weathered face. Times like that, it seemed like he was back, untouched by the disease robbing him of his memory.

He slapped a hand on my knee. "Hell of a game last week, Son."

Aaaand there it was.

I stayed silent. I knew it didn't do any good correcting the timelines in his fractured memory.

"How exciting!" Lark skated over the lapse in his memory. "You must be very proud."

"Damn right." Dad smiled at me again. "Now where's that cute girl of yours?"

Funny.

He seemed to always remember Penny was my daughter, but it never occurred to him that the overlap of her and his mind perpetually believing I was still in college didn't quite add up.

"She's out back, Dad. Probably finding some trouble."

"That's good. That's good. A little dirt's good for kids."

～

DINNER HAD BEEN EXACTLY like I'd remembered it as a kid. Tootie loved to feed people, and it wasn't uncommon to have a table full of friends and family. It also helped that she was an excellent cook. Roasted chicken, mashed potatoes and gravy, and vegetables straight from her garden. It was hearty and so much better than anything I could whip up.

I was full and satisfied, and as the conversation flowed, I had been able to sneak a few glances at Lark without worry someone would notice. I patted my stomach. "Aunt Tootie, you outdid yourself. Dinner was amazing."

"Yeah, thanks, Ms. Tootie. The chicken was delicious." Joey smiled at her, and I was proud that my team was made up of decent, respectful kids. The boys plopped themselves onto the couch and started flipping through channels, while my brothers and I began clearing the table.

Tootie beamed with pride as we all stood to clear our plates. "Just you wait for dessert. I made my specialty—blueberry pie."

I turned to Duke, who was responsible for the family farm. "Good season?"

He nodded and flipped a rogue piece of chicken to the shaggy dog at his feet. "Getting there. Could use a rain or two."

Duke was never a man of many words, and if I was considered grumpy, he could be downright unpleasant. Not that I didn't understand. When Dad had gotten sick, he'd shouldered much of the burden, taking over operations at the blueberry farm as well as making sure Dad was taken care of.

Duke turned to Tootie. "I saw tire tracks on the west field. Were you out there?"

Tootie frowned. "Wasn't me."

Duke's jaw clenched and Lee jumped in. "Kings?"

"Could be. I got wind they're scoping out the Tillerman farm, and it butts up to one of our fields."

Lee's typically happy demeanor soured. "You know they also bought out Reed Jennings and his fishing charter. And Tootie let it slip that they made another lowball offer on the Highfield House."

"I see the littlest one sometimes," Dad offered from his spot on a recliner. The woman he referred to was a nurse at Haven Pines and often took care of Dad, despite the fact he was a Sullivan.

"MJ," Lee offered with a shrug.

"They're all scoundrels, the lot of them." Tootie grabbed a stack of plates from Lee. She called back over her shoulder as he walked away. "But MJ is a good egg."

"What's the end game?" Lee asked. "Buying up all the property in Remington County. Expansion probably, but why the boats? Doesn't make sense."

"It's never enough for those greedy motherfuckers." Duke's voice carried a hard edge, but I agreed with him. The Sullivans were hard workers and had fought for everything we got—all the way back to my great-grandfather, who'd started the farm.

A low simmer of anger bubbled in my chest. "It's not enough they stole Great-Granddad's patent, but they have to go run roughshod over all of Outtatowner now?" Being away for so long meant I'd missed all this. Things were changing, and not all those changes were good.

Lark looked awkwardly between my brothers and me, her eyes wide as we lamented the Kings. Tootie threw her hands in the air and blew out an exasperated breath. "I'm so tired of you boys and your grudges. Lark, come help me in the kitchen, dear?"

She looped her arm into Lark's and guided her away from the dining room. We all stood around, frowning and thinking about the Kings. I couldn't believe how much had changed in the years I'd been away. It seemed the Kings had been busy scouting local businesses in trouble and paying low dollar to bail the owners out.

Just didn't sit right with me.

I looked around Tootie's house. The paint in the dining room was faded, and the floorboards squeaked under my foot. The place was literally crumbling around her, and it would be only a matter of time before the Kings got wind of it and stole her house from under her.

"Anyone talked to Katie lately?" I looked at my brothers, who avoided my eyes and shook their heads.

I lowered my voice. "You know Tootie doesn't listen to anyone but her." I stretched my arms wide. "Look at this place. It's too big. She can't keep it up. Maybe it's time we call Katie and see if she can talk some sense into her."

"Think she'll come back?" Duke asked.

Lee shrugged. "Worth a shot. She loves Montana, but school's almost done for her. I can call her tomorrow."

Duke looked around the old farmhouse. "I can call in a favor to Beck. See if he knows anyone who'd be willing to help us out."

Beckett was Duke's best friend and owned a successful construction company, but his family would be a complication after what had gone down with their beloved son Declan and Katie. We were running out of options. If we could get someone he trusted, along with Kate smoothing things over with Tootie, we could have her home up to code, and I'd worry a hell of a lot less about everything.

Sold on the idea, I nodded. "Just let me know how much."

Duke looked at me. "We'll all take care of her."

In solemn agreement, we nodded at each other.

Just then Penny burst through the side door and hustled into the kitchen. When I followed her, I saw her peering into a shoebox. She clamped the lid down tight at the sight of me.

"Lark, how much did Aunt Tootie pay you to come to Bowlegs's funeral?"

"Pickle," I warned.

Penny dipped her hands in the pocket of her skirt and held out several coins in her little hand. "What? I just need to know. I want to hire her."

Lark's eyes danced with amusement. "Hire me?"

Penny shifted the box to her hip and looked up. "If you could all please come outside."

We eyed each other warily, but over my shoulder I nodded. Tootie looked at me as I glanced at Dad, settled on the couch, and she smiled. "We'll stay behind."

One by one, Lark, Lee, Duke, the boys, and I followed Penny out to the backyard. Across the grass, near an old oak tree, there was a small hole.

"Pickle, did you dig up Tootie's yard?"

"Shh." She frowned at me. "This is a serious time."

My eyebrows popped up. "Oh. Sorry."

Rounding the old oak, Penny adjusted the small shoebox. She held it high above her head. "This is Eggburt the chicken."

My stomach dropped. "Oh my god. Pickle, is there a dead animal in that box?"

Lee stifled a laugh, and I shot him a look. Duke stood stoically beside him with his hands clasped in front of him, but a smile pulled at the corners of his mouth. Kevin, Michael, and Joey looked on, horrified.

"Is this what you needed my help for?" Lark asked.

Penny nodded. "I want to give Burt the burial he deserves. Can you help?"

Lark looked to me, but I had no clue what to say. "Sure." She smiled.

Penny gently laid the shoebox in the too-small hole. "Here lies Burt. Lark will now say a few nice things."

Surprised but composed, Lark took one step forward. "Oh, well . . . okay." She cleared her throat. "Burt was a good chicken. His life was . . . peaceful here. There were many sunny days, and he was loved. Though we will miss him, I know he's in a better place." She stepped back and leaned over to Penny to whisper, "How was that?"

Penny's mouth twisted in subtle disappointment. "Can you cry a little?"

At that, I coughed to hide my laughter. Lark's eyes whipped to mine before clearing her throat. "I'll work on it."

We stood, silent and staring down at the shoebox.

I really hope there's not an actual dead chicken in there.

Lark blotted at the fresh tears in the corner of her eyes. After a moment of silence, Penny nodded, satisfied that Eggburt had been properly honored.

"Thank you, everyone."

We slowly started walking back to the main house. "Pickle, what was in the box?"

She looked up at me. "Eggburt."

"Okay . . . what happened to him?"

Penny rolled her eyes at me like I was the simplest human on the planet. "Daddy . . . we ate him!"

Lee's barking laugh erupted into the evening air while Joey turned and puked into Tootie's rosebushes.

Having a casual dinner with Wyatt and his family was easy.

Too easy.

I could feel that Red's condition made Wyatt uneasy, but for me, I loved listening to stories about when the Sullivans were little, especially hearing the pride in Red's voice when he talked about Wyatt.

There was so much love there.

The fact Penny had stolen the chicken carcass from dinner and forced us all into an unexpected chicken funeral had me giggling the rest of the night. I couldn't get over the look of horror on Wyatt's face. Poor Joey had lost his composure and ended up throwing up all over Tootie's rosebushes. He recovered once he learned that the chicken was store-bought and not one of the cute little hens that milled around Tootie's backyard.

We also had the best blueberry pie I'd ever tasted.

After dessert, Penny had begged and pleaded to have a sleepover. The boys took off to a late-night beach party, and

Duke and Lee parted ways, presumably bringing Red back to his place at Haven Pines.

The silence in Wyatt's car was deafening on the ride back. I fiddled with the hem of my skirt.

When he caught my movements, Wyatt adjusted the air-conditioning. "Are you hot?"

I only shook my head. Truth was, I *was hot*. Hot and bothered.

The drive was quick, and once I'd wrapped my head around the fact that the crushed limestone path connected the two properties, I had a much better sense of where each home was located within the greater boundaries of town. Bit by bit I was learning more about Outtatowner and feeling more comfortable in my temporary hometown.

When we stopped on the driveway between my apartment over the barn and Wyatt's house, he didn't make a move to get out. I looked up at him in the fading evening sunlight.

He cleared his throat, and I stared a moment too long at his chiseled, stubbled jawline. Wyatt reached into his pocket and opened his hand. On his palm was a key. "This is for you."

I reached over and plucked the key from his hand, careful not to touch him. "Oh. Thanks."

"Use it any time."

"Um . . . okay."

Fuck, this is awkward.

I wanted Wyatt to lean in, grab the back of my neck, and kiss me again. Part of me knew he wanted it too. His eyes darted to my lips, and I licked them. Our steady breaths were the only sounds filling the interior of his car.

But he didn't inch forward.

"Good night, Wyatt."

I unfolded myself from his car and took the steps to my upstairs apartment two at a time. Clutching his house key in my hand, I pushed through my own front door and leaned against it.

I was flustered. Annoyed.

Why wouldn't he just kiss me again?

You know what? No. I took care of his schedule, his players, his daughter. He'd invited me to a family dinner, and his family members were so amazing my heart ached. The way we were acting around each other was ridiculous. We were adults. I could tell he wanted to kiss me but wouldn't do anything about it. He was a grouch, and he was happy to live in his grouchy little trash can.

Nope.

Not today, Oscar.

Gathering my courage, I opened my front door and bounded back down the stairs. With purposeful strides, I walked across the driveway and up to his front door.

One knock. Then two.

I leaned in but heard nothing through the heavy wood door but silence.

Do I use the key?

That felt like a weird invasion of privacy, so instead I knocked again and tried the handle. Unlocked, I opened the door only slightly to peek my head in.

"Wyatt? It's Lark. Can I come in?"

I listened again. Silence.

No. Not silence, but something else, coming from the back.

"Wyatt?" I tried again.

A low moan floated down the hallway.

Was that? Oh god—

Excited and feeling brave, I slinked through the door

and closed it quietly behind me. I dropped the key Wyatt had given me on the small table at the entrance and slowly crept toward the sound.

I heard it again. An unmistakable soft, low groan of pleasure.

My toes tingled. My nipples hardened beneath the flimsy fabric of my dress. My heart raced as my feet carried me toward the sound.

At the end of the dark hallway, a bedroom door was open. The bedside lamp was glowing, but otherwise the room was cloaked in darkness. Across the bedroom, a light shone through the open bathroom door.

My feet were bolted to the floor.

In the mirror, Wyatt was naked. Glorious lines of cut muscle as he hunched over, one hand gripping the edge of the sink and the other . . .

The other was fisted around his cock.

"Fuck." He groaned again as his hand moved up and down his length. "Lark."

Holy shit. Holy shit!

He pumped into his hand. Long, hard strokes as his hips pushed forward. A guttural moan slipped from his throat, and my hand moved to my neck in shock. My pulse pounded beneath my fingertips.

I stood, watching Wyatt stroke himself, my name on his lips. It was wild. Wrong. But *such* a turn-on. I could feel myself get wet.

My throat was thick, but I stared directly at him. "Wyatt."

His gaze whipped to mine, but he didn't stop. The rich flecks of amber in his eyes darkened, and the sharp muscles of his jaw clenched.

He looked out of control, lost in his desire, and it was

my name that he was stroking himself to. I wanted to tear my dress apart and give myself to him based on that look alone. Wyatt continued staring through the mirror as his fist pumped and his thumb brushed over the head of his cock again.

"Wyatt."

He groaned. His abs flexed, and I could see the veins in his forearms as he worked himself in long, smooth strokes. "Again." His throat bobbed as he swallowed. "Say my name again."

I bit back a smile and swallowed. "Wyatt."

"Oh fuck." His head fell back as his strokes became harsh and frantic. He was close. I wanted to see him finish— to see him come apart with my name on his lips as I watched the most gorgeous man I'd ever laid eyes on stroke his long, thick cock.

My fingertips found the hem of my dress and brushed up my thigh, but I didn't move from the doorway. Grazing over the fabric of my underwear, I knew they would be damp. Wyatt's eyes landed on the spot between my legs where my dress hid me from him, but my hand disappeared. My other hand skated across my hard nipples.

God, I want his mouth there. Everywhere.

My whole body was burning up. I wanted to feel him, every delicious inch, as he moved over me and split me open with that monster cock.

His back muscles rippled, and I knew he must be dangerously close.

"Again, Lark. Say it again." Wyatt's voice was thick and gravelly as he pumped himself over and over.

"Come for me, Wyatt. Please. I want it." Teasing the edge of my panties, I didn't let myself push past that barrier to fill the aching emptiness between my thighs. After seeing his dick, I knew nothing else would satisfy me and that my fingers would be a sad letdown.

"Wyatt, please."

My quiet, pleading whimper sent him tumbling over the edge. His hips bucked as he came. Long, thick ropes erupted from him as he shuddered. "Yes, god yes, Lark."

Tingles prickled at the base of my spine. I had just walked into my neighbor's—no, my *boss's* house—and interrupted him while he was jerking off to *my name.*

It was the kinkiest, wildest thing that had ever happened to me. In the heat of the moment I hadn't felt an ounce of shame, but suddenly, watching Wyatt unravel had me worried that I'd not only invaded his privacy but completely blown up the perfect summer gig I'd been building.

I needed to go. To get out and take a cold shower and find my vibrator. Maybe I could pretend it was Wyatt and ease the tension that was pulled taut inside me. Whatever I did, it wouldn't involve looking Wyatt in the eyes and admitting that I'd totally spied on him.

Frantically, I moved through his dark house and burst out of the front door. The screen door slammed behind me, and I ran up the steps to my apartment and flung myself inside.

"What the hell was that?" I whispered into the darkness.

Your hot boss just came to you calling out his name and pleading for him to finish.

Behind me, a loud pounding at my door had me yelping, and I jumped.

"Lark. Open the door."

I brushed back the stray hairs at my forehead and took a

deep breath. My body ached with need, and based on the growly tone in Wyatt's voice, he was *not happy*.

Time to get fired . . . and probably arrested for being a creep or something.

I slowly pulled open the door. Wyatt leaned with one hand against the doorframe and the other in a fist at his side. I tamped down the thought of where that hand had just been. He was wearing only low-slung jeans and no shirt. His feet were bare, and *damn* that was so hot.

I lifted my chin and tried not to freak out.

"You ran away."

I brushed away another stray hair and tried to steady my voice. "Look, I'm sorry. I shouldn't have barged in, and then when I saw you, I—"

Wyatt invaded my space, pushing the door open and stepping inside the apartment. His mouth was hot on mine before I could even finish my sentence.

Our lips broke apart, our pants mixed in the sliver of space between us. "You ran away. Before I could get my mouth on yours and make you come as hard and good as I did."

A moan rattled through my throat, and Wyatt kissed me again. His tongue moved over the seam of my lips, and I opened for him as he gripped me and pushed us farther into my apartment.

After weeks of simmering tension, want and need flooded my system. I pressed against his hard chest as his rough hands moved over my hips to grab my ass.

He pulled away to run one hand down the length of buttons at the front of my dress. "You teased me all fucking night with this dress. I was stroking my cock thinking about what you'd look like with it splayed open just before I fucked you."

I was breathless. The room was spinning. "I'm sorry. I shouldn't have—"

Wyatt stopped my halfhearted apology with another brutal kiss. I lifted on my toes, wanting to rub every inch of my body against his.

He dropped to his knees.

"What are you doing?"

He lifted the hem of my blue dress. "You got to watch me while I came. Now I get to taste you while you do."

Heat rippled through me as my core clenched around emptiness, wishing to be filled. Wyatt licked and sucked my skin as he moved up my thighs and toward my underwear.

"You wouldn't let me see this pretty pussy either."

Over the soft material of my panties, Wyatt nuzzled me with his nose and teased me with gentle kisses.

"Wyatt, please."

"That's right. Beg for it."

"Oh my god, please. Please."

His hands pulled my underwear down to my knees, and his tongue dragged a long, slow path through my pussy. My hands found his shoulders as I steadied myself. He lowered himself to go even deeper. He stroked me with his tongue. Teased my clit until I was shaking.

"More. Please, more."

Two thick fingers circled my clit before his mouth clamped over me and his fingers slipped inside. My hands tangled in his hair. I should have been ashamed or embarrassed, but I wasn't. I was grabbing his hair and riding his face while he devoured my pussy. I could feel his fingers, his tongue, the vibrations from every moan he made.

As I was right on the edge, he reached around to grab my ass, pushing his face deeper between my thighs to lick and suck my clit. The room dissolved as I came apart. His name was on the tip of my tongue, but I couldn't speak.

After one final shudder, he stood, towering over me. Lust raged a war in his eyes, and a cocky smirk played on his lips. With my underwear still at my knees, Wyatt bent and hoisted me over his shoulder. I let out a giddy shriek, and my hands flew to my skirt to cover my bare butt.

Wyatt's wide palm came down with a playful smack, and he laughed as his hand slid under my skirt to smooth the stinging skin on my bottom. He gripped a handful of ass as he stalked toward the back bedroom.

He knew exactly where it was, and I bounced when he plopped me on the bed. As he stood over me, grinning, Wyatt slipped a condom from his back pocket.

I lifted an eyebrow. "You came prepared."

"I walked up those stairs knowing I was going to fuck you."

My thighs scissored. Aching need raced through me as I undid my dress, button by button. Wyatt watched as my fingers moved lower and lower until the dress was open and draping at my sides.

He unbuttoned and unzipped his jeans before dropping them to the floor and stepping out of them. I watched in fascination as he freed his cock and made quick work of rolling the condom down his thick length.

On the bed, Wyatt stretched over me. My legs parted. He gripped the base of his cock, guiding it to my entrance.

"You have no idea how long I've been thinking about this. I am not going to fuck you soft and slow. Are you okay with that?"

My hips tipped forward, begging him to enter.

"Tell me, Lark." His eyes burned into me.

I was already coming undone beneath him. I finally

found my voice. "Hard."

Before that single syllable was out, he thrust forward, filling me and stretching me open. I cried out. He didn't give me any time to adjust to his size before he began thrusting his hips into me.

"Oh god Wyatt. This dick—" He was setting a delicious, brutal pace, fucking me hard, just as he promised.

"Maybe next time I'll even let you gag on it."

I couldn't believe the filthy things coming out of his mouth. *I love it.* His dirty words made me only wetter, and I wanted him to go deeper, push harder. My body adjusted to his size, and I dug my heels into him, urging him to give me more.

An incoherent stream of pants and *omigod, please fuck me* and *yes, yes, yes* filled my bedroom.

Wyatt felt incredible. I couldn't remember the last time I'd been so filled. So *used*. So cherished. Despite pinning me to the bed and railing me into next week, his mouth was gentle, his tongue hot, and his hands touched every nerve ending. Sparks shot through me as he adjusted his angle and allowed the base of his cock to grind against my clit.

My nails raked across his back as I thrust my hips up to meet his every long stroke. A hard line formed between his eyebrows, and the mean, grumpy look on his face had my pussy quivering all over again. Wyatt gripped the back of my neck as he pumped hard into me. With his forehead pressed to mine, his cock throbbed, and the tension melted from his shoulders.

For long moments, we breathed the same air.

Panting and sweating, I was gloriously used up.

If fucking your boss and neighbor was always like *that* but also meant lighting your entire life on fire? Then hand me the matches.

18

WYATT

When my vision finally cleared and I could see straight again, I lifted my forehead off Lark's. I peered down at her beautiful, smiling face. Her neck was red and splotchy, her cheeks were a glorious shade of pink, and her breasts rubbed against me with every ragged breath she took.

I steadied my arms on either side of her head but didn't pull my cock from her.

Not yet.

"That was— Are you okay?" As far as first times go, we'd crossed a lot of boundaries without having talked about it first. I was rough. Brutal, even.

Lark smiled up at me. "I'm fantastic. But I could use a snack."

She laughed, and the worry eased from my shoulders. "I can manage that." The thought of taking care of Lark, not just making her come but truly taking care of her, made my heart skip a beat. After how hard we just went, she deserved a little pampering. Tenderness.

Worry trickled in, knowing I wasn't that guy. Her nails tickled at my back. Lark was warm and soft and *perfect*.

I stifled a groan when I slipped out of her. She was still half-dressed, her tits barely hidden under the lace of her bra, and her dress was open and rumpled at her sides. I pulled my hand through my hair. That didn't go at all how I'd imagined it.

That's a fucking lie.

It actually went exactly how I'd imagined it—taking Lark rough and hard. Punishing her for all the times I imagined what it would be like to feel her, taste it. Now that it had happened, I felt like a prick.

"I, uh . . . I'm just going to clean up."

Lark pulled the sides of her dress closed. "Down the hall and on the right."

I nodded and scooped up my jeans. I had been in the apartment a thousand times. In the bathroom, I disposed of the condom, washed up, and slipped my jeans back on. In my rush to stop Lark from bolting, I hadn't even bothered with underwear or a shirt.

When I stepped back into the hallway, Lark was waiting, her dress still pulled together over her body. She offered a meek smile and slipped past me into the bathroom.

Though the apartment had been the home of nearly all the Sullivan kids at one point or another, it was Lark's home now, so I didn't know what to do with myself. I didn't want to leave, but staying felt like crossing yet another line. My life was complicated enough without adding *budding relationship* to the mix. I sighed, knowing we'd have to have the dreaded *Does this change things?* conversation.

I was awkward. And shirtless.

Annoyed at myself, I stalked to the kitchen. Lark was hungry, and making her some food was the least I could do.

Unsurprisingly, Lark's fridge and pantry were well stocked, so finding something to whip together was easy enough.

I eyeballed a nub of ginger root, pulled herbs from the pantry, started to boil water, and got to work.

When I heard Lark's light footsteps behind me, I stared down at the cutting board and continued chopping.

"You stayed."

I smirked at the scallion I was mincing. "Kicking me out?"

Her gentle laugh made my insides go tight. "Well, I would have deserved it after I ran out of your place."

I risked a glance at her over my shoulder. Her dress was buttoned and her hair gently tousled. A light flush stained the delicate skin on her chest, and it hit me again how rough I had been with her.

I grunted and slipped my hand into the front pocket of my jeans. I pulled out the key she'd left at my place and tossed it onto the kitchen counter. "You left that."

She walked up and smiled down at it before picking it up. "Thanks for returning it." Lark dragged her fingertips down my triceps to my wrist before moving to put it away. Heat raced up my arm and through my chest at her touch.

I continued assembling and chopping and tried to focus on anything but the mass of complicated feelings that were running through my mind.

"Whatcha making me?" Lark gave me space but hopped up on the countertop to watch me cook.

"Ramen." I used the chef's knife in my hand to point at her. "The good kind."

In my many years as a bachelor, I'd learned to make a pretty wicked dish with instant ramen, some aromatics, and an egg.

Lark eyed the ingredients I was lining up on the

counter. "You know some people think cooking is a love language."

I frowned at the water that was refusing to boil. "Love language?"

"Yeah . . . acts of service. Love languages. It's how people give and receive love." Lark talked with her hands, and it hit me just how cute she could be. "Let me see. There's that, gifts, words of affirmation, physical touch—"

I pointed the spatula at her. "That one. That one's mine."

She rolled her eyes and tossed a slice of scallion at me. "Says every guy ever."

I moved to stand between her knees and tipped her chin with my fingers so her eyes would meet mine. "I'm feeding you. It's the least I can do after how rough I was with you."

"You can call it whatever you want as long as it means you standing in my kitchen half-naked, cooking for me."

I ran a hand across my bare abs. "Do you have a shirt I can borrow?"

She grinned. "Nope."

I growled and nipped at her neck, causing an eruption of giggles that shot straight through me.

"And for the record, you weren't too rough," Lark added. "In fact I'm a little bummed you didn't just rip this dress open."

I raised an eyebrow at her teasing. "Is that so? I'll remember that for next time."

The muscles in her neck moved as she swallowed hard.

"So about that . . . next time."

I shifted, focusing on finishing her food and not on the shift in the conversation.

"I wouldn't mind that, but I think we need to talk about it a little. Ground rules?"

I nodded. "I agree."

"Maybe we don't say anything to Penny. I wouldn't want her getting confused or having too many questions."

I dumped the noodles into the water and continued working as she rambled on.

"Or the guys—they don't need to know. And I feel like if Tootie knows, then the whole town is going to be talking, so maybe we just . . . keep this between us?"

It felt an awful lot like she wanted to hide whatever was developing between us. I should have been relieved. Thrilled. I couldn't quite place why it didn't sit right with me.

I checked the noodles and went to work on the broth. "If that's what you want."

"It's for the best, don't you think?"

"Absolutely."

Lark stayed quiet but watched me cook. In a bowl I layered the noodles and a dark broth. I sliced the soft-boiled egg and smiled at myself.

Nailed it.

I slid the bowl toward Lark. "Fancy ramen."

She beamed up at me, and for a second I wanted to tell her to screw her plan. If we were going to keep fucking, there was no way I wasn't going to want to show her off in public, claim her as mine, and treat her like a fucking queen.

But she was right.

In Outtatowner that meant questions and unsolicited opinions and having to explain casual relationships to my seven-year-old.

Fuck that.

Right now, with the way my life was running off the rails, I'd take Lark in whatever capacity she was willing to give.

I opened the silverware drawer and plucked out a pair of wooden chopsticks.

Lark scrunched her nose at me. "How do you know where everything is?"

I grinned and leaned against the counter next to her as she began eating. "Lived here. All of us but Katie did at some point. It's how I knew to tell you to avoid that green recliner."

It was the first time I noticed it was missing from the living room.

"What's the deal with that chair, anyway?" Lark took another bite, and the soft moan of appreciation was a shot to the gut.

"Lee lost his virginity in that chair, and then for a while it became his 'lucky chair.'"

"Oh god." Lark burst out laughing, and the happy sound rippled through me. "I moved it into the spare room, but now I think I should just burn it."

The laughter between us died down, and awkwardness took its place. Satisfied that she was well fed, I cleared my throat. "I should get going. The guys will be back soon."

Lark set the bowl to her side. "Yeah, good idea. See you tomorrow?"

I nodded and rubbed my hands down the front of my jeans, unsure of what to do with them.

I took one step away but then leaned back to drop a kiss on her cheek before heading straight for the door.

By Thursday night, I found myself comfortably surrounded by the chatter of the Bluebird Book Club. Prepared this time, I brought a tray of mini pastries I had begged Huck to set aside for me. For some reason, I really wanted to make a good impression. Though I knew I wasn't staying in Outtatowner long term, I sought their approval—their acceptance of me into their little secret society.

MJ wasn't there, which was a shame. She was quiet and sweet, and the whole rivalry between her family and the Sullivans was fascinating.

Annie breezed into the book club. Her contribution was a bottle of champagne, and I happily accepted a fizzy paper cup full to the brim.

"Are we celebrating?" I took a sip, and the bubbles tickled my nose.

Annie lifted a shoulder and smiled. "Life is always a celebration at book club."

"Fair enough." I lifted my paper cup and tapped it against hers and sipped. "Mmm. This is really good."

Annie's grin widened. "I got it from Charles Attwater.

He's some award-winning sommelier from New York, and he's opening a new wine shop a few storefronts down. When I bumped into him and we started talking, he gave me a bottle to try. His place is going to be upscale. Small bites and wine pairings, that kind of thing."

"Seems pretty smart. In a tourist town like this, he'll make a killing."

"Wine and cheese won't be the only reason women flock to the store. He's *gorgeous*. All charming smiles and tight shirts, and when he starts talking about tasting notes" —Annie sighed—"I get all mushy inside."

She took a healthy gulp of the champagne. "Thank god he's not a King." Her eyes immediately flew to Bug, who was on an emerald-green settee a few spots down. "No offense."

Annie shifted in her seat and focused on me. "So what about you? Settling in? Word around town is you're getting pretty cozy with our resident golden boy." She winked as she teased, but I could already feel the heat coloring my cheeks.

"Penny's great." Deflecting was a skill I'd mastered a long time ago. "The boys are pretty easy. Tutoring Kevin has taken up a good chunk of most days, but it also keeps him out of trouble."

"And Wyatt?" Annie smiled innocently.

"Busy. He says the upcoming season should be a good one. Practice will start up closer to fall, but for now it's a lot of meetings, I think."

A flash of Wyatt pausing to kiss my cheek before he left my apartment tumbled through my mind. After all that had happened between us, it was the sweet little kiss that had haunted me for days.

"Mm-hmm." She was not buying my *play it cool* bullshit. "You realize you have intimate access to one of the Midwest's most eligible bachelors, and I am not believing for one second you haven't thought about seeing him naked."

I nearly choked on my champagne, and Annie laughed. After I recovered, I sighed. "I guess I'm just not interested in becoming one in a long string of women throwing myself at him."

Let's not forget that's pretty much exactly what you already did. Such an idiot.

Annie shook her head. "Wyatt's not like that."

Curiosity got the best of me. "He isn't?"

"He's no Lee, if that's what you're asking." Annie rolled her eyes. "I think he had a steady girlfriend all through high school. I've known Wyatt my whole life, and he's never been a womanizer, as far as I can tell." She made a grumpy face and deepened her voice. "He's far too serious for that."

I laughed at her spot-on impersonation of Wyatt. My budding friendship with Annie was easy. Fun. Though she was practically a Sullivan herself, it was so nice to have a girlfriend to confide in.

I leaned in close to whisper. "He does look pretty good naked, though."

Annie's arm shot up, champagne sloshing over the rim of the paper cup. "I knew it!"

Immediately, I shushed her and pulled her arm down with a giggle. "Stop! It's not a big deal. We're just friends."

She laughed again and leaned in. "Yeah. *Naked* friends!"

"I'm serious. Penny and the boys don't know. I'm here for the summer, and he's got his hands full."

"Hands full of that ass, maybe."

We cackled again, drawing curious eyes our way. The champagne was definitely already going to my head.

"But tell me." Annie wiggled her eyebrows. "Good, right?"

I exhaled and bent over. "So, so good. And he cooked for me afterward."

"Oh, that sounds super casual." Annie sighed wistfully. "I wish I had someone to cook for me."

I elbowed her. "Maybe that hot new wine guy."

Annie's smile grew as she finished her cup. "Maybe. Around here, you never know."

WHEN MY PHONE rang and the number that flashed across the screen had an LA area code, my stomach dropped. I looked over at Penny, who was on her scooter and making her hundredth lap around the playground; then I picked it up.

"Hello?"

"Good afternoon, is this Lark Butler?"

"It is."

"I'm from the Grinstead Casting Agency. We reviewed your video slate. Would you be available for an in-person callback?"

In person? As in LA . . .

"Oh, I, um . . ." Penny caught my eye and waved wildly. "I am not currently in California."

"I see. I do have it in my notes that we would accept recorded callbacks; however, any advancement beyond that would require you to be in person."

I breathed a small sigh of relief. A lengthier video audition I could definitely handle. If by some small miracle I made it past that round, I could figure out my next steps.

"Of course. I would be honored to submit a recorded callback."

"Lovely." The woman on the other end was robotic, as though this call was anything but lovely. "Also, any recent references." She provided brief details of what was required, and I scrambled to write it all down on the back of a crumpled receipt from my purse.

It wasn't a huge role, but it was already all over Twitter and Instagram that Chase Singleton had been cast as the series' leading man. If I got the job, I would be playing his bitter ex-girlfriend in some pivotal character arc scenes. The woman at the agency also explained that depending on my performance and the direction the showrunners took the series, the part had potential to expand to a series regular. It meant getting in front of the right eyeballs and standing out from the crowd of thousands of LA hopefuls. In this industry, that was ninety-nine percent of the battle.

I hung up the phone and tried to loosen the knot that had formed in my throat.

Holy shit.

I hadn't landed the gig yet, but I'd made a huge step in the right direction. I bet Aunt Tootie could provide a reference for my *latest performance.* The Grinstead Casting Agency didn't need to know that it was for crying at a funeral—or that I was now embedding myself into their little community. I tapped my feet in a little dance of excitement, and Penny rode up.

"What are you doing?"

"Dancing!" I exclaimed. I held my arms out to her as I stood. "I got great news today!"

Penny hopped off her scooter and gave me a big hug. I rocked her side to side and started tap-dancing again.

Penny's giggles were infectious as we celebrated and had our very own dance party. A niggling little pinch formed under my ribs when I thought about leaving Penny to do an in-person audition.

I swept the thought away. Thousands of actresses, those working every single day in LA, were vying for such a small number of roles. The likelihood of me getting the job was so slim I couldn't let it bother me. I had learned the hard way it was best not to get your hopes up at all.

For now I was personal assistant to *the* Wyatt Sullivan, tutor, college-athlete wrangler, and nanny extraordinaire.

I laughed and hugged Penny again.

That gig was pretty dang amazing.

"WHAT DID I TELL YOU?" My mom was so satisfied with herself. "Goddess will provide."

"You did say that. Although Goddess still has a little work to do. It's just a callback." I held the phone between my shoulder and ear as I looked over my appearance again.

"I'll continue to help manifest greatness into your life."

I smiled. "Thanks, Aubergine. I have to run. I'm already late for dinner with Wyatt and Penny."

"Yet another good thing my intentions have brought into your life."

I laughed. She was always taking credit for anything positive that happened. She called it *raising her vibrations*. Truth was, she did pretty much get what she set out to do, so part of me couldn't find it in me to tease her too much. "You're the best, Mom."

After we hung up, I huffed out a breath and fluffed my hair again.

It's just dinner—Penny invited you.

I pressed a hand to the flutters rioting in my tummy. I was being silly. It was just dinner, but there was something about being in his home, outside of me working for him that felt . . . intimate.

We'd done a pretty good job of keeping things between us strictly professional. Wyatt had a string of meetings in St. Fowler, and with me helping Kevin cram for an upcoming exam, the days were busy.

One last swipe of lipstick and I headed down the stairs and across the gravel to their house. The door was open, but I still rapped my knuckles on the screen door.

"It's open." Just his voice sent ripples down my spine.

I stepped inside, drawn in by the warm smells coming from the kitchen. I set the bottle of red wine I was clutching down on the table.

"You didn't need to bring anything, but thank you." Wyatt's eyes lingered on my mouth a fraction of a second too long, and I felt my temperature rise.

"Annie introduced me to Charles Attwater; he's opening the new wine shop in town. I guess they've become friends."

Wyatt grunted in response as he turned back to the stove. "Lee said that guy was a tool."

I bit back a smile. I might have been the only one in town who seemed to think there was some mutual pining simmering between Lee and Annie. Or maybe they had just been friends for so long I was seeing something that wasn't really there.

Penny moved around me, placing three forks next to the plates already on the table. "Just us?" I asked her, curious where Michael, Kevin, and Joey had run off to.

"Dad gave them money and told them to get lost."

My eyes flew to Wyatt's when I saw him frown. "It wasn't *exactly* like that."

I stifled a little smile and helped Penny finish putting down plates and silverware on the small farmhouse table.

During dinner, Penny drew most of the attention, sharing little snippets of our adventures over the past several days. I knew she missed her dad when he had to work long hours or travel back to St. Fowler, and even though he'd already heard of our dip in Wabash Lake and of Joey trying to convince me he could do a backflip off the rocks, Wyatt listened to her every word. Thankfully, I had challenged Joey and Michael to a race to the shore, and Joey had been easily distracted from going through with the backflip.

"Thank you for that." Wyatt sighed as he no doubt thought about Joey's reckless nature. "He's going to get himself killed, one random injury at a time."

"For an athlete, he is surprisingly clumsy." My affection for the three boys had grown in the past weeks. They were good kids. I couldn't help but wonder how life might change for them if they continued to have successful football careers—or didn't.

Joey's confidence was unwavering, Kevin seemed determined to make professional football his life path by sheer will, and Michael always talked about life after football as if he had a feeling pro ball wasn't in the cards for him.

I crossed my legs, and my knee brushed against Wyatt's thigh. As I adjusted, his warm hand landed on my knee and gave it a quick squeeze. His eyes were still tuned to Penny, deep into another story, and before I could discreetly put my hand on top of his, it was gone.

My body hummed with how close Wyatt was, but always just a millimeter too far away. My fingertips itched to rake through his hair. We'd agreed to keep our growing attraction between us, but in the intimate space of his home, it was becoming nearly impossible.

After salad and pasta alfredo and garlic bread, I stood to help clear the table. Penny raced down the hallway, prompting me to speak up. "Nice try, Pen! We all help out."

She popped back around the corner and into the kitchen with a smile. "Sorry. I forgot."

I wrinkled my nose at her and pulled her into a one-armed hug. "You're the best. You know that, right?"

Penny beamed up at me. "Yeah."

I glanced at Wyatt, who stood still, holding two plates, staring at us. The tight line of his lips had a rock settling into my stomach.

Shit.

Hours and hours spent with Penny had made me really comfortable around her, and while she was a good kid, she was seven and needed help with manners and remembering to pitch in. I offered him a small smile, hoping I hadn't overstepped.

Wyatt turned and started rinsing the dishes.

Double shit.

"Is that good? Can I go play?" Penny innocently looked for me to answer.

I smoothed her hair and looked at the expanse of Wyatt's back. "Um, that's up to your dad, kiddo."

"It's fine." Wyatt didn't look up from the sink, where he was now stacking the dirty dishes into the dishwasher.

"Come on, Lark. Let's play." Hoping to smooth things over, I stepped toward him and placed my hand at his back.

His head turned toward me, and when the corner of his mouth lifted to a grin, my insides went liquid. "Go have fun. I'll be done with this in no time."

Penny showed me a game on her iPad, something about fashion design for cats. When she got bored with that, we sat on the floor in front of the coffee table in the living room and colored.

Wyatt walked in with a kitchen towel slung over his shoulder, looking devastatingly at ease and altogether handsome. I swallowed hard and tried to quell the entirely too-domestic thoughts that raced through my mind.

I didn't need to think about how easy it felt with Wyatt and Penny. How natural.

"Daddy, can we watch a movie?" Penny continued to draw what I assumed was Aunt Tootie's house, complete with a chicken coop and a little chicken tombstone next to it.

"It's late, Pickle." Wyatt dried his hands on the towel, and I tracked the movements of the veins that ran down his forearms and across the backs of his hands.

God, I wanted those hands on me again.

"But it's the *summer*!" Wyatt's shoulders slumped, and I knew she had him worn down with simple seven-year-old logic.

I shrugged but continued looking down at my own coloring. "I could stay for a little bit."

When I chanced a look up, Wyatt had turned up his grin and aimed it right at me. My stomach whooshed, and I had to busy myself with organizing the crayons to hide the blush I could feel creeping onto my cheeks.

Penny had chosen a family-friendly movie about a football team who faced tragedy but made an epic comeback with a dog as their wide receiver. Throughout the movie, Wyatt grumbled and commented more than once on the lack of accuracy with the plays, uniforms, and coaches.

One time he even asserted, "That's not at all how that works," and finally Penny rolled her eyes and said plainly, "We know, Dad." She gestured at the television. "He's a *dog.*"

I couldn't hold in my laughter.

Penny sat between us, and I focused on the ridiculous plotline and not on the way Wyatt's muscular arm stretched across the back of the couch. Absently, his fingers found the base of my neck and drew little circles, teasing the baby hairs there and sending chills racing down my back.

When I glanced over at him, his eyes were tuned to the movie, but the barely there flick of the corner of his mouth made it obvious he knew exactly what he was doing.

The sun set, and Penny's eyelids got heavier and heavier. She fought sleep, but before she could see the final touchdown scene, she was lightly snoring against Wyatt's chest.

A knot formed in my throat at the sight of them. She was peaceful and safe, snuggled up against her dad's chest, and he appeared the most relaxed I'd ever seen him.

He looked over at me and whispered, "I'm going to put her down."

I nodded, not wanting to wake her up. As he stood, I also stretched my legs and glanced toward the front door.

"Don't go." His low, rough tone rooted me to the spot. Happy little sparks danced through my stomach.

I turned to the kitchen and kept myself busy by emptying the now-clean dishes from the dishwasher. I could feel Wyatt's energy before he stepped into the kitchen, and my nerves jumped.

"She asleep?"

"Out cold." He took one step in my direction. Then two.

I smiled as I turned to face him. "I'm not going to lie, that movie was . . ."

"Oh, it was goddamned awful." He took another step toward me in the dimly lit kitchen.

Together we laughed quietly. He rubbed his hand across the back of his neck. His biceps flexed, and I looked away, suddenly nervous to be alone with him. I turned back to the dishes, but his hand on my arm stopped me. "Hey, leave that. I'll get it later. Come here."

I turned to face him, wrapped in his arms. The smell of his skin was clean and masculine. Our closeness had my heart thrumming and my mind racing to dirty, delicious places.

"You look gorgeous. I couldn't stop touching you." His wide palms ran up my sides, settling around my rib cage.

"I noticed. It felt good."

His hand found my face, and his thumb brushed across my cheeks. "*You* feel good."

My heart raced. Any alone time with Wyatt had been scarce, and a deep, achy need was taking over.

I wanted to lean into him, press my chest to his, and let him kiss me. I'd been thinking about his mouth on mine for the last forty minutes of that god-awful movie. Every stolen touch had amped up my neediness, and I was desperate for him. He leaned in, closing the inches between us.

"I've been thinking about you." Wyatt's nose stroked down the side of mine, and I sucked in a sharp breath as tingles buzzed down my back. "I think about you too much."

"You do?" My limbs were heavy. My body was tuned into him and molding to his thighs as he held me.

"I can't even tell you some of the things I want to do to you."

Wyatt's words were hard and laced with indecency. I desperately wanted to know, to hear what he wanted to do with me.

"You can show me." I was breathless. At the edge.

"Hey, Coach, we—oh shit!" The screen door banged as it closed, and Kevin's shocked face turned red as I pulled out of Wyatt's arms and immediately started fussing with the dishes.

"Hey, hi." Wyatt tried to recover, but it was painfully obvious we'd just been caught in a very risqué embrace.

Behind Kevin, Michael tried to look away, while Joey had a shit-eating grin on his face.

"Lark and I, um . . . Lark was . . ."

"I was just leaving!" Unable to look anyone in the eyes, I wove around a dumbstruck Wyatt and three grinning college kids.

I'd been seconds away from climbing Wyatt like a tree and had been caught. Despite Wyatt calling to me, I raced outside and up the stairs to my apartment.

So much for keeping things between us.

20

WYATT

"You see, sometimes . . . when two adults have feelings for each other, they . . ." I pulled my hand through my hair as Joey, Michael, and Kevin leaned on the kitchen table and I paced in front of them.

"Really, Coach? It's a little late for the birds-and-the-bees talk." Joey's grin still hadn't left his face.

"No, it's not . . . that's not what I'm doing. I just . . . forget it." Annoyed, I exhaled and slammed the dishwasher door shut.

"Sorry we ruined your date." Michael shrugged and turned to head upstairs. I didn't have the energy to tell him it wasn't a date.

It definitely wasn't a date. Right?

"At least someone's getting some." Joey grumbled under his breath, and I pinned him with a hard stare. His grin only widened. *Little shit.*

Kevin followed his teammates but paused before going up the stairs. "You know you should probably go talk to her, right?"

I dropped the kitchen towel on the table. "Yeah, I know."

"'Night, Coach."

I lifted my chin in a good-night motion and pulled my phone from my pocket. I'd been so keyed up with Lark in my arms that I hadn't noticed Michael's car pull down the driveway.

What if Penny had caught us or the guys had been a few minutes later? I had been a fraction of a second from wiping that coy little smile off her face with a kiss.

I pulled up Lark's phone number.

> Sorry about that.

I watched as the bubbles appeared and disappeared three times before she finally responded.

LARK
> It's okay. Good night, Wyatt.

I frowned at my phone. I had been surprised at how simple things felt over dinner with Lark. Penny adored her, and even when Lark had corrected Penny to help with dishes, I wasn't my typical overprotective self. I actually felt . . . relieved. It was nice knowing the parenting wasn't solely on my shoulders, and for a brief moment I had someone else carrying the responsibility with me.

It rattled me. I shouldn't be having those feelings, *any feelings*, for a woman I shouldn't trust because she had already told me that she would be leaving. It was the exact opposite of the stability I was trying to create for Pickle.

But with only the moonlight in the kitchen, Lark was irresistible. Rational thought had flown out the window when she was warm and pliant in my arms. She'd felt it too.

I was sure of it. The way her pupils dilated and she melted against me told me everything I needed to know.

I needed five more minutes. An hour, tops.

Just to get her out of my system.

I knew it was bullshit even as I typed out the message.

> I'm coming up.

I stopped at Penny's door and listened one last time. She didn't stir, and her slow, steady breathing let me know she was sound asleep.

I ground my teeth as I stomped through the darkness. I tried to pretend I didn't know exactly what I was doing as I pounded up the wooden stairs toward her apartment.

The reality was, I planned to fuck Lark Butler. Use her up and satiate the clawing need she seemed to drag out of me. A need I didn't have time for and definitely didn't want —but which was there nonetheless.

Handling things on my own, getting shit done and not asking for help, had worked for me so far, but lately I had caught myself asking for her opinion, wondering what she would think if I got home late or made a tough call to cut a player.

It was maddening.

It had been years since I'd let a woman in, and I didn't realize how badly I craved the closeness of another person. The intimacy of a family dinner and a night on the couch watching a shitty movie.

Lark had managed to wedge herself into my life, and she hadn't planned on staying.

A bitter part of me wanted to grab onto her, shake her, and make her see what she was doing to me. To us. Because it wouldn't just be me who would be broken and bruised when she finally walked away. Penny was already attached to her, and the closer we got, the harder it would be to pick up the pieces when Lark eventually moved on.

My fist paused in midair before landing with a resounding bang on her front door.

Fuck it.

The door swung open, and the wisps of her hair blew back.

"Wyatt—"

I surged forward, swallowing her gasp as I lifted her and pulled her legs around me so I could feel the heat of her pussy press into my aching cock. I wanted to rut into her, show her exactly how unhinged she was making me simply by existing.

My hands met her ass and squeezed, pulling her into me, rubbing her against me as I slid my tongue into her mouth. That spicy cinnamon and citrus I knew so well assaulted my senses as I left a trail of wet kisses down the column of her neck.

Her moan thrummed under my mouth, and I licked and sucked the pulse point under her thin skin. Lark's hands moved up my chest and over my shoulders as she pulled me closer. Through her jeans I could feel the heat of her pussy, and a core-deep longing pulled a guttural moan from my body.

Lark found my belt buckle. I pulled back, enjoying the lust flash in her eyes and how her lips were already puffy from my kiss. In one swift movement, I whipped my belt through the loops and let it fall with a clatter to the ground.

My hands found her tits, her nipples already hard beneath my thumbs as I teased in slow, rough circles. Her nails scraped against the thin skin of my stomach as she undid my jeans and worked the zipper down.

Lark flashed a mischievous grin as she lowered to her knees. I gripped the sides of her arms. "Hey, I—"

Before I could stop her, she smiled. "Shh. I want this." Lark freed my cock and pushed my jeans and underwear down my thighs. "Didn't you say you'd let me gag on it?"

I swallowed hard. "Is that what you want?"

She licked her lips and nodded.

"Tell me," I demanded, desire flooding my bloodstream as she looked up at me, teasing and gorgeous and perfect. "Tell me you want me to feel the back of your throat with this cock."

Lark took me in one hand, then smiled and licked the bead of precum from the head of my dick. "I want it. I want every inch of you."

"Is that right? You want me so deep you gag and then I feed you another inch?"

"Yes." She practically whimpered, and on a moan, Lark pulled the head of my cock into her sweet mouth. It was tight and hot and wet.

Emotion flickered through me as her eyes met mine. I was holding back. My words were harsh and demanding and bold, but I would go only as far as she would let me.

She licked and pumped me with her hand as her mouth and tongue sucked me deep.

I ran a hand across her cheek, brushing the hair away from her face so I could watch her lips stretch around my cock.

"Fuck." My hand moved to the back of her head, gently holding her while she bobbed and moaned as she sucked me off. My entire body hummed with pleasure as I watched.

With a languid stroke of her tongue, she pulled back, and I ached to bury myself inside her again.

"Now," she said. "Hold my hair back and watch as I take you deep."

I could barely breathe. Lark was fully in control, despite the fact I was desperate to hammer into her.

This woman is everything. "You want me to fuck that pretty little face?"

"Yes. Please, yes."

Her desperate whimper snapped the last cord of my control. With both hands, I cradled her head, lightly fisting her hair as she took all of me into her mouth. I tipped my hips forward but let her set the depth. Her hands gripped my bare ass as she pulled me forward. The head of my cock pushed against the soft palate at the back of her throat.

I froze.

Determined, Lark's mouth moved up and down my length again, pulling me impossibly deep. I felt her throat close and her gag reflex kick in. My cock was aching to finish in her mouth.

She pulled back to catch her breath and sucked me deep again. I groaned and watched as saliva dripped from her stretched lips.

And I snapped.

I needed to bury my cock into that tight little pussy and unleash on her.

"Get up." My voice was hard and demanding.

I helped Lark to her feet, and the back of her hand swiped across her chin. I brushed a strand of hair from her face. "You are so fucking beautiful it hurts to look at you."

Her lashes swooped down, and she offered me a shy smile. I pulled my pants up so I could bend at my knees and scoop her up. I playfully tossed Lark over my shoulder and stomped toward the bedroom.

After dropping her on the bed, I peeled off her jeans

and socks, letting my fingertips stroke down the smooth skin of her thighs. Her underwear was damp, and my cock surged at knowing how wet she was from being on her knees for me.

"Did you like that?" My fingertips ran across the wet spot at her front.

"It was deliciously naughty." Lark tried to cross her legs as I teased her, but I only planted a hand on her knee, spreading her open for me. My hands moved up her rib cage, pulling her shirt up and over her round tits.

I ditched my shirt and pants before getting my hands back on her smooth skin. Every inch of her was perfect to me. "There are so many naughty things I can do to you."

Lark wiggled out of her bra, making her tits bounce, and she grinned up at me. "Like what?"

She liked when I was vocal—told her exactly how I wanted to use her, worship her. I moved forward and pressed my hips into her as I climbed higher.

My hands massaged her chest, teasing her puffy nipple through the lace of her bra. "For one, I wouldn't mind slipping my cock between these."

Lark bit her lip and her eyes met mine.

She likes the idea of that.

I dropped a kiss in the hollow of her collarbone.

"But tonight I want to stretch open this pussy." Her sharp intake of breath was a shot of adrenaline to my system. She arched and moaned as I gave her only featherlight touches. "I want to fuck you long and hard. Then I want to watch my cum drip out of that pretty little cunt."

Her legs wound around me as her back arched and her head tipped to the ceiling. "Oh my god. You are so filthy."

My hands had a mind of their own, memorizing every dip and curve of her body.

"I want that."

My eyes flew to hers, and I raised an eyebrow. *No condom?* I fought an internal battle as every safe-sex talk, warning from coaches about women looking to get knocked up by a professional football player, and even Penny's mom, Bethany, flashed through my mind.

But somehow, with her, I was unafraid. I wanted this, wanted *her*.

Lark could see my hesitation, and she added, "I'm on the pill. You can pull out if you want."

I gripped her hips and pulled her closer to me. "I trust you."

My fingers teased her pussy, and my balls tightened when I felt how wet she already was for me. My thumb found her clit, and she arched off the bed to meet my caress. With slow, teasing touches, I made sure she was ready for me.

Her brown hair fanned out, and her hips gently rocked, bucking up to get more from every touch. I gripped my cock, sliding it through her pussy and teasing her with the tip.

I bit back a groan. If I wasn't careful, I'd blow my load before I even had the chance to sink balls deep inside her.

I wanted her that badly.

Finally, I placed one hand on her hip and another on my cock, guiding it into her entrance. I watched as her gorgeous pink pussy stretched to accommodate me. Her low moan was intoxicating. I needed more of her—all of her.

Lark did too. "More. Yes, more."

A grunt vibrated in my throat. "I want to hear you beg like the greedy little thing you are." Encouraged by her moans of approval, I slowly pumped into her, feeding every last inch until I was fully seated and sheathed deep inside.

Lark gasped. I groaned and had never felt more connected to another human being.

She was everything.

Her hands moved across my chest, and I bent down to embrace her. I needed every part of her touching every part of me as I poured myself into making her feel good. With long strokes, I pumped into her, her body clamped around me. I lifted to gaze down at her perfect features, scrunched with pleasure, and I poured every touch, every unspoken word into her.

Despite his filthy words, Wyatt's tenderness came through loud and clear.

He never rushed but made sure each measured stroke was designed to light my nerve endings on fire.

The rough edge of his whispers against my ear made me dizzy as I pulled him deeper into me. When both of us were sweating and spent, I curled into him, stealing his warmth and being comforted by the slow, steady rhythm of his breathing.

Wyatt's hand moved in lazy stretches up and down my back. The grip he had on my heart was tightening.

The wild look in his eye when he finished and made good on his promise to watch his cum seep out of me was dirty and delicious. The possessiveness that filled his gaze had my heart tumbling, and when he swiftly moved to help clean me up, my throat grew thick.

After a long stretch of minutes, I walked him to the door. Indecision was warring in his eyes—he didn't want to leave any more than I wanted to see him go, but we both knew it was for the best.

He had Penny to look after, and whatever was blooming between us was supposed to be casual. Friendship with a side of lewd and deliciously naughty sex.

Wyatt stroked my face before he kissed me gently, and I tried my best not to swoon against the doorframe. Watching him leave was yet another poor decision. He stopped on the driveway, lit only by the moonlight and the glowing bulb at the base of the stairs. He looked up, smiled, and placed a hand over his heart.

I needed to remind myself that this was temporary. I had a whole life ahead of me that didn't include professional football players or sexy single dads or even men who know how to balance dirty sex with tender touches.

Still, it was hard to not let myself get lost in wondering what it might be like to be chosen by a man like Wyatt Sullivan.

∼

"PROP IT THERE. TO THE LEFT."

"Dude, you're in my shot!" Joey balanced my phone on a little cooler, a novel, and my beach bag before stepping back. Michael and Kevin were looking at the lines I'd scribbled on paper and checking themselves out in the camera.

I looked around again. "Maybe I should do this somewhere quieter." We had found a little alcove with massive sand dunes looming over us, providing a little bit of privacy, but I still felt incredibly shy and awkward.

"No way. It's authentic." Joey stepped back and nodded. "It's perfect."

I smiled at him. "Ready for your directorial debut?"

"Director and leading man," he corrected with one finger pointing at me.

I rolled my eyes at him. "Yes, of course. How could I forget? Ready, Pen?"

I had only just confided in the players that I needed to record a scene to submit for the upcoming television series. Surprisingly, they had jumped all over it and were determined to help. Joey had even asked if I could introduce him to Chase Singleton when I got the role. I laughed and rolled my eyes but was also touched at his confidence in me.

Penny grinned from her seat in the sand, ready to push the record button. "Let's do it!"

I cleared my throat and dipped my chin to signal that I was ready.

We bumbled and laughed through seventeen takes.

Michael and Kevin were taking their roles of background beach bums so seriously. They pointed off in the distance, inspected seashells, even splashed together in the surf.

I dissolved in a fit of giggles when Joey walked up, looking like a young Johnny Depp with pursed lips and brooding eyes.

He sighed and planted his hands on his hips. "You aren't very good at this. Stay in character."

His annoyance only ratcheted my laughter higher. My sides and cheeks hurt from laughing so hard. I had to get it together.

I cleared my throat and tried again. "You're right. I'm sorry."

"Do you want this job or not?"

I laughed again and pushed away the tiny little thought of *eh, not really* that popped into my head. "Of course I do. I'm used to performing in person. I think the camera is messing with my head."

Joey planted his hands on my shoulders. He was a

running back—a fast thinker, quick on his feet, and strong. His lanky frame loomed over me, but his young face made my heart soften. Despite his carelessness at times and flippant attitude, he was a really good kid. My grin was cheesy, but I couldn't help it.

"You're right." I schooled my face. "I'll be serious. I promise. From the top?"

It took another eleven tries before Director Joey was satisfied. It was a simple scene where I was supposed to frantically ask another beachgoer if he had seen my missing child. Very emotional and slathered with drama. I imagined little Penny in the role of my daughter—lost and in danger—and it was surprisingly easy to drum up the emotions I needed to give a convincing performance.

Together we watched the final playback.

"Dude, are you guys holding hands in the background?"

Kevin and Michael grinned. "We were being an authentic beach couple. What about it?"

As the clip ended, I hugged our group and thanked them again for their help. It was perfect. I slipped the phone back into my pocket. I could decide later if I would even send it out. "All right. Lunch is on me. Sand Dollar or Derpy Dogs?"

Penny's little fist shot straight up into the air. "Derpy Dogs!"

THE NEXT WEEK at book club I no longer felt like an outsider. Welcoming smiles greeted me as I pushed open the door to Bluebird Books. While I was still most comfortable sitting near Annie, I'd even ventured out and made friends with the other women, who'd become my weekly girl-time comrades.

Bug was delightfully grumpy, but women flocked to her for advice. Anything from fertility to child discipline to trouble with your in-laws—Bug had an answer.

Mrs. Fritz was always working to bring fresh new ideas to Outtatowner. She worked with other nearby towns to have representations at local festivals, publish newspaper articles about our local farmers, and even organize events from the towns' business owners. If Outtatowner was going to stay on the map, Mrs. Fritz would surely have a hand in it.

Mostly we avoided the conversation of bubbling tensions between the Kings and the Sullivans, but it was becoming harder and harder to ignore as summer wore on. More and more the town was becoming divided over the Kings' apparent takeover of many local businesses. Some saw it was a hostile takeover, while others viewed it as a way to bail out small business owners that were otherwise in trouble.

I landed somewhere in the middle. Impartial. Switzerland.

But maybe partially dipping a toe onto Team Sullivan.

"Looks like being Wyatt's personal assistant agrees with you." Cass, the reporter and Huck's fiancée, smiled at me as she balanced a small plate of fruit on her lap.

Though I bristled a little at the label *personal assistant*, it was hard to deny that, essentially, that was exactly what I was. I smiled back. "Huck was a great boss, but I truly was a disaster. He's probably still finding shards of broken dishes somewhere."

Affection took over her face. "That man has the patience of a saint. Settling in, then?"

I looked around, surrounded by friendly faces. I had never felt so at home in a town I was supposed to just be passing through. Every woman in the room had a story, a whole life beyond the bookstore, but once we were inside, the stressors melted away. We laughed and chatted and drank too much wine.

"I like it here." Admitting it out loud felt dangerous. Real.

She pointed a blackberry at me and winked. "I warned you . . . something in the water."

Recalling my first meeting with Cass, she was right. Though she'd worked in Chicago for a newspaper, Outta-towner—and Huck—had soon claimed her as their own. Perhaps I should have listened to her playful warning more carefully. Day by day the town and its quirky residents were tightening their grip on my adventurer's heart.

I sighed. It was silly to get lost in the what-ifs. I had a whole plan already in motion. I certainly couldn't hang around and be Wyatt's *personal assistant* for the rest of my life.

What a joke.

Wanting anything but to talk about what it truly meant to be Wyatt's assistant, I leaned in close. "So as someone who doesn't pick a side . . . whose side are you really on?"

Cass grinned. "Depends on the day." She crossed her legs and leaned in to whisper. "The King men are trouble. Rough and ready to fight at the drop of a hat. But it's hard to deny that they don't have a hold on this town. They're smart businessmen. And holy shit, have you seen them in suits?" Cass whistled low and smiled. "But then you have the Sulli-vans. Strong, hardworking. Real salt-of-the-earth men. If you need a job done, and done right, you call a Sullivan."

I looked around, finally getting some intel on the true

underbelly of this strange little town. I craved more. "So what's the real deal? Why do the Sullivans and Kings hate each other?"

She shrugged lightly. "It's anyone's guess."

Disappointed that she wasn't sharing more, my lips twisted. Then Cass looked around and lowered her voice even further. "But there are rumors . . ."

My eyes widened.

"Some say Red's grandfather ran off with a King and started the whole thing. That seems unlikely, because as far as I can tell? The rift really started with Red's dad and Amos King."

Red's dad? Wyatt's grandfather.

I nodded for Cass to keep going. She was a local reporter, so maybe she'd been looking into the whole thing. I needed to know more.

"See, Red's dad, Henry, was a farmer but also a tinkerer and businessman. I found some really old public records that Amos King and him were *partners* at one time."

"Partners?" I whispered. "So it was a business deal that went wrong?"

"I think it was more than that. Something about patent rights. Whatever it was, it's buried."

"Are you investigating it?" My eyes went wide.

Cass looked around. "Not officially. Huck would be pissed if he knew I was sticking my nose into the Sullivan–King rivalry, but I can't help it. I just know there's something there."

"Something where?" Bug's voice ripped through our cozy cocoon of whispers.

I withered under her harsh stare, but Cass only smiled and popped another piece of fruit into her mouth. "Bug! It's good to see you. Loving your new haircut."

The firm line of her lips cracked enough for me to release the breath I was holding.

"Can I get you ladies any more refreshments?" Bug asked.

I did my best to give a genuine smile and shook my head. Cass had been brought into another conversation, and I was disappointed that I couldn't hear more about Wyatt's family and the mystery of the town's infamous rivalry. It seemed everyone knew about it, acknowledged it, and even took sides, but talking about it was strictly off-limits.

For the rest of book club, I couldn't stop thinking about the possibilities. Forbidden love. Backdoor business deals. It was all too scandalous to ignore.

22

WYATT

"You don't think this is too . . . I don't know, casual?" Lark looked down at herself as my eyes raked up her body. Annie had invited her out for a night downtown at the Grudge, and Lark had chosen a blue-and-white shirt dress with short sleeves and a matching belt. The long vertical stripes made the perfect path for my eyes to trail over her. The dress was almost to her ankles, but she'd left the line of buttons open starting at midthigh, and wedge heels made her legs look a mile long.

She'd have the attention of every man in town.

A hard lump lodged in my throat. "No."

"You look so pretty, Lark!" Pickle beamed up at her from the couch, and they shared a smile that nearly broke my heart.

"Thanks, Penny! Are you excited for movie night?"

"Aunt Tootie said we could watch *Die Hard*!"

I pointed at my little girl. "Not. Happening."

Tootie came up behind me and patted my back. "Don't you worry. I'll fast-forward through the bad parts."

When my scowl deepened, my aunt and Lark erupted in a fit of laughter.

"That Bruce Willis . . ." Tootie lifted the front of her shirt to fan herself. "He is something."

Lark walked over to Penny and ran a tender hand down her hair. The simple maternal gesture looked so natural. "Maybe one of the live-action Disney movies would be a better choice."

"*Beauty and the Beast*!" Penny chimed in.

Lark nodded. "Solid choice."

It was surprising, and kind of nice, not to be the bad guy ruining everyone's *Die Hard* fun. "Almost ready?" I asked Lark.

She turned and hit me with her million-dollar smile. We said our goodbyes, and as we left, I held the door. For a casual night downtown, it felt an awful lot like a date.

Once we were in the car, Lark shifted her legs, and the slit up the side draped open, exposing the long, smooth column of her thigh. My hand immediately landed on her silky skin. Our eyes met, but neither of us said a word. Lark only settled herself into the seat and smiled.

"Are the guys meeting you at the bar?"

I nodded as I pulled out of the driveway and headed down the dark country road toward downtown Outta-towner. "We'll grab a beer or two before Duke gets itchy and wants to bolt. Head down to the beach for a bonfire." I risked a glance at her, from the sharp line of her collarbone to the soft swell of her breasts in the vee of her dress. "You could come, too, if you'd like."

Lark gave me a soft smile as her eyes lowered to where my thumb was drawing soft circles on her skin. "You mean you're not sick of seeing me every day?"

I chuckled. "Not yet."

The tension in the car was palpable. Though my hand stayed on her leg, I wanted to run it higher, explore her body again.

I hadn't planned on asking Lark to come out to the bonfire, but the moment the words left my mouth, I was glad I had. A tiny wave of disappointment washed over me when Lark tipped her head and smiled. "Girls' night."

"Got it."

Lark's long fingers toyed with the hem of her dress. Her nails were painted a soft cotton candy pink—one I recognized from Penny's collection of nail polish. My own toes were painted the exact same shade.

"I like your nails."

She smiled. "Thanks. We had a spa day." Lark grew quiet, and I pulled the soft perfume of her hair deep into my lungs. "Hey . . . um, I'm a little worried about her. Penny."

My jaw went tight.

When I didn't comment, Lark continued. "So I noticed that she hasn't really made any friends. I know she's new here, and I'm sure she'll have a ton of friends once school starts, but . . ."

I nodded, my jaw working overtime.

Lark gently cleared her throat. "And I love hanging out with her, don't get me wrong. But I was thinking that maybe signing her up for one of the activities at the library or a summer camp or something might be a good way for her to meet some girls her own age."

Worry flickered through me. Penny and I had moved around a lot in the last few years, and while I worried about her making friends, it had never seemed to be an issue until now. Penny had always gravitated toward adults, particularly any babysitters or nannies that had come into our lives.

My hand squeezed her thigh. "Thank you."

Lark gave herself a little satisfied smile, and I couldn't seem to get over how perceptive and good-natured she was. I realized that maybe I had been too quick to judge her when we'd first met. God knows she had been surprising me left and right lately.

When we pulled into a parking space, we walked side by side toward the local bar. The crowd was picking up, and a little jolt of pride ran through me when Lark entered and immediately turned to the west side of the bar to sit with the Sullivans.

With one last smile just for me, Lark peeled off and joined Annie at a table with a few other women. Lee was at a high-top table with Duke, who was already looking uncomfortable and ready to bolt. Lee lifted a hand to signal me over and slid a cold beer in front of me as I walked up.

"You look hungry." Lee's grin spread across his face.

I picked up my beer and tipped it toward him. "You mean thirsty?"

His smile widened as he looked over at Lark. "Nah."

What a shit.

Duke looked up from his phone. "Beckett is driving in. Said we can meet him at his place in an hour or so. He'll have the fire all set up."

I nodded. Beckett's family had summered in Outta-towner for much of his life. One summer he and Duke had struck up a friendship, and they'd kept in touch over the years. Beckett had taken a job as some big-shot contractor in Chicago but came back every few months to visit. His little brother, Declan, was the piece of shit who strung Katie along and broke her heart. I tried not to hold it against Beckett, but it was hard not to when Lee so accurately recalled how hard she cried over what Declan had done to her.

Their family owned one of the large beach houses along

the shore. Built into the side of a dune, it was massive, and the entire wall that faced the water was made of glass, but the beach was private.

While we drank our beer and made small talk, I was acutely aware of Lark. Nothing about her seemed out of place in my little hometown. The women laughed and talked and danced along to the music coming from the band. Any outsider could easily mistake her for someone who'd been a part of our community forever.

Across the bar, I spied the King brothers. Mostly they seemed to be keeping to themselves, shooting the shit like we were. I didn't miss the way Royal's eyes locked onto Lark as she and her friends danced. The familiar wave of jealous possessiveness coursed through me, but I only gripped my bottle tighter. I wouldn't embarrass either of us by starting shit and ruining Lark's night.

"You ready?" Duke had drained his beer and was already wanting to leave.

I tipped my bottle to my lips and set it down with a hard clank. Leaving was a good idea, because if I stayed any longer, I wouldn't be able to help myself. I was pretty certain it was only a matter of time before I wound my arms around Lark and pulled her into me on the dance floor.

And I never danced.

~

MITCH

I think I met a girl.

Oh yeah? Another one?

MITCH

Dick.

Something different about this one.

Jersey chaser?

MITCH

Sure hope not.

Good luck.

THE FIRE CRACKLED in front of me as the sun slowly dipped into the water on the horizon of Lake Michigan. Orange and peach faded into deep indigo as the sun set into the water. Barefoot, I dug my toes into the soft sand.

Lee plopped into the Adirondack chair next to me and handed me a beer. It was some fancy IPA from the local brewery, one I hadn't tried yet. I scowled into my beer as I sipped.

"What's got your panties in a twist?" Duke sat diagonally across the fire from me, Beckett to his left.

Lee was next to me and bumped my arm as he leaned in. "He's pissy that we left the Grudge, and Royal was there eyeballing his woman."

I pushed his arm off mine. "Fuck off."

Lee laughed as though my reaction confirmed his suspicions. "Told you."

"You should have danced with her, man." Lee loved the Grudge and the attention from townies and tourists alike.

My jaw tightened as I thought of her on the dance floor. "Probably. But I don't care about that arrogant prick." *Lie.*

Lee tipped his bottle toward the fire. "You cared enough to stake your claim against Royal King and nearly knock his head off his shoulders the first time she stepped into the Grudge."

"That was different. She was new and didn't know how things are here."

"Seems she's figuring it out," Duke added.

I stretched my legs. Relaxing at beach bonfires with my brothers, just shooting the shit, was something I had missed. There was a sliver of comfort in our shared history, no matter how depressing it was. Despite the fact that I was fundamentally disconnected from them, in the growing darkness, we shared the peaceful silence of the fire crackling and waves lapping against the beach.

I stared into the bonfire, watching the flames lick the wood and dance in front of me. "I don't want Pickle getting too attached."

"Like you're not already attached?" Duke shook his head. I didn't miss his implication that it wasn't solely my daughter whose feelings for Lark were changing.

"We're *all* attached. Lark is great. Is that a bad thing?" Lee asked.

I shook my head, ignoring his comment that Lark had already woven herself into the fabric of my town—and my family—with her grace and sunshine. "Maybe not. Lark is really sweet with Penny. It's just . . . the last nanny we had was her only real friend. Then she met one of my teammates, and when he got traded, she went with him. It was hard on Penny."

And now I'm fucking this one just to make it extra complicated.

"It was bound to happen, though, right? It's not like she's got a lot of women around her." Duke's comment was particularly insightful, and it grated on me.

"Yeah, we see the news," Lee chimed in. "You don't date. Ever."

Beckett took a pull of his beer. "Probably smart."

The reality was that after Penny and the demands of a high-profile career, there wasn't much left to give anyone else. The women who were happy with next to nothing were the same ones I could make happy with money instead.

Lark is nothing like them.

I couldn't get my gorgeous brunette and her flirty summer dress out of my head. "Lark's . . . thoughtful and kind. Aunt Tootie loves her."

"Tootie loves everyone," Lee quipped.

I saw the opportunity to turn our discussion away from Lark and the warm, fuzzy feeling that I was certain was from more than just the bonfire. "I offered to build her a new house. Right there on the property—knock down the old one and start fresh."

"No shit?" Lee looked into the fire as though he was considering my very logical solution to our problem.

I nodded. "She laughed in my face."

Duke sighed. "Well, we need to do *something*. I think she's holding on to memories of Dad from that house or . . . I don't know."

"I can do it." Beckett looked up from the fire and around at us. He lifted a shoulder. "The reno. I can handle it."

Duke reached over to clamp a hand on his best friend's shoulder. A tightness seized in my chest when I realized I was jealous of their easy, lasting friendship.

Something like that took time to cultivate. It meant staying in one place long enough to set down roots. Permanence. Something I'd learned, city after city and team after team, was never going to happen for me.

23

WYATT

I FLIPPED THE LAST PIECE OF FRENCH TOAST ONTO THE plate and doused it with maple syrup. "Blueberries?"

"Are they Uncle Duke's?" Penny was very serious and very loyal about her blueberries lately.

"Of course they are, Pickle."

"'Kay. Then yes." She sat at the table, ready to devour her breakfast. Kevin sat next to her, cramming for another exam, and when I set her plate down, he plucked a ripe berry from the top and popped it into his mouth.

Penny stuck her tongue out at him and grinned.

A squeeze tightened in my chest and wouldn't let up. I stacked the dishes in the sink. I hated to leave them, but if I didn't head out in five minutes, I'd hit traffic and be late. I stared down at the sink as indecision gnawed at me.

"I'll get 'em, Coach." Kevin tipped his head toward the dirty dishes.

"Thanks. You're a lifesaver."

He shook his head. "Just remember this when you're making the starting lineup."

"You got it." I grabbed my hat and sunglasses before

swiping my keys off the table. When I walked toward the door, there she was.

Lark twirled the small bundle of wildflowers—the ones I had collected from the edge of Beckett's property and left on her doorstep—under her nose as she walked into the house. It hit me that she didn't bother to knock anymore, and a strange part of me didn't mind that in the least.

The honey flecks in her eyes sparked to life when she saw me approach. "Morning!"

I swallowed hard. Lark was always so happy. Lately I'd felt pretty damn happy too. And worried. All this seemed a little too good to be true.

"Hey, I'm sorry but I gotta run. Do not do the dishes."

Lark offered me a cute little salute. "Yes, sir."

I sidled up to her, cocooned in the privacy of the small entryway. "I'm serious. If I find out you did them, I'm going to have to punish you."

Fire danced in Lark's eyes. I loved that she was a bit of a brat and liked to push my buttons. She walked her fingers up my chest before tapping the end of my nose. "Noted."

The smirk on her lips told me exactly what we'd be in for later, if I had any say. "You're still coming up later?"

"Three o'clock, right?"

I dropped my keys into my pocket and secured my hat on my head. "I'll be at the field anytime after noon. You and Penny can watch the practice if you're bored."

Lark stepped up to me. Her hand went to my hat and turned it backward with a grin. "*Much* better." She leaned in closer. Her warm breath floated over my ear and made me swallow back a low groan. "*So hot,*" she whispered, then slapped me on the butt and laughed as she turned toward the kitchen. "Have a good day, dear!"

THE SHIT-EATING grin didn't leave my face all day.

The summer sun was high, and it was brutally hot. I made sure the other coaches were cautious. It was Friday and we had a field full of high school students for a one-day summer training camp.

Pride coursed through me as I looked out onto the field. These kids would have the opportunity to be trained by some of the finest coaching staff in the country. The kids could see the university, tour the facilities, and hopefully be eager to join our ranks in the fall. I wanted them to feel like our school was a special place.

But that didn't mean we went easy on them.

The kids were grouped by position and ability. I had worked hard to make sure that no one group far outmatched another. Those with less skill could learn from the technically skilled players. I also found that players who weren't born ready had a tenacity that others lacked. I liked mixing those groups together—building up their confidence while also stretching them as players. Their attitudes also played a major role in whether our scouts would pay special attention to them.

Depending on their positions, each player had the opportunity to work on passing, skill and combo drills, and scrimmages. As I walked on the field, a group of comically large kids—the big dogs—were ready to start work with my lineman staff. I nodded at them as I passed, ignoring the whispers as I found the group of coaches running the individual training squads.

"Great turnout, Coach." Ricky, my offensive coordinator, crossed his arms and looked out onto the field.

"As it should be. We've got one of the best teams in the

country." My eyes skated over the small clusters of hopefuls. If they were lucky, maybe one or two would have a shot at the NFL. If that were the case, they had four years to prove their worth, and it all started right here. "Maybe we'll round up a few more before fall." I clamped a hand on Ricky's shoulder. "Let's get 'em started."

"Should I run the dog piss out of them?"

I huffed a small laugh. "Nah. We'll go easy on them for now. Normal warm-up."

Ricky nodded and blew his whistle. I scanned the schedule on my clipboard, making notes on how I'd spread my time over the one-day training camp. It was important to me to meet each player. Hear a bit about his story. The way he spoke about his high school career, future goals, and even his family told me a lot about a player.

The university had struggled in the past with players getting too big for their britches—kids thinking they were hot shit on campus and ruining any chance at the pros over drugs, reckless nights, or injuries.

Things like broken pinkies.

I shook my head at the sheer ridiculousness of Joey's injured hand. So far the best thing for him had been to hang low in Outtatowner and stay out of trouble, but his cocky smile and carefree attitude still made him very popular with the girls.

I also need to talk with him about that.

My eyes scanned the nearly empty stadium. It was only a few minutes past noon, and even though I'd told Lark to show up around three, I looked for her.

For hours, I looked for her.

We ran the kids hard. They needed to know that university ball was a step up from their small towns and high school glory days. At Midwest Michigan University, you didn't fuck around—not while I was coach.

After a grueling afternoon, I was ready to give them a break. The coaches gathered the players in a semicircle, and I stepped onto a small platform so I could look out onto the field. Several of them had a lot of potential, and a few even caught my eye. I'd be having some serious conversations with the other coaches, comparing notes and deciding whether we'd be making any offers for the open positions.

As I began my speech, my eyes snagged on Pickle, grinning and waving wildly from the first row of stands. She was across the field, but her little arms were flying above her head. My heart pitched and I smiled, but I continued to speak with the players and field questions.

One kid, a quarterback from Iowa with serious potential for greatness, raised his hand. I pointed at him and nodded for him to speak up.

"So what's the secret, Coach? How do we make it onto the team?"

The players around him laughed. That was what *everyone* wanted to know—how to make the team and make it big.

I watched Lark walk up behind the players, Pickle bouncing in front of her and my father at her side. My stomach tightened as I watched them and considered the quarterback's question.

"Always work hard. Never give up. It's a game, have fun." Those were words my dad always said to me before a big game or a big decision. I gestured toward Dad and the players' heads turned in his direction. "That's what he'd always tell me before every single game."

Dad looked at me with clear eyes and a smile, and the

roiling in my stomach settled for the briefest moment. "If you can figure that out, you'll be successful on my team."

As I stepped down, Ricky took over, instructing the players how to sign out and where to go for the tour of campus. I jogged toward my family.

My family.

The errant thought hit me like a ton of bricks, and my steps faltered on the turf. Thankfully, I scooped Penny into a hug to hide my nerves.

"This is a surprise." I smacked a kiss on Penny's cheek and smiled at Lark. She looked nervous, so I shot her a wink.

"Penny and I went to see Red this morning, and he wanted to tag along. I hope that's okay. I read somewhere that exercise is good for . . . you know. A walk around campus is just what we need, right, Red?"

Dad stepped up to shake my hand. "Fine speech you gave, Son. Nice to know my talks didn't always land on deaf ears."

My throat tightened, and I couldn't find the words to respond. Dad was here, in my element, without that confused, dazed look in his eyes. It was clear Lark had also looked up or talked with his nurses about his condition, and that left my chest feeling tender and strange. Lark was shifting things, and I wasn't altogether sure how I felt about that, but deep down I knew it wasn't all bad.

"Papa Red, they have *snacks*!" Penny pulled my dad's hand and led him to the table stacked with Gatorade, water, chews, and energy bars to keep the players hydrated and energized during the grueling day.

"Just one, Pickle. Those are, like, ninety-nine percent sugar and caffeine."

Her eyes bugged with forbidden delight. *Wrong thing*

to say.

I turned to Lark. "She'll be bouncing off the walls."

Lark swatted the air in playful dismissal. "Ah, it'll be fine. We can always make her run laps."

I'd grown to love playful banter with Lark, and she could always find the silver lining in situations that would normally piss me off. Penny was stuffing energy bars into my dad's pocket when I gestured toward them.

Lark chewed her lip. "I hope it's okay. The nurse said he was having a great day."

I leaned in to bump my shoulder against hers. "More than okay. Thanks for showing up."

"I like seeing you in your element. All your brooding charm is starting to make sense."

"Brooding charm?"

She laughed. "Yeah. Always in charge. Always in control. It makes the times I see a crack in your grumpy facade that much more fun."

I crossed my arms. "I'm not grumpy."

"You kind of are, Daddy." Penny looked up at me with serious eyes.

I deepened the furrow in my brow and growled at her. Pickle screamed a peal of laughter and took off running before I chased after her and scooped her up in my arms. I bounced her high in the air and didn't give a single fuck who was watching or that I was supposed to be the man in charge.

None of that mattered.

What mattered was that I had had a great day with the players, my kid was happy, and Lark and my dad were around to share it with me.

For the first time in what felt like forever, everything seemed to be clicking into place.

24

LARK

Cold water splashed on my fingers as I set the wet cup down, sweating from the summer heat. I pasted on a smile and tried to swallow down the sudden wave of nausea. I stood awkwardly a foot or two away from Wyatt, Penny, and Red, who were at the entrance to the stadium.

Penny's hand was tucked into Wyatt's, but as an electric-blue sports car pulled up to the circular drive, she looked up at him with a huge grin. Wyatt looked back at me. I'm sure he was wondering why I was being weird and standing away from the group, but as a woman stepped out from behind the driver's side, I swallowed hard again.

Wyatt's ex.

Penny's mother.

She was stunning, a mature and gorgeous version of Penny herself.

I shouldn't have been surprised that handsome, charming Wyatt would have exes that had dazzling smiles and were built like Wonder Woman.

I tugged at the hem of my cutoff shorts and the

discarded Midwest Michigan University T-shirt I'd stolen from Wyatt's laundry basket and cropped into a cute top.

"Mom!" Penny stepped forward to embrace her mother, and the woman's arms wound around Penny's back.

"Hey, Penny. I've missed you!" She smiled at Wyatt. "Thanks for making this happen."

"'Course." His voice was softer as he looked at the woman and Penny. "Glad you could make the trip."

The woman looked at Red, who didn't say hello or seem to recognize her. "Hi, Mr. Sullivan. It's good to see you again."

My heart ached for them, as it was clear as day Red didn't recognize her.

"I'm Bethany. Penny's mom? I visited you a few times with Wyatt. Remember? Of course you do!"

"Yeah. Yes. Of course." Red shifted his weight, and I worried that he'd get frustrated and agitated, as MJ had warned often happened when he was pushed to remember fuzzier details.

Thankfully, or maybe unfortunately, the woman's eyes landed on me. "Oh. Hi. I'm Penny's mom, Bethany."

I stepped forward and offered my hand and a wobbly smile. "Lark. I'm, um . . ."

I looked to Wyatt for help.

Am I the nanny? Personal assistant? Fuck buddy?

It was Penny who provided the details as the awkward silence filled the air. "She's our neighbor and my very best friend! She also works for Daddy."

Penny's delighted eyes met mine, and I winked at her as Wyatt nearly choked next to me.

He cleared his throat. "Lark's been a lifesaver this summer, what with me juggling the new job, the team. She's the only reason a few of my players will be eligible in the fall. Penny likes hanging out with her too." He ruffled her hair.

Bethany's smile was nothing but genuine, and I relaxed a little. "I still can't believe you moved back to the middle of *nowhere.*"

Red grumbled at her tiny jab. Her words weren't malicious, but it was obvious she was a city girl, through and through.

Bethany stood, holding on to Penny and looking at Wyatt. The weird, jealous feelings I hated to admit to having started to bubble up, so I took the opportunity to bail.

"Hey, Red, how does a walk sound?"

Relieved gratitude flickered over Wyatt's face, and my throat went thick. Bethany was pleasant. Nice, even. I knew I wasn't the first woman Wyatt had ever been with, but the fact that he *never* talked about Penny's mom made me burn with curiosity.

Red and his fractured mind felt safe. He didn't recall much, if anything, about Bethany, and that meant I couldn't torture myself with peppering him with questions in search of answers.

I smiled at Penny as I looped my arm through Red's. "Have a great time, Pen."

Penny surged forward and wrapped her arms around my middle. "See you Sunday night. Love you."

Sudden, unexpected tears pricked at my eyes as I rubbed her back. "Love you too, kiddo. Have so much fun."

Before I could look at Wyatt's face and dissolve into a puddle of unwelcomed emotion, I gave Red a watery smile and led him down the sidewalk.

Red patted my hand. "Kids always know how to punch you in the gut, don't they?"

I blew out a breath and squeezed his arm. "They sure do, Red."

THANKFULLY, my muddled-up feelings stayed in check for the rest of the afternoon. Wyatt still had things to wrap up after the football camp, so I'd texted him that I was taking Red home and would chat with him later.

Within seconds he responded.

WYATT

Seeing you on the field was the best part of my day.

My insides went gooey. I'd managed to quell my irrational jealousy on the drive back to Outtatowner. It had been a very long time since a man had made me as mixed up and dizzy as Wyatt had managed to do in a few short weeks.

I dropped Red back at Haven Pines and helped make sure he was settled in his room before wishing him a good night. I was beat from the long day, but keyed up.

As I pulled into my driveway, I paused. Lee was sitting at the base of the steps that led to my apartment. He stood when I pulled the car to a stop.

"Hey!" I smiled back when a goofy grin spread across his face. "Wyatt's still not back from work. What's up?"

Lee unclasped his hands and lifted his palms. "Here to see you."

I closed the car door behind me. "Okay . . ."

"I need someone who isn't a townie to help me for a little while. You game?"

I crinkled my brows at him. "What's up?"

Lee rubbed a hand across his chin. "On a scale of one to ten, how opposed to a little small-town troublemaking are you?"

I smiled. "I don't know . . . I guess that depends. A two, maybe?"

"I can work with that. Let's go." Lee reached into the small duffel bag that hung crosswise against his body and tossed something at me.

I caught it, revealing a black knit stocking cap. "Seriously?"

Lee winked, and I looked back at Wyatt's darkened farmhouse before walking toward his truck. "Just get in," he said.

LEE TURNED DOWN A SMALL, dark road and flipped off his headlights. My eyes went wide, and my skin prickled.

"It's fine. I promise. I'll have you back to your place in thirty minutes. An hour, tops." He nodded toward the stocking cap in my hands. "Put that on."

I pulled the knit hat over my head and peered into the darkness. "Where are we?"

"Just an old two-way stop." Lee shrugged. He climbed out of his truck, and I followed him toward the truck bed.

We were cloaked in darkness, but down the dark country road, headlights appeared in the distance. I held my breath but exhaled when the vehicle turned.

Lee pointed left and right down the road. "You're the lookout. Yell if you see anyone coming. Yell louder if you know for sure it's a King."

Confused, I watched Lee pull a tool bag and a long rectangular piece of metal from the back of the truck.

"What is that?"

Lee's childlike excitement was palpable, and my stomach flipped. He turned the sign around, and it read, Poor House Road. I glanced up at the existing sign, which read, Pour House Road.

"I know a guy who works for the road commissioner." He shrugged and grinned. "In the sign shop. He married a cousin, so technically he's a Sullivan and did me a favor."

I narrowed my eyes at him, already knowing the answer. "And who lives down this road?"

Lee's grin widened.

A King.

Replacing the sign to the house of the richest family in town with Poor House Road?

"This is so childish." I tried my best to make it sound like a reprimand, but I couldn't help the laughter that laced through my words.

Lee motioned down the road with the big metal tool. "Just keep your eyes peeled."

I peered down the dark roadway. It was still warm from the day, but a chill raced across my chest as my nerves started to get the better of me. Far into the darkness, a pair of headlights turned onto the road.

"Lee! Hey, someone's coming!"

Lee had already removed the old sign with a hammer and another tool he used to punch out the rivets. He was working fast to attach the new sign with bolts. "Almost. Almost there."

I leaned against the side of the truck, trying to make myself invisible. "They're still coming. I have no idea who it is. Lee!"

The car approached, and my stomach sank to my shoes as the familiar outline of a police cruiser came into view. I straightened as Lee kicked the tool bag away and stepped to my side.

An officer climbed out of his vehicle, and I froze. "Evening. Car trouble?"

My eyes grew wide as he scanned the roadway by us.

"No, sir," Lee answered smoothly. "Lark here is new, and I was just showing her some of the sights." He looped his arm across my shoulder, and I could only look at him with horror as I realized what he was implying.

The officer stifled a knowing laugh as I shot daggers at the side of Lee's head.

"Well, you two best move on. This is a dark stretch of roadway, and it's not safe to be parked without lights."

"Yes, sir." Lee guided me toward the passenger side and opened the door. "We'll head out."

Satisfied, the officer nodded and returned to his cruiser. I watched as Lee took his time rounding the hood of the truck. When the police officer pulled away, Lee ducked down to retrieve the tool bag and the old road sign. Hurrying, he tossed them into the bed of the truck and hopped into the cab.

He grinned his devilish grin at me and turned on the engine. "That was a close one. Are you coming?"

I moved around the open door and climbed inside. "You idiot! We could have been arrested!"

Lee laughed and leaned closer. "Nah. The cops are always trying to scare people away and keep them from making out on dark country roads." He wiggled his eyebrows at me.

I rolled my eyes and pushed him away, laughing.

"What do you say I buy you a beer for your trouble?"

I looked at my phone. Still no text from Wyatt. "Sure." I pointed my finger at him. "But no more breaking the law."

Lee smirked as he pulled down a road and headed toward Main Street. "No promises."

I KNEW IT WAS A SETUP THE MINUTE DUKE TEXTED ME, asking to go out for a night on the town at the Grudge Holder. Duke hated the bar scene, especially during the height of tourist season. Truth was, I wasn't a big fan of it myself, and I was hoping for some alone time with Lark.

Joey had invited Michael and Kevin to his parents' house for the weekend, and that meant, for the first time, I was officially responsibility-free.

My plan had been to fuck Lark on every surface of that damn farmhouse until she cried out for more.

Except I still hadn't heard from her. I shot her a quick text anyway.

> Heading out for a beer with Duke. Please give me an excuse to see you.

LARK

> Good news. I'm already at the Grudge with Lee and I'm having to practically beat down the wave of women who keep coming up to him to dance. Come save me.

I smiled down at my phone and dialed Duke's number. "Yeah."

"Almost to your place. Are you planning to stay out a while?"

"I was thinking so. Maybe have a dance or two."

It was then I knew those assholes were up to no good. Duke was never a dancer. "You feeling all right?"

"Shut it. Come pick me up."

I laughed and set the phone down. Duke lived a stone's throw away from Tootie's house down Boogertown Road. He was waiting for me on the porch when I rolled up.

With a tip of his chin, he climbed in.

"Are you wearing cologne?"

Duke grunted, and we made our way up the lonely country road. As we passed Aunt Tootie's house, it looked even more dilapidated in the low lighting.

I sighed. "We've got to do something about that house. It's not safe."

Duke shook his head. "I know it. She won't move out. Won't sell it. I also talked to Beckett, and I think it'll work out. He's moving to the area, so if we can convince Tootie, he'll do the whole place up."

"I know you have your hands full with the farm and operations. Lee's schedule is totally fucked, and I'll be swamped once the season starts. Are we going to be able to make this work? Especially with Dad?"

"Dad's in good hands where he's at. Lee talked to Katie. She's coming home, man."

A knot twisted in my gut. Katie had run off to Montana to get away from the drama of Outtatowner. Start fresh. Somewhere no one called her *Catfish Kate*. I laughed a bit to myself at the childhood nickname she had never managed to shake. A part of me felt bad for being the one to call her that because of her big round eyes. I never expected my teasing to stick with her so long.

"It'll be good to see her again."

Duke nodded. "She might be pissed, though."

"Because of Declan?"

"That little fucker hasn't shown his face around here since he broke her heart, but Beckett's his older brother, and Katie holds a grudge."

I nodded and turned down Main Street. "That she does, brother. That she does."

"Beckett's a good guy. He'll do solid work on the house and won't overcharge. She'll just need to get over it."

When we pulled up to the Grudge, it was a quiet night. I parked next to Lee's truck and walked with Duke to the front door.

We went inside and were greeted with friendly faces and waves. Duke walked in first, toward the Sullivan side, and I scanned the room, looking for Lark.

I watched as Duke's eyes also scanned the entirety of the room, and his frown deepened. It was almost like he was hoping to see someone out tonight and was disappointed the person wasn't there. When I asked him as much, he only responded with "Fuck off."

I finally spotted Lark, and my stomach dropped to my shoes. She was so beautiful, sitting at a high table and watching as people danced around the small wooden dance floor. After our eyes met, her big white smile widened, and I struggled to catch my breath.

Lee was chatting with a woman who was swirling the straw in her drink and looking up at him with big, hopeful eyes.

Duke stomped toward the table and nodded a greeting

to Lark. Then he turned and tapped Lee on the shoulder. "Let's go."

Lee scrunched up his face. "What do you mean, 'Let's go'? You literally just got here."

"Tired. Just drive me home."

Lee looked at me and I only shrugged. Whatever Duke was hoping to find here wasn't at the bar, and he was done.

Annoyed, Lee excused himself from the conversation he was having and turned to the table. He looked at Duke, who was growing more and more uncomfortable with every passing second. "Fine, but you owe me."

We said our goodbyes, and Lee held out his fist to Lark. She bumped it and smiled. "Hell of an accomplice," Lee said.

Her eyes grew wide and darted to me.

"What does he mean? Accomplice?"

Lee howled with laughter and headed straight out the door.

I turned back to Lark. "Accomplice?"

She lifted her hands. "I had no idea, I swear. I was an involuntary criminal."

Lark looked so innocent and scared that I laughed and pulled her beer bottle toward me. I put it to my lips and took a deep drink. "Sounds like I'm gonna need a beer for this story."

～

BEING out around town with Lark was effortless. Natural. Just like everything else with her, she brought levity and fun. With her I didn't have to worry so much about the upcoming season, whether Pickle and I would have to move, or how the drama of Outtatowner was going to inevitably fuck up my life.

She had been content to watch the people dancing, and after a popular song came on, she lifted her brows at me. I pretended to resist, but when she pulled me from my stool, I was happy to hold her in my arms while we moved to the music. I could feel the eyes on us, but I didn't care if that started a slew of fresh rumors. As far as I was concerned, Lark was mine and I was hers.

At least for now.

After the dance, we left the Grudge to wander down Main Street. It was bustling with tourists and townies alike. The café had string lights illuminating their outdoor patio, and the warm glow bounced off Lark's skin, making it irresistible. I pulled her under my arm and enjoyed how perfectly she fit as we walked side by side.

"How do you feel about ice cream?" I had already started heading toward the shops that lined the waterfront.

Lark smiled up at me. "I feel good about that."

We continued our lazy path down the sidewalk and toward the marina. She looked at boats bobbing in the water and asked questions about the people who owned them. A lot were from tourists who parked for the weekend or the season, but I pointed out the ones I did know and filled her in on which side of the Sullivan–King feud they landed. My teeth ground together when we passed a fishing boat with Noble King Fishing Tours freshly painted on the side.

I recognized the sleek lines of the fishing boat my father once owned. Back when he was himself and operations on the farm had run so smoothly he was branching out into other tourism opportunities. The boat, and Dad's dream of hosting guided fishing tours, had flown out the window when he'd gotten his diagnosis, and things had gone to hell fast. It pissed me right the fuck off to see the King name on *Dad's boat*.

Russell King wasn't a businessman like his father, Amos. He was a scavenger. Even after all our families had been through, he was greedy enough to capitalize on our misfortunes. I hated him for it.

I hated that the Kings had the ability to sour my mood without even being there. I refocused my attention on the gorgeous brunette at my side and how I hoped she was as excited for an evening alone together as I was. The fact that she had inadvertently helped Lee piss them off was the icing on the cake. As childish and reckless as it was, I wished I could have been there to help pull off the prank.

We stepped into Sweet Sundae, the old-fashioned creamery shop, and I motioned for Lark to step ahead of me. Her eyes danced with delight as she scanned the menu.

When it was our turn, Lark smiled at the server. "Cherry chocolate chunk in a waffle cone, please!"

The young girl behind the counter looked up at me. "Rum raisin. Sugar cone, please."

Lark snorted beside me.

"What?"

"You are such an old man."

I rolled my eyes at her. "Whatever. It's a classic."

"I swear if you have a hard candy in your pocket, I'm going to lose it."

I stared at her as I reached a hand in the front pocket of my jeans. I held my hand in front of her and slowly opened it, revealing a Werther's Original Penny had asked me to hold on to earlier in the day.

Her laughter settled over me, settling between my ribs, and I moved to stand behind her. My arms wrapped around Lark's shoulders, and I pulled her close to me as we waited.

Her cinnamon-and-citrus scent swirled with the sticky-sweet aroma of the ice cream shop.

Happy memories of getting ice cream with Mom and Dad and walking down the pier flooded my mind. I nuzzled into her neck and felt her hum at my affection.

This will be another good memory to add to that.

The young server handed us our ice cream, and I paid. "Hey, let's take these to go."

I led Lark out of the ice cream parlor and toward the beach. Families and kids hanging out near the pier walked past us as we enjoyed the warm summer night. The road ended, and we stepped on the pier. At the end, the old lighthouse stood tall, its beam of light stretching out over the dark waters of Lake Michigan.

The closer we got to the rocky outcropping at the base of the lighthouse, the fewer people there were to interrupt us. I found a quiet corner and gestured for Lark to sit. Enjoying our ice cream, we sat in comfortable silence, looking out at the waves that disappeared into the horizon.

She leaned into me and held her cone out. "Want a bite?"

I eyed it skeptically, like I wasn't sure if her choice in ice cream was up to my standards. Lark playfully rolled her eyes at me. I leaned forward and lowered my mouth to her cone.

Then she squished cherry chocolate chunk into my face.

What a shit.

I sighed even as my chest began to shake with laughter.

Her melodic giggle was infectious as she tried to pull herself together. I simply stared at her, doing a shit job at keeping a straight face while melting ice cream dripped from my chin. "Mmm. It's really good. Can I have a little more?"

A fresh round of laughter burst out of her as I leaned down and aggressively bit off the top half of her ice cream.

"Hey, that's too much!"

Deep, hearty laughter felt strange in my chest as I wiped at my chin. "That's what you get."

She licked one side of her cone to try to straighten it out, but it was hopeless, and I mopped up the mess on my chin with napkins.

"Can I try yours?" She wiggled her eyebrows at me, and I huffed at how fucking cute she was.

I held my cone up, and she leaned in for a bite. I jerked my hand, and when she pulled back, my unrestrained laughter rang out.

"I'm kidding. I won't." I narrowed my eyes at her. "Even if you do deserve it."

In that moment, the full force of Lark's breathtaking smile was just for me. I wanted to bottle it up, save it, and tuck it away so no one else could have it.

I held my hand steady as she lowered her head. My eyes tracked how her mouth moved. How her lips closed over the creamy ice cream. The hum of her throat as she closed her eyes and savored the bite.

My heart clunked.

A dot of ice cream clung to her lower lip, and I couldn't resist.

"You missed some." My voice had dropped, turning thick and gravelly. I leaned forward, and instead of wiping away the drop with my thumb, I swiped my tongue across her full lower lip.

Her soft exhale brushed across my mouth. I moved in again, closing the fraction of space between us as I took her mouth. It was cool, sweet, and delicious. I moaned into her, thinking of all the depraved things I wanted to do with Lark.

I wanted her—needed her—unlike anyone I'd ever met.

And I needed her *now*.

I was sure I looked crazed when we broke apart, but I pinned her with my glare. "We're leaving."

26

LARK

Wyatt kicked open the front door to his farmhouse, and the screen door closed behind us with a slam. Our mouths were frantic—hungry and seeking.

Barely inside the house, Wyatt had me pressed against a wall, my legs wrapped around his waist as his hands tangled in my hair, controlling the kiss. Need and passion radiated from him, and I was just as eager to soak up every last drop.

I planted my hands on his shoulders to break free, and his mouth captured my neck. "Wait. The kids."

Wyatt's voice was heady and deep. "Gone for the weekend." His arms tightened around my back. "You're all mine."

Desire coursed through me. Thrilled at the prospect of a house alone with Wyatt, I arched into him, accepting his kiss and reveling in the way his teeth scraped against the thin skin of my neck. It drove me wild.

Wyatt walked us through the foyer and turned the corner into the kitchen. He tipped me backward, depositing me onto the kitchen table, and yanked away my cutoff jean shorts. My hands went to my T-shirt.

"Did you wear this for me?" His hands smoothed up my exposed ribs, looking over the university tee I'd cropped just for him.

I nodded and smirked.

"Leave it on."

Bracing my hands behind me, I thrust my boobs in the air and wrapped my legs around his waist. He crushed his lips to mine. We were frantic for every touch, every taste.

Wyatt leaned back, and I released him from my hold. His hand went to his belt, and when he whipped it off in one smooth motion, a choked squeal of delight escaped me. He reached behind his head and removed his shirt in the sexiest, most manly way possible. I could feel my pussy go slick. He took off the rest of his clothing and stood in front of me, butt naked and utterly confident.

Goddamn he's beautiful.

The intense furrow in his brow made me only hotter. I couldn't wait until he unleashed all that pent-up frustration and grumpiness on me. He gripped his dick and stroked his length. I slipped my hands inside my tee to remove my bra.

Wyatt's hungry eyes watched me as he continued to pump himself. I absorbed his gaze in eager anticipation.

"What do you want, Lark? Tell me. You can have anything you want as long as you say it."

"I want it." My eyes moved up to his, and I suddenly felt shy voicing exactly what I wanted. "Bare again."

A cocky grin spread as he stepped forward. My legs wound around his hips and held him close. Wyatt gripped his cock as he teased me through my underwear. "Like I said, anything you want, baby."

My head lolled back as he tortured and teased me. I clenched, wanting to be stretched and filled. His thick erection found the edge of my underwear.

"Pull those aside."

Heat poured through me and I did as I was told. I released a small squeak as he lowered to his knees.

He shot me a wicked grin. "You didn't think I was going to fuck you without tasting this pussy first, did you?"

I moaned as his mouth clamped over my heat. Not only did he use his tongue to lick and tease, but he used what felt like his whole damn face. He moaned into me, and the vibrations sent shivers up my back. My hips tilted on their own will, begging for more. Wyatt's hand reached up and slipped below my T-shirt to play with my nipple, while the other teased my entrance.

It was an onslaught of heat and pleasure, and with every pulse of his tongue I was closer and closer to coming. "Oh god. Don't stop."

My hips were moving and grinding against him and—bless that man—when I was close, he didn't stop or change speeds or do something different. He continued to suck and lick and tease in exactly the way that hurled me closer and closer to the edge.

As I cried out, his mouth clamped down on my clit, and he tweaked my nipple. I held my panties to the side as I unraveled. Soaked and humming with pleasure, I rode the wave of my orgasm as he continued to moan in approval and devour me.

I collapsed on the table, overtaken by the intensity of my orgasm.

"Uh-uh." Wyatt rose and leaned over me, planting hungry kisses down my neck. He looked at me, his gaze dark and devious. "We're just getting started."

His rough hands gripped my hips, sliding my ass to the very edge of the table and slipping my underwear down my legs. "I'm dragging you down the hallway to my bed, but I'm doing it with your pussy milking this cock."

I clutched him, burying my face in his shoulder as his wicked words made my nipples impossibly harder. With one hand, he gripped his rock-hard cock and pulled me onto him.

I cried out into the darkened kitchen as he filled me.

Supporting my weight, Wyatt made good on his promise and carried me, his cock still buried deep, down the hallway to his bedroom. He gently laid me on his bed, his frame moving over me as his hips pumped.

I could feel his massive dick throb inside me. I stretched my arms over my head, reveling in the way he made me feel cherished and wanted and used up all at the same time. His hands shoved my top up, letting my chest bounce, and he started dragging his length from me before stuffing himself back in.

Over and over he pumped into me as his hands explored every inch of my body. His thumb found my clit, and I cried out over a string of his curses. My hands reached for his abs, and I explored every hard peak and valley. Tension built in his muscular shoulders, and he rocked into me.

Wyatt leaned back, looking down at where our bodies were connected. "Your pussy is so pretty when it's taking my cock."

He reached down and wound his hand around the back of my neck, supporting it as he lifted me up. "Look at it. Look at how well you take me."

Pleasure flooded my system as his praise sent buzzy warmth pooling between my legs. I watched in awe as his cock disappeared inside me. Deep and full. Over and over he brought me closer to the edge with every thrust of his hips. He increased his pace, and I fell back onto the mattress. Wyatt gripped the bed as he continued to fuck me. His body slammed against my ass as he drove into me.

I was there, right there with him.

"Fuck, Lark." His simple, guttural outcry forced me over the edge. My inner muscles clamped down hard around him. I circled my hips, begging for more.

"You feel so fucking good." Wyatt stilled as he came, and when I squeezed down on him, he groaned louder. He collapsed on me, his dick pulsing and spasming inside me. I tilted my hips.

"No. Stop. Don't move. It's too good."

I stifled a laugh as he stroked my side and kissed my shoulder. His heart hammered against me, and he was as breathless as I was. We stayed, locked together, catching our breath for long moments.

He laughed and my chest squeezed. I'd grown to love that sound. "You're trying to kill me, woman."

Leaning to the side, Wyatt rolled, slipping from me and onto his back. His hand was on his chest as it rose and fell with every labored breath. I propped my head on my elbow, energized by my own orgasm. A sliver of moonlight slanted through his window and washed the bedroom in pale light. It cut across the floorboards and allowed enough light to see his satisfied smile.

His hand trailed up my thigh, catching the remnants of his orgasm as it seeped out of me. "So fucking hot." His thick fingers teased my pussy. He wasn't shy, but rather proud, of the mess we had made together.

I pressed my knees together, capturing his hand, and I pointed up at him with a smile. "You are so filthy."

He winked at me and stood. "Baby, you have no idea."

Wyatt returned quickly with a warm, wet washcloth and made quick work of cleaning us both up. As he smoothed the warm cloth over my body, he whispered sweet compliments and dotted kisses along my sensitive skin.

Then he lay on his bed and gathered me close, holding me against him. I listened as his heart thumped against his ribs as he stroked my back.

With Wyatt I was warm. Safe.

My limbs were heavy, and I cuddled into his protective warmth. He worked so hard to make me feel wanted and cared for. A surge of protectiveness swelled in me.

His grumpiness. The wariness and mistrust of new people. The more I got to know him, the more it made perfect sense.

He'd learned to protect himself.

I shifted to rest my chin on my hands as I looked up at him. His face was calm, but his eyes stayed pinned to the ceiling.

"Hey."

He looked down at me, and a soft smile lifted his lips. "Hey."

I scooted up to kiss him, to pour into him every ounce of affection and appreciation I felt for him. For us.

I was falling for Wyatt Sullivan.

Hard.

While I didn't know what it meant and couldn't quite find the words, I could show him with my kiss. It started soft and slow but turned sensuous and deep. A hard, raspy moan moved from his throat into me.

My heart ached at how sweet and perfect that man was. Strong, honest, short tempered, and kind. The man who had believed for so long that his performance on the field equaled his worth. The man who had been told time and time again that his best was just short of being enough.

You are more than enough.

I squeezed my eyes tight as I continued to kiss him and scream the thought in my mind over and over—*You are more than enough.*

Finally, I broke the kiss and swallowed hard. My hand swept the stray hair from his forehead. "I'm here. I'm here with you."

It was all I could do to not blurt out the feelings that were growing wildly out of control. Like a vine you knew might be trouble but had suddenly overtaken everything and nothing was the same.

Wyatt's gravelly voice echoed through the dark room. "I am the luckiest man in the world."

I preened at his praise and attention.

My inner critic was blissfully quiet, and I enjoyed the stillness his comforting words brought me.

I settled into the nook of his arm, and we spent lazy hours exploring each other without having to rush or hide or be quiet. Our hands roamed. We found each other in the darkness, coming together to make love and cherish each other with unspoken words.

SOMETIME IN THE early morning I awoke, tangled in Wyatt's arms and legs. My eyes burned from lack of sleep, and my body was swollen and sore, but I couldn't keep the smile off my face. Wyatt barely moved as I shifted to lift some of the weight off his heavy arm.

I smiled at him. *Out cold.*

I used the protection of the dim room to stare at his perfect face—his straight nose, the dip in his upper lip. I gently smoothed a finger over the spot where a line usually creased between his eyebrows.

Thoughts of my unsent callback slate flickered through my mind.

How could I leave now?

I laughed at myself. Aubergine would be proud that I was *acting as if* by assuming I'd get the gig, it would force me to leave Outtatowner to film in LA. Thankfully, I didn't have to worry about that, since I hadn't mustered up the courage to even send in the video clip yet. My insides went to war over whether I was being foolish for not even seeing if the casting director would be interested in me. The day player role was perfect—everything I'd been working for and trying to land since I'd left my first year of college and driven 457 solo miles to Los Angeles with nothing but a few thousand dollars and a hopeful naivete.

But just thinking about it left me . . . uneasy.

On one hand, the chances of me getting the role were slim, and even then I could always turn it down. On the other, Wyatt and I had been operating under the assumption that I was staying in Outtatowner only for the summer. We hadn't talked long term. At all.

Bubbles of worry fizzed in my belly.

I couldn't think clearly while I was surrounded by Wyatt's scent and wrapped in the most expensive bedsheets my ass had ever touched. I lifted his arm and quietly padded to the en suite bathroom.

After I finished, I washed my hands and patted my face with the cold water.

"Sneaking out?" Wyatt's voice was heavy with sleep. He leaned against the doorjamb, and I stepped forward to wrap my arms around his middle.

"'Course not." *Well, not now that I was totally busted.*

"Good." He dropped a kiss to my head, and I crawled back into the bed that still held his warmth.

After a minute, he crawled back into bed, too, lying behind me and tucking my back against his front.

His breath was heavy in the darkness. "It's quiet when she's gone."

I smiled to myself. For such a grump, he was awfully tenderhearted. "She's lucky to have you."

Wyatt squeezed me a little tighter. "I just worry. Bethany doesn't see her a lot, and when she does, I start to worry that Penny will get scared sleeping there or not have her night-light or forget that she's the best kid in the world."

My thoughts turned to Wyatt's ex. "She's . . . nice. Pleasant even."

"It's taken Beth a long time to get used to the idea of being a mom. It's a work in progress, but I know that when Penny's there, she's cared for. Took a long time for me to come to peace with that."

"I have to admit I was a little worried." I shrugged and tried to hide my nerves. "Even if I am just the nanny."

"You know damn well you're not just the nanny." His nose nuzzled into my neck. "Keep saying that and you're going to piss me off."

My insides turned to mush, and I scolded myself for letting myself fall a little harder.

Get a grip, Lark.

"Right." I stifled a giggle as his naked body pressed into mine. "Personal assistant."

He grunted in response, digging his hips into me. "Not that either."

"Well, an actress is nothing if not adaptable. I can be whatever you need." I turned inside the circle of his arms and batted my eyelashes at him.

"Right now, the only thing I need is you."

27

WYATT

Sunday night ended with wearing down the paint by walking circles on the front porch when Bethany was three hours late dropping off Penny. Between the unanswered texts and the missed phone calls, I was worried and thoroughly pissed off.

Lark and I had spent the morning sleeping in after pulling another all-nighter, exploring each other well into the night. My body was tired, but somehow I still craved her. She tried to break away and go up to her apartment, but I was able to convince her that a shower at my place—together—followed by a pair of my sweats and a T-shirt was the much better option.

She had looked damn good in my clothes, and a fresh wave of protectiveness coursed through me any time I looked at Lark. It was late by the time we rolled out of bed, but I made coffee and fried-egg sandwiches. She dipped hers in ketchup, which was fucking gross. When I told her as much, she only laughed and commented, "Words of affirmation must not be your love language." I huffed and reminded her that it was physical touch. Twice.

As the late morning bled into early evening, I had been stressed about Penny coming back and being ready for the upcoming week. I was also worried about the boys driving back from Michael's house. I'd tried not to let it show, but Lark had the uncanny ability to read my moods, and she'd called me out on it.

It was then she insisted on leaving me to pick up groceries for both herself and me while I waited for Penny. Getting help taking care of my shit was strange, and I didn't really like it, but as I debated and looked at the clock, Lark pulled the grocery list from the refrigerator and left me staring after her with a smile.

To be honest, having one less thing to do was a huge relief. Lark had returned by the time the boys got back, and they'd helped unload groceries.

By then Bethany was already late and I was fuming. When she finally returned my calls to let me know she was only a few minutes out of town, Lark had excused herself to her apartment. I'd been relieved. She didn't need to see me lose my shit.

Bethany's blue sports car rolled down the driveway. After she stopped, Penny shot out of the car with a huge smile on her face. "Hi, Dad!"

She crashed into me, and the relief I felt nearly brought me to my knees. I squeezed her harder. "Hi, Pickle. I missed you."

"I had so much fun! We got our nails done and went shopping for some school clothes and Mom got me a hamster!"

My eyes whipped to my ex.

She looked appropriately sheepish, and I was seething.

Penny went to the back seat and pulled out a small plastic cage with colorful tubes sticking out of it.

Jesus.

"Isn't it great, Daddy! I named him Cheeto."

"Wow. Cheeto." I swallowed hard as I fought the urge to raise my voice at Bethany. *What the hell was she thinking?*

"Why don't you take him inside."

Penny smiled at me before setting the cage down on the ground. She ran to Bethany, squeezing her middle. "Thank you, Mom."

Over the top of Penny's head, Bethany shot me a smug smile.

I faked a thin smile at Penny as she walked back and brought her new hamster into the house.

"Really, Beth?"

Her eyes went wide. "What?"

"A hamster? And you're late. Three *hours* late."

Bethany pursed her lips. "It took longer to buy all his supplies than I expected. It's fine."

"No. It's not fine. You didn't call. You didn't text. Do I have to remind you that you . . ." My voice was rising, and I had to keep myself in check. I didn't want Penny to see or hear me lose my shit at her mother.

I lowered my voice and stepped forward. "You gave up your parental rights. This weekend was because Penny means everything and she loves and misses you. I think it's great you made an effort this weekend and got your nails done and went shopping, but you can't buy her love, and you *definitely* cannot disappear for three hours without calling me. I can't believe you thought it was okay to buy her a pet."

Bethany let loose an annoyed sigh as she opened her car door. "Fine. Then tell her she can't have the hamster."

"And make me the bad guy here?" Anger and frustration wound together in my gut.

She shrugged and raised her palms as if to say, *Well, if the shoe fits.*

"It's not about the fucking hamster. It's about respect . . . and communication."

I got an audible sigh and a heavy roll of her eyes.

It hit me how different it was from the times Lark smiled and rolled hers at me. Those times were playful and lighthearted. Bethany's dripped with impatience and disdain. Contempt.

I hated comparing the two, but my emotions peaked. I glanced up at the apartment and then over my shoulder, hoping Penny wasn't watching me have an emotional meltdown in our driveway.

My shoulders slumped. "Look, I'm not doing this. Next time just have her home when you're supposed to."

I turned my back to her and stormed into the house.

AS THE WEEK WORE ON, my frustration with Bethany and how the weekend ended started to fade. Throughout the week, Lark and I found stolen moments. I craved every secretive, hot look, as well as little things like brushing the back of my hand against hers when we passed.

It was nice for the house to not feel so empty, but it was something more than that. It had become impossible to ignore that Lark filled my house with sunlight and joy and laughter.

While it pissed me off that we separated each evening, the long moments kissing each other goodbye on the front porch made me feel like a teenager again. If Lark had been staying longer than a single summer, I would have sat Penny down and let her in on my growing feelings for Lark. But with her plans to leave, I couldn't bring myself to get attached, only to break Penny's little heart.

It would be hard enough on her to watch Lark drive away.

I already knew it would be hell for me too.

After I wrapped my work for the day, I returned the missed call from Duke.

It rang only once before he picked up. "You busy?" His voice was rushed and harsh.

I glanced at the clock. I had hoped to swing by the market and grab some flowers for Lark and maybe a treat for Penny, but it would have to wait. "Nah. What's up?"

"Rough day. Meet me up at Dad's place."

I hung up the phone and drove straight to Haven Pines. I sat in the parking lot, gathering the balls to walk inside. I hated that as a family we couldn't get it together enough to care for Dad and that he had to live in a nursing home.

Duke buried himself in farm and operations work.

Lee was reckless and wild.

Katie had found a college scholarship in a town I'd never heard of.

And then there was me. Football had been my ticket to a new life, and I'd taken it without hesitation.

Only now it didn't seem fair to leave everything up to my siblings when I was not only financially secure but also *living* in town.

I sighed again. *This is why I left in the first place.*

I hated the antiseptic smell even more, and it hit me as soon as the automatic doors opened. The receptionist at the front desk looked up with a smile, and when she recognized me, it grew wider.

"GB! Good to see you."

I offered a terse nod. *Stupid fucking nickname.* "Duke called. Said there was some trouble with Dad."

Her face fell. "I'm sorry to hear that. The memory-care wing is down that hall. You can go in through the double doors. The nurse at the station will buzz you in." I nodded and she smiled again, but it didn't reach her eyes. "Give Red my best."

I stalked in the direction of the memory-care ward and met up with Duke outside the nurse's station.

He nodded in greeting as the nurse gave him a rundown of the situation. He turned to me as I walked up.

"I guess it's been an all-around bad day. He started in on a new nurse—yelling at him and generally being an asshole. Apparently the guy didn't get Dad's breakfast right and it all went to hell."

"Is the nurse okay?"

"Shaken up, I guess, but otherwise fine. The afternoon wasn't much better. Trashed his room, so they called me."

I gestured toward the locked double doors that kept the patients secured in the facility and prevented them from wandering. "After you."

We could hear the yells before we even got to his room. Two security guards stood outside the door as a large male nurse backed away with his hands up. Dad's yells were a string of insults and curses. I didn't know what to do, so I looked to Duke, who'd gone pale too.

As we approached the chaos, the little King girl—AJ or TJ, something like that—walked up in a nurse's uniform with a gentle but determined look in her eyes.

Duke stopped short as she intercepted us. "May I?"

He only stared, the muscles in his jaw working, so I

spoke up. "Yes. Thank you. We just got here, so we don't really know what's going on."

Her voice was calm and soothing. "It'll be fine. Give me a few minutes."

She slipped past the male nurse and security guards with a friendly smile.

"You know her?"

Duke stood a little straighter and lifted a shoulder in dismissal. "She works here, doesn't she?"

"But she's a King, right?"

He nodded once. "MJ."

I frowned and strained to listen. Inside Dad's room, there was arguing, but he was already quieter. I could hear only snippets of the conversation, but MJ spoke in calm tones, reassuring Dad, and when they both laughed, I relaxed a little.

It didn't even take the full five minutes before she was slipping back out into the hallway.

"Hey." She addressed me and seemed to ignore Duke's brooding attitude as he crossed his arms. "I think he's fine now. He's resting. I'm sorry they called you all the way down here. I just got on shift."

Clearly, this wasn't the first time MJ had had to pull Dad back from the ledge. "Does this happen often?"

She looked nervously between us. "Umm . . . sometimes? There are several personal items that were broken today. That's unusual, but we'll do what we can to fix them up for him."

"Thank you." Duke's voice was strained.

"Of course." MJ smiled again and left us, followed by the male nurse and the uniformed guards.

I sighed and pressed my back against the wall, sinking to

the floor. Duke joined me, and our legs stretched into the empty hallway.

What a fucking day.

I pulled my attention back to my older brother, who was looking at his clasped hands. "What do you know about love languages?"

Duke's mouth twisted, and he slanted his head toward me. His expression communicated, *The fuck?* loud and clear.

"Forget it. It was just something I was reading about." I blew out a heavy breath. "Are we doing the right thing here?" I wasn't sure if I was asking him or myself, but I let the question hang in the air.

Duke sighed, defeated. "I don't know. I think so."

"I didn't realize things had gotten so bad."

Duke's work boots looked worn against the clean carpeting, and his shoulders slumped. "Yeah."

We sat in silence, each lost in memories of Dad. I thought about how he'd always been bigger than life. When Mom died, he was raising four kids on his own and doing whatever he could to keep the farm afloat. He was tough and demanded perfection from all of us. Tootie had stepped up to be like a mother, especially to Katie, who was so young she probably didn't remember much about Mom.

"I'm sorry I left." The words were out before I could rethink them.

Duke shook his head. "Don't be. You deserved to live your life."

"And you didn't?"

"Ah, c'mon." Duke bumped my shoulder in a rare attempt to lighten the mood. "I got to tell everyone my little brother is that hotshot quarterback they see on TV."

I saw his joke for what it really was—deflection of my question regarding how *his* life had turned out.

"Should we go in and see him?"

Duke's lips flattened into a grim line, and he shook his head. "He won't know us today."

~

MY SULLEN MOOD dogged me the next day as I stomped out onto the football field. It was an optional workout and practice for our special teams players to develop their long-snapping skills, and it pissed me off that only three kids bothered to show up.

I ran them hard. When they screwed up, they ran again. When my thoughts drifted back to Dad, they ran. Whenever an image of Lark getting in her car and leaving Outta-towner for good popped into my head, they ran.

"You're gonna run the dog piss out of those kids." The warning and disappointment in Ricky's voice was clear.

I ground my teeth together. I knew my coach was right.

I blew my whistle twice to signal the end of the run, and the players groaned in relief and dragged their feet back to the center of the field.

"Look alive. Fast feet! Fast feet!" I barked at them.

Jesus, I sound just like him.

Memories of hours rehashing game video and sitting silent while Dad pointed out all the things I'd fucked up flooded back to me. I needed to run faster. Throw harder. If a pass was five yards, it should have been seven. A touchdown was fine, but not if it was sloppy.

At the time, I'd hated him for it. That hate morphed into gratitude when, in college, I realized I could get on top, not just on natural skill, but on my willingness to outrun, outthrow, and outwork every other player on the team.

I looked onto the beaten-down faces of my players. I didn't want to be that kind of coach, so I offered the only words I had wished to hear from my dad for so many years.

"You worked hard today. You didn't give up. You each gave your best, and I want you to know that your best is good enough. I'm really proud of you."

THOUGHTS OF LARK consumed me on the drive back to Outtatowner. My feelings were getting away from me. Something about being back in my hometown, about having family around to know and love Penny, about how easy and natural things felt between Lark and my daughter.

It almost felt too good to be true. I'd learned a long time ago that vulnerability led only to failure—a hit you didn't see coming.

I couldn't let that happen.

When my phone buzzed and my sister's name flashed across the screen, I smiled and connected it to my car's Bluetooth. "Catfish Kate!"

"Jesus, Wyatt. Really?"

It was so easy to get a rise out of my little sister. "To what do I owe the pleasure?"

"Duke told me about Dad, and Lee has been nonstop about Aunt Tootie's house."

I paused, giving her space to finish, hopeful she had finally made a decision about coming back.

"So are you staying in Highfield House for a while?"

I smiled. Katie was coming home. "That's the plan."

I actually didn't have a plan beyond the summer, but

the longer Penny and I had stayed at the old farmhouse, the more it had felt like home. If Outtatowner really became home again, I'd have to sublet my apartment, move my things out of storage, figure out how to enroll Penny in the elementary school . . .

The tasks should have overwhelmed me, but instead, my body hummed with excitement.

"I haven't made any concrete plans, but Penny and I are going to be staying a while," I said, making the decision out loud. I smiled and couldn't wait to let Pickle in on the news.

Kate huffed on the other end, her annoyance coming over the speaker loud and clear. "Awesome."

"What's up?"

"Don't get me wrong—I think it's great you're back home, and I can't wait to see you. It's just that I was hoping to stay at Highfield House." She exhaled again. "I guess I will stay with Aunt Tootie after all . . . like a loser."

"You're not a loser. You're doing us all a favor by helping. You know she doesn't listen to anyone but you."

That got a laugh out of my little sister. "She doesn't listen to me either. I just have a way of getting things done and helping her think it was her idea."

"Exactly."

Katie huffed a breath. "If the house is as bad as Lee says, I need to start calling contractors and getting them lined up if we want some of the work to happen before winter sets in."

Guess Lee hadn't told her the plan to have Beckett Miller do the work.

We'd all talked about how pissed Kate would be once she realized it was her ex-boyfriend's older brother who'd been hired. I wasn't about to be the one who broke the news to her.

"So when do you leave?"

"Soon. My friends are throwing me a goodbye party. I think the entire town is coming." Her embarrassed laughter made me smile. My little sister had always been popular, but the kind of girl who never let it go to her head.

"It's hard to believe you found a place *smaller* than Outtatowner."

"Turns out Tipp was exactly what I needed, especially after what happened with *he who will never be named*, but I do think I'm ready to be home."

I exhaled as I turned down my driveway and looked at the farmhouse. My heart squeezed behind my ribs.

Same.

I watched Wyatt sit in his car and look at the farmhouse from the kitchen window of his home. Tootie had stolen Penny for an afternoon, reading to the animals at the Outtatowner animal rescue. I'd spent my solo afternoon cleaning the apartment I now used only for sleep and tidied up the farmhouse. It was amazing how many dishes and socks three college-aged boys could go through in a day or two.

When Wyatt still hadn't come in, I snagged two beers from the fridge and walked out onto the front porch. The movement from the screen door caught his eye, and he climbed out of the car.

I dangled a bottle from my fingertips and held it up. "Looks like you could use one."

He sauntered up, a playful smile on his lips, but it didn't quite reach his eyes. "I could use you."

Wyatt's arms wrapped around my waist, and he buried his nose in my neck. Big, giddy feelings bubbled up in my chest, and I did my best to calm them.

"Careful." I laughed. "A girl could get used to a greeting like that."

Wyatt pulled back, a frown on his face.

Shit.

With every day that passed, we were flirting with the end of summer, and so far we had been careful not to talk about what that meant for me.

For us.

I faked a bright smile and brought a bottle to my lips. I swallowed away the knot in my throat and handed Wyatt his beer. "Sit with me."

I sank down on the top step, and he sat across from me. Wyatt's long, thick legs stretched out in front of him. I wanted to crawl into the cradle of his embrace and smooth away the lines of worry that seemed permanently etched into his forehead.

Tonight was not the night for big, growing feelings or talks about how I was totally falling in love with him. He'd had a long day and needed someone to help brighten the mood.

A little sunshine.

"So, good news or bad news?"

Wyatt eyed me carefully. His jaw worked once, and he took a swig of his beer. "Might as well hit me with the bad news."

"Penny isn't home. She's on a lady-date with Tootie until around dinnertime."

A slow grin started on his face as his hand found my thigh. "That's terrible news."

I smiled back at him and scooted a little closer.

"So what's the good news then?"

"Good news is Cheeto is no longer missing."

He nearly choked on his beer. "*No longer* missing?"

I lifted my shoulder and did my best not to laugh. "He *may* have gotten out of his cage today and spent the morning on a little adventure. Thankfully, Penny's idea of crushed-up Cheetos—the snack, not the hamster—actually worked. Turns out he's a big fan."

Wyatt rubbed his eyes with one hand. "I think we need to work on your understanding of good news–bad news."

When he laughed, the tightness in his shoulders eased. I liked being the one who could bring him a little humor after a long day. His wide palm rubbed up and down my leg, and warmth pooled low in my belly.

"So Penny is out having fun. And the boys?"

Excitement danced through me. I knew that primal look in his eyes. "Michael and Joey are working. Kevin promised to study at the library for at least an hour before meeting up with them."

"So what you're saying is . . ." Wyatt gripped the belt loop at my hip and pulled me onto his lap. "I get to have my way with you?"

I was breathless and loved being manhandled into his lap. I stared down at his lips. "What did you have in mind?"

His fingers tickled the skin above my jean shorts as he smoothed them over my hip and moved down to squeeze my ass. "I don't want to be gentle."

There was a roughness, barely contained, that I hoped he'd unleash on me. I knew he would never hurt me, but if after a long day he wanted me to be his release, I'd happily do it.

"That's perfect, because I don't want you to be gentle either."

"That's good." Wyatt wound my legs around his hips so I was straddling him, my boobs pressed against him. "Real good because I want to watch your tits bounce while I fill this cunt."

My whole body shivered as we tore at each other's clothes and Wyatt made good on his promise.

~

"I WANT to tell Penny about us." Wyatt carefully pushed a strand of my hair across my forehead and tucked it behind my ear. After the entire population of Remington County heard me screaming his name from the front porch, we'd continued our fun inside. Now tucked into his arms on top of his bed, Wyatt looked at me with a tenderness that made little sparkles of energy crackle under my skin.

"Us as in . . . special friends?"

Wyatt laughed. "I don't care what you want to call it. I just don't like being in the same room with you and feeling like I can't touch you."

"Oh." My nerves were getting the best of me. These were the kinds of talks that made things real. Committed. *Dangerous.*

"Is that okay?" His fingers paused the lazy circles they had been making on my back.

"Yeah, no. Of course. I don't like the secrets either. I just don't, you know, want her to be confused is all."

"Confused?"

"Well, like, *Am I the nanny? Am I the personal assistant? Am I the fuck buddy?*—not that that's how you would phrase it. I just . . . I don't know. You know what? It's your kid. You know what's best!" The fake cheeriness I tried to infuse in my words was hollow.

Wyatt saw right through it. "I was going to tell her that

we were dating so that if I held your hand or kissed you, it wouldn't be a surprise."

"Yes. Great. That's better." Embarrassment stained my cheeks. Wyatt was being so sweet, and I'd made it awkward and uncomfortable.

I looked at the clock on the wall and found my exit strategy. "Oh shit. You know what? I have the Bluebirds tonight and haven't even made something to bring to the book club. I should go."

I untangled myself from Wyatt and gathered my clothes in my arms. I slipped on my underwear and jean shorts before pulling on my shirt. In two swift steps, I pressed a quick kiss on his lips before he could even get out of bed. I practically ran through his house and up to my apartment.

Way to go, Lark. That was handled spectacularly.

I groaned in frustration and looked out my kitchen window, down at the farmhouse. My heart pounded as I considered Wyatt saying that we were dating.

Were we dating? When did that happen?

As someone who had moved from town to town without a care, the idea of *dating*—being committed, making promises, expectations—felt big. Real.

I wanted it, especially with Wyatt, but I also knew that kind of love was for other people. Lucky girls who weren't cursed at Renaissance festivals. My sad string of unfulfilling relationships proved that it never lasted.

My phone buzzed in my pocket. When I saw the text from Wyatt, I laughed in relief.

> **WYATT**
>
> I'm going to try really hard to not take your graceful exit personally.

> You mean that time you said we were dating and then I immediately bolted? Definitely not related.

WYATT

> Well that's a relief. Have fun at book club.

> Thanks.

WYATT

> Oh, and on the off chance you are Words of Affirmation—you make our lives better. I care about you.

> Would have been nice to say that to your face before you ran out the door in a panic.

My heart clunked and I couldn't breathe.

Wyatt had listened to my ramblings about love languages? Holy shit.

> I care about you too. Next time I'll try not to run.

WYATT

> It's okay if you do. I'll chase you down.

THE BLUEBIRDS WERE in rare form tonight. As soon as I'd walked into Bluebird Books, the chitter died down, and a sea of owl eyes stared at me. I wiped at my mouth, wondering if the remnants of my lemon blueberry scone were still stuck to my face.

Bug looked irate, and when she turned back to Tootie, the conversation picked right up again. I hustled in and set the bottle of wine I'd picked up on the table. My phone buzzed in my pocket, but I ignored it when I saw Cass.

Cass lifted her hand in greeting, and I hurried to her side. "What's going on? Why is everyone so mad?"

Cass grabbed my arm and lowered her voice. "Trouble."

"What kind of trouble? Is everyone okay?"

Cass shook her head. "Some kids down at the Sand Dollar got into it. They were arrested for fighting on the beach. Kings and Sullivans. *Again.*"

Worry swirled in my stomach. "What do you mean some kids at the Sand Dollar? What kids?"

Cass only shrugged, and I stood. "Excuse me, Tootie? What's going on?"

She turned from the tense discussion she was having with Bug and a few other ladies.

"This is getting out of control." Mrs. Fritz shook her head. "People are going to stop coming to Outtatowner if it becomes a town that isn't safe. Where people are *fighting* on the beach where families are trying to enjoy our town!"

Tootie stepped forward and gripped my shoulders. "There was trouble at the beach. It may have been one of Wyatt's boys, but I'm not certain."

Oh no.

Dread pooled in my stomach, and I could feel the blood drain from my face. I needed to call him—warn him if one of the boys had gotten into trouble.

After I pulled my phone from my pocket, I saw a slew of missed texts from Joey.

Shit.

JOEY

We need help.

Don't tell Coach.

Kev and Mike got arrested. I don't know what to do.

This wasn't good. *Double shit.*

I grabbed my bag and headed straight for the door. "I have to go," I called out to no one in particular.

Once there, I looked left and then right. I had no idea where the police station was. Across the road, I spotted Bootsy and called out to him.

I ran up, breathless.

"Is there a fire?" He looked concerned and his eyes darted around.

"No, I'm sorry. But there is an emergency. Where is the police station?"

Bootsy raised a weathered finger and pointed down the side street. "Head that way. I saw a mess of Kings arguing outside. You be careful, with you being a Sullivan and all."

I took off running before I could let his words truly sink in. "I owe you! Tomorrow—lunch on me. You just pick the place!"

I raced down the sidewalk without looking back and headed the few blocks toward the police station. A small crowd was already gathering outside the entryway. I recognized Sylvie and a few of the King men, but no Sullivans.

Sylvie offered me a terse, sad smile, but she was tucked behind a wall of Kings. When their accusing eyes raked over me, I straightened and calmed my breathing. If I had to represent the Sullivans, I'd do it with my head held high. Moving through them, I opened the door to the station and immediately saw Joey sitting in a brown leather chair, his shoulders slumped and one leg bobbing up and down.

After the bell on the door caught his attention, he looked at me and shot to his feet. "Lark."

I ran to him, pulling him into an awkward hug. "I'm so sorry. I just got your messages. What happened?"

Joey shook his head. "We were working. Everything was

fine. Then we saw Kevin shove some guy on the beach, and they started fighting. Michael stepped in. I would have jumped in there, but I couldn't get hit in the face."

I shook my head and couldn't worry about Joey and his precious face.

I moved to the counter. "Excuse me? Can I speak with someone about Kevin Williams and Michael Thompson?"

The elderly receptionist nodded. "You kin?"

"Um . . . they are in my care."

She pursed her lips and my heart sank. Both Kevin and Michael were adults. I wasn't certain anyone would talk to me, especially given the fact that it seemed like they were in serious hot water with the Kings.

"I'll send an officer out."

After what felt like an eternity, a female police officer with long black hair and a smug smile called me back to her office.

"Stay here." I pointed at the chair, and Joey sank into it. When I followed the officer and walked into her office, my eyes scanned down to her name plate.

Amy King.

Crap.

Her hard eyes held my worried ones. "Hi, I'm Lark Butler. Michael and Kevin have been staying with Wyatt Sullivan, and I'm his, um, personal assistant. The boys have kind of been in my care. Can I ask what happened?"

"You are aware they are adults, correct?"

I swallowed hard and tried to make light of the situation. "I mean, if you can call any nineteen or twenty-year-old boy an *adult*, then sure . . ." I laughed.

Officer Amy King did not find me amusing. She only lifted an eyebrow as the ice in her stare chilled my bones.

I cleared my throat. "Are they okay?"

"Miss Butler, those boys were involved in a physical altercation on public property. I have several witnesses that report Michael Thompson assaulted—"

"Assaulted?"

Her voice dripped with impatience. "Yes. Assault. That is the charge being brought against them."

"Charges? Oh no. No no no. I'm sorry." I smoothed my palms on her desk as I tried to wrap my head around the situation rapidly spiraling out of control "What is happening?"

"The boys in your care? They assaulted a man. Broke his nose and caused a very frightening scene on a very public beach."

My breaths were helpless little pants.

This is bad. Really, really bad. "What can I do?"

Officer King let go of the folder she was holding, and it dropped to her desk with a plop. "Unless you can convince Lucian King, the guy with the mangled face, to not press charges? Nothing."

I stood from the chair. "Thank you."

I went straight to Joey. I grabbed his arm gently and lowered my voice. "Tell me what happens if anyone finds out about this."

He looked around. "We have a code of conduct. This is big. They could be suspended from the team. Indefinitely."

I worried the skin on my thumbnail. "I figured as much." I gestured impatiently. "Tell me the worst-case scenario."

"Kevin's in position to be an early-round NFL draft pick if he gets his grades up. An arrest like this could ruin his entire life. And football is everything to Mike. He doesn't really have a plan B yet. This is really bad. Do we have to tell Coach?"

"Are you kidding me?" I hissed. "In this town? *Everyone already knows!*" I took a calming breath. "It's fine. Everything is fine. I will take care of this."

I clamped my teeth together, and with a nod, I left Joey behind to head straight outside and into the crowd of Kings. When I spotted Royal, I mustered my courage and pointed directly at him. "Can I speak with you for a moment?"

A cocky smirk flashed on his face, and he stood tall from where he was leaning against the brick planter. He let me lead him a few steps away so I could talk to him in private.

I swallowed hard and hoped this wasn't the worst idea I'd ever had. "Royal, I need your help."

"He was black with little white boots and the cutest, tiniest stripe down his nose."

I smiled down at a sleepy Penny. "He sounds cute."

"The cutest." She pouted as I tucked the covers around her shoulders. "And he was all alone, but when I read him *The Wonky Donkey*, he curled into my lap and purred *so* loud, Daddy."

"I'm glad you had fun. I'm sure he was glad to have a friend for the day."

"But Figaro wants a *home*." Penny looked up at me with big round eyes. I knew exactly what she was getting at, and there was no fucking way we were getting a cat.

"His name was Figaro? Like in Pinocchio?"

"His name was Darryl, but I changed it because he totally looks like a Figaro."

She named the cat. I was going to kill Tootie.

"So tell me about Cheeto's adventure today?" I raised an eyebrow at her, and she looked sufficiently sheepish.

"He got out."

I nodded and kissed her cheek. "I heard. And don't cats eat rodents? We wouldn't want to put Cheeto in danger."

"Figaro would *never!*"

"I'm sure that's true. How about this? It's not a no forever, but a not right now. Can you work with that?"

Her sleepy frown deepened. "I guess so."

I couldn't help but smile. "You're the greatest kid in the world, you know that, right?"

Penny rolled to her side to face me and nodded. "I love you, Dad."

"Love you too, Pickle."

"I wanted to talk to you about something, Pickle." I pressed a kiss to her forehead and rubbed her back.

"Am I in trouble?"

I laughed. "No, not at all. I just wanted to talk to you about Lark. It's nice having her around, don't you think?"

"Usually, but I'm mad at her right now."

Taken aback, I considered my words. "Mad at her? What happened?"

"She tattled on me about Cheeto getting out."

"Oh, babe. She didn't tattle—that's when you tell on someone just to get them into trouble. She was sharing about the day, and your name didn't come up once."

"So she didn't tell you that I was the one who left the door to his cage open?"

I shook my head. "Nope."

"Now I feel bad. I was just having bad thoughts about her."

"Oh, Pickle. You are a sweet girl. Maybe you can be extra kind to her tomorrow, since we both like having her around."

"Are you going to get married?"

My mouth dropped. "Um, no. I like Lark, and she likes

me. I want to take her out to eat and hold her hand some-times. That's all."

For now.

I pushed away the errant thought.

"With me too?"

I nodded. "Sometimes. But sometimes I would like to take her out just the two of us. Like a date."

"Could I hang out with Uncle Lee when you do that?"

I laughed. Penny was so smitten with her fun-loving uncle. "I'm sure he would love that."

"Lark likes it when you leave the flowers for her."

I paused the back scratches. "Oh yeah?"

"She always puts them in a little cup of water and smiles a lot when you do that."

I kissed her on the top of her head as I stood. "I'll keep that in mind."

"One more, Dad." She was nearly asleep, and love for her rushed through me. Our lives were finally feeling settled. Lark had had a huge part in that.

When I clicked the door to Penny's bedroom closed, I walked down the hallway. Whispers coming from the kitchen caught my attention, so I headed that way.

Lark was pacing the floor. Sitting at the table, Michael was shirtless and icing his side, while Kevin looked down at his hands and Joey scrolled on his phone.

When I walked into the room, the hushed whispers stopped, and they all stared at me.

"What the hell is going on?"

Lark stepped forward when Kevin spoke up. "I got into a fight and was arrested."

The roar of blood rushing to my head was deafening.

"Me too." Michael lifted the bag of frozen vegetables

from his side to inspect a fresh bruise blooming across his ribs.

"Arrested?" My voice rose, and I looked over my shoulder toward Penny's room. My eyes sliced back to them and landed on Lark, who stood behind Michael with her hand protectively on his shoulder. "Did you know about this?"

"I was at book club when I found out. I took care of it. The charges were dropped."

"Charges? Took care of it? What do you—" I started stomping back and forth across the kitchen as thoughts of the university board finding out about this hounded me. The boys could get kicked off the team, and there wouldn't be anything I could do about it. Their scholarships. Their futures. Key players in my starting lineup. Not to mention how bad it would look that they had been arrested when it was my job to keep them out of trouble.

"Look, Coach, they were talking shit and—"

"I don't want to hear it. You don't understand how *bad* this is! For all of us!" My voice boomed in the small kitchen, and Lark took another step in my direction.

"You don't have to raise your voice!" Hers was pitching higher as she came to their defense.

I sighed in defeat.

Lark put her hands out. "I'm sorry. We're all on the same team here."

"Team? I'm just finding out about this now."

"It happened really fast, and when Joey called me, I took care of it. I'm sorry I didn't call you, but they were in trouble, and I fixed it."

I was unsure of exactly how she'd managed to fix this shit show, but the way she wasn't revealing exactly *how* she'd managed to fix it made me uneasy. In my gut, I knew there was something more to it.

My eyes moved over my players. "This is unacceptable." They nodded in solemn understanding. "There need to be consequences, but for now . . . I don't know. Just go to bed."

Looking more like twelve than twenty, the three boys quietly left the kitchen and headed to their room in the loft. As he passed Lark, Kevin reached out and hugged her. My heart felt tight in my chest, and a thousand emotions rolled through me.

Alone in the kitchen, I looked at her. "What the hell, Lark?"

"I know. I'm sorry."

I shook my head. Deep down I knew it wasn't her fault and that I'd let my temper get the best of me. I had so many questions, and the anger was still just below the surface. "Tell me what happened. Everything."

I told Wyatt everything. *Almost.*

Sitting across the table from me, he was fuming, desperately trying to rein in his temper, but it was there, simmering under the surface. He was pissed. Disappointed. Worried.

"A fucking fight. After everything I've talked to them about. How much I've stressed that eyes are *always* on you when you're rising to the top. There's always someone there waiting to cut you down, and they just *handed* it right to them!"

I kept my voice calm. "I really don't think anyone outside of town is going to find out about it."

"You think the most gossipy town in the Midwest is going to stay quiet about this? What if Kevin is drafted? You don't think someone's going to remember this and offer the story up to the highest bidder? Reporters would salivate over exclusive dirt on a rookie with as much talent as him."

My brows pinched together. "I don't think you're giving your hometown enough credit. From what I've seen, they take care of their own here."

"Exactly. They take care of their own. *Townies*. Kings and Sullivans but not hungry college kids whose dreams of a professional career are just as impacted by reputation as they are by actual skill. You don't understand how this works, Lark."

My frustration with his stubborn attitude bubbled over. My hands slapped on the table. "Why can't you trust me on this? Come on, Wyatt. This doesn't have to be a big deal. Royal gave me his word—"

Ah, fuck.

"Royal? Royal King?" Wyatt stood from the chair. "What does he have to do with this?"

I sighed. "It was Lucian King who Kevin and Michael got into it with. Apparently they made a crack about the day the boys were helping me with an audition tape on the beach. Teasing them and making fun of me. They came to my defense, but when Lucian made a crack about *you*, Michael lost it. He threw the first punch."

"Wait a minute. Slow down. Audition tape?"

Sweat started to prickle in my hair. "I got a callback, and they are accepting a taped audition. Surprise!" My weak attempt at a joke landed flat.

A hard line formed between his eyebrows. "When are you leaving?"

My heart pounded. He wasn't asking *if* I was leaving, but when. "I haven't sent out the tape yet."

He pinned me in place with his stare, the one that said, "Cut the shit." I used to love that stare and get a kick out of pestering him a little bit, but I couldn't bring myself to joke. I stalled by shifting in my seat and picking at a piece of invisible lint on my shoulder.

"Why not?" he finally ground out when I still hadn't answered.

*Because I'm in love with you and your daughter and I
don't know that I have the guts to leave.*

"I don't know." It was all I could manage.

I wanted him to fight for me. To tell me that he was
choosing me and that he wanted me to stay with him in
Outtatowner. Somehow the quirky lakeside town had
become a part of me. I was settled and grounded for the first
time in my life, but it was nothing without Wyatt.

He pulled me from my thoughts. "And Royal?"

"I talked with him after the boys were arrested. He said
he could talk with Lucian and get him to drop the charges.
He did."

Wyatt scoffed. "Just like that?" He shook his head.
"Nothing comes from a King without strings."

"I'm telling you, he just . . . agreed. I told him how
damaging this could be and how silly it would be to ruin
their futures over a little fight. It wasn't a big deal. He kind
of laughed and said that he'd been in plenty of stupid fights
and that he'd talk with Lucian."

"You should have talked to me first." Visible tension
rose in his shoulders and neck.

"I didn't have time. It all happened really fast. Royal
was right there at the station, and he talked with Lucian. I
made the best call I could in the moment."

"And now you're indebted to Royal fucking King."

I rolled my eyes. "You make him sound like some larger-
than-life Mafia kingpin or something. It wasn't that big of a
deal. In fact, he was kind of . . . nice."

Wyatt dismissed my statement with a disgusted sound
and shake of his head. Heavy moments passed, tense and
silent. My palms felt damp. I rubbed them together, looking
around his farmhouse.

This night, this *entire* conversation, was too intense. Too close to a real relationship with its ups and downs. Every part of me craved that connection, but it was clear that the lines between personal assistant and girlfriend were blurred, and Wyatt wasn't sure what to make of it either.

I stood and took a few steps toward the front door.

"Stop." The hard, grumpy tone of his voice halted my feet. "Don't go."

I froze, my heart beating wildly.

"I owe you an apology."

I glanced over my shoulder but didn't turn back. "I get it. Tonight was . . . a lot. It's fine. Everyone just needs a little time to cool off."

Wyatt stood and took a step toward me. "It's not fine. I was a dick. You didn't deserve that."

A tiny smile played on my lips. Wyatt's arms wound around me as he pressed my back against him. His warm breath moved over my ear. "Can you forgive me for losing my cool and being a jerk?"

I lifted my shoulder and shot him a playful look. This I could control. When we were lost in each other, I knew exactly where I stood. "I dunno. I guess that depends on how you'd like to apologize."

He grunted, low and deadly, as his hands moved down my sides and over my skirt. "What would you say if my apology included bending you over this table right now and showing you just how sorry I was."

"Wyatt Sullivan," I hissed, a blush staining my cheeks. "There's a house full of people."

His fingers teased my exposed thighs, dragging higher and higher, dipping beneath my skirt. "Then you'll have to work extra hard at keeping quiet."

A thrill danced through me. "If you're doing it right, I shouldn't be able to keep quiet."

His teeth nipped the base of my neck. "Exactly."

I bit down on my lip and tried to listen for any sign of the boys or Penny. Through the ceiling I could hear the low drone of their television and no sign that Penny was awake.

My heavy breaths rattled through me as I considered just how desperately I needed to connect with Wyatt. To use my body to show him all the pent-up feelings I was too afraid to voice.

As Wyatt continued to kiss my neck, I gathered my skirt in my hands. Wyatt was just as impatient because he dropped to his knees and used his strong arms to bend me at the waist. With one hand pinning me in place, my chest pressed flat against the wooden table.

I could feel his face close to my pussy and then the drag of his teeth across the line where my thigh met my ass.

I let out a small, desperate whimper.

"Quiet now." Wyatt's teeth clamped down on my inner thigh, and I pressed my lips together to keep from moaning. His tongue darted out to smooth over my skin, and his strong fingers flexed over my lower back.

His hand left my back, trusting that I'd stay in place while he explored my body. Both hands trailed up the back of my thighs as his mouth teased and sampled. Finally —*finally*—his hands looped into the top of my damp thong and yanked the fabric down.

Hard.

A strangled sound escaped my throat, and I clamped a hand over my mouth. My hips tipped backward, urging him to put his mouth on me. Begging for it.

His large hands gripped my butt as he spread me open. Wyatt dragged the flat of his tongue through my pussy with an aching slowness. Every nerve ending was on fire, and my body arched and pleaded for more.

I could feel the rattle of his own groan as he spread me wider and devoured me. My knees wanted to buckle. I shifted my weight, pushing my pussy into his face.

"Yes," he growled into me. "More."

My hips swiveled, and I lost all sense of time and space after his mouth found my clit. Wyatt was so good, sucking and lapping up every part of me. I wanted to float away.

But not before I felt him inside me.

"Wyatt, please," I whispered and pleaded. "I want to come on your cock."

My dirty, wanton words had him pulling back with a sexy groan. "Jesus."

He stood and gripped my hips, then pressed his erection to my exposed pussy.

"I like hearing you beg."

I swiveled my hips and ground into him.

The sound of his zipper sent waves of anticipation racing through me. In one aggressive move, Wyatt's thick cock pushed into me. A startled cry threatened to escape me when his hand clamped down over my mouth.

He continued to fuck me with hard thrusts. His hand pressed over my mouth as he banged me against the table with every brutal drive of his hips.

"You're so fucking wet for me."

My eyes squeezed together as I reveled in the harsh way he took me, his hand keeping me quiet.

Exhilarated. Grateful. Stretched.

With Wyatt I was free. It wasn't wrong to like being fucked hard or that his grumpy attitude was a total turn-on. My ears were acutely aware of any noises, and outside of the wet, sloppy sounds of our bodies coming together, the farmhouse was silent.

I pushed my hips into him, soaking up every sensation that rolled through me.

My legs started to quiver. My pussy tightened, and it was Wyatt who stifled a quiet groan. His spare hand left my hip and dove under my skirt to move down over the bundle of nerves between my legs.

His other hand moved over my mouth, and his fingers pushed past my lips. I brazenly sucked on them while he fucked me from behind and teased my clit.

The thought of it all—the reckless, delicious reality of getting thoroughly fucked in his kitchen—sent an orgasm tearing through me. I tucked my forehead against the table, doing everything I could to stay silent as the waves of pleasure crashed over me.

Two hands gripped my hips, and Wyatt pumped into me. His cock swelled, and with one final push, as deep as he could go, he came.

The stillness of the kitchen blanketed us. Only our low pants filled the silence. His hands were gentle as they caressed my lower back and over my hips.

"I don't think I can move," I whispered. My unsteady legs shook beneath me. "Do you think we were quiet enough?"

His touch was gentle as he slipped my thong back up my legs and smoothed my skirt back in place.

He kissed me on the ass before chuckling softly. "I think we're okay. You were a good girl, but you bit the shit out of my finger."

I turned to face him and smiled, gripping his hand. I brought his finger to my mouth and held his gaze, then kissed the side of it before swirling my tongue around it and sucking.

I had never been so bold, so openly sexual with anyone, and it was delightfully sinful. Wyatt grabbed the back of my neck and pulled my mouth to his.

After he kissed me breathless, he warned, "From now on, no more favors and promises to any other man but me."

As far as I could tell, Outtatowner had kept its promise, and word of the fight between Lucian King and the boys hadn't gotten beyond the small-town rumor mill. It seemed people were more interested in drumming up speculation about a potential love triangle between Lark, Royal, and me than some college kids getting into a stupid fight.

It also didn't help that Royal had an arrogant smile plastered on his face when I saw him driving through town.

What a dick.

I still felt it was my duty to remind the boys of how serious something like a fight was, which was why they were all standing in front of me, looking appropriately chastised.

"Now, I want to tell you something."

All three had their heads hung low and shoulders slumped.

"Your actions were reckless, stupid, and dangerous. You need to think about how every choice you make will influence the next ten years, not just the next ten minutes."

The boys answered in sullen unison. "Yes, sir."

"If you're going to haul off and pop someone, it better be

for a damn good reason."

Michael's head whipped up. "But Coach—"

I raised my hand. "I'm not finished."

"Like I said, it better be for a damn good reason. Defending a woman, or a friend, might be reason enough."

They all looked up at me, surprised.

I let a small smile twitch at my mouth. "Another good reason is putting a King in his place." Slowly their grins matched mine. "It was stupid, but I'm proud of you. Just don't let it happen again."

"Yes, sir." Their response was significantly more upbeat. I gestured with my head toward the door. "Now get out of here. Lee needs your help at the fire station."

All three mumbled a *thanks* and rushed toward the door, letting the screen close with a bang. They needed a consequence, but my heart wasn't really in it, so I'd talked to Lee, and he'd agreed the boys could wash trucks and clean the fire station. If it ever came up, I could say that they'd received a punishment, but I wasn't all that worried about it. I hadn't heard a thing from the athletic board.

Penny and Lark had run off for a day at the beach, and before they'd left, I'd teased her to avoid the dunes. She'd smiled and I'd winked.

Trying to focus on work and not on the way Lark's smiles had a way of sticking with me, I used my phone to check the calendar. I smiled at the color-coded days—work from home. I had a few meetings to work around but nothing too pressing. If I was lucky, I would be able to join them on the beach.

In the office, I went through several emails, watched recruitment films of potential athletes, and returned calls from parents eager to give their players a leg up on the upcoming season. Overall, I felt good about our lineup, and if no one got into any more trouble—*or broken pinkies, for Christ's sake*—we would be ready to start the fall season strong.

Despite the mindless tasks, I still couldn't focus, overwhelmed by thoughts of Lark and where she fit into the whirlwind life of a football coach and his family. Before this, she'd had a whole life before blowing into Outtatowner and upending my world.

What would that even look like once the season started?

September to December would be the busiest time of the year—the actual football season. Then we'd go right into bowl-game preparations and meetings with other coaches across the country. By January I'd be traveling the US, prime recruiting season, scoping out potential players to fill the roster.

Thoughts of her sunny smile on the sidelines in MMU red and white as she, Pickle, and I celebrated a victory heated my chest. Even nights after a loss, it would be nice to come home to someone who would understand and listen to me bemoan the nuances of the game. Maybe even unleash some of that pent-up frustration by burying my face between her thighs.

But not just anyone. *Her.*

I loved Lark. That much was painfully obvious. Pickle had already told her so much. It had all happened so fast and without me realizing it. Lark had swooped into our lives —organized it and infused it with joy and laughter. I hadn't acknowledged how much we'd needed that.

But it was selfish.

I did nothing but take, take, take from her. *Organize* my *schedule, watch* my *kid, be nice to* my *dad, keep* my *players out of trouble.* I had done nothing but take and then ask for more.

Did I love her or love what she could do for us?

I felt sick at the thought. I had unknowingly done to her what Bethany and so many others in my life had always done to me—used her because it was convenient.

I have a knack for that—feeling alone even in a crowded room, right next to someone.

Lark's words flooded back to me, and I was ashamed of how epically I had failed her. From the beginning, she had quietly understood a fundamental part of me.

I didn't deserve her sunshine or her smiles or sitting together in the dark feeling completely fulfilled and at peace.

Even if she did stay, our relationship was unbalanced. I had already pursued my dreams—set goals and gone after them relentlessly until I succeeded. Eventually she would realize that she deserved better. So much more than *me*.

I frantically looked around my desk and scooped up my keys. I needed to talk with someone and figure out how the hell I was going to make this right.

I STOOD for what felt like hours outside the room, staring at the small plaque next to the door that read HAVEN PINES ROOM 1102. My thoughts raced, and indecision rooted my feet to the ground.

"He's not in there, you know."

I turned at the quiet voice and noticed MJ, Dad's favorite nurse. *The King girl.*

With so many things roiling in my gut, I didn't have the heart to even care that she was a King.

She smiled again. "He's in the courtyard feeding the birds."

"Thank you." I frowned and turned back to the heavy wooden door to his room.

"He talks about you, you know." I turned back toward her as she leaned an elbow on the small rolling computer cart.

I huffed a humorless laugh. "I'm sure you hear all about the Fairfield game."

She smiled. "It does come up a lot. *Hell of a game.*" She imitated the gruff nature of Dad's voice in an attempt to ease the tension between us.

I nodded. It was one of the memories that seemed to be on a loop in his head.

"But he also has the nurses google your name. He likes to read the articles."

"Really." The word came out incredulous, and I didn't attempt to hide my doubt.

She lifted a shoulder. "On the good days." MJ smiled and pushed the cart down the hallway before knocking on a door and disappearing through it.

The new information of Dad keeping tabs on me and my career, of wanting to know the man I had become and not just the player I was, did painful things to my insides. Nothing seemed to fit in my chest.

I stomped down the hallway until I found the corridor that led to the courtyard. It was a large, wide-open space in the middle of the building. Sun streamed overhead, and there were picnic tables and benches dotted throughout the sunny courtyard. Small flower beds had been planted, and there were several bird feeders hanging from shepherd hooks. I spotted Dad in the far corner, sitting on a bench and tossing birdseed onto the brick pavers.

When I approached, he offered a friendly, if not slightly distant, smile.

"Hey, Dad. Can I sit?"

He made room for me on the bench, and I settled in next to him.

I didn't know where to start. "Duke came up yesterday. He told me you had a great day. He's working hard on the farm, keeping it afloat for us."

I recalled the doctors and nurses telling us that it might be helpful to anchor the conversation with cues or names and memories we once shared. Apparently it was important to show him that I knew who he was, even if he had trouble recalling his own son.

Dad nodded. "Got his hands full." Dad squinted up at the sun. "What day is it?"

"June twenty-eighth."

"U-pick will keep him busy. Out of trouble."

I laughed at that. "It's Lee who needs to stay out of trouble."

Dad tossed a few seeds, and the timid birds poked and hopped around us. "He's always been a wild one. Just like his mother."

For a moment I let myself imagine that Dad's mind wasn't fractured. None of this was his fault, and it was exhausting to carry around the anger that this had happened to him—to all of us—when we'd all been through so much after losing Mom.

"Katie's coming home. She's not looking forward to moving in with Aunt Tootie, but she's going to be helping to fix up the house."

Dad turned to me. "What's wrong with the house?"

The way his voice deepened and he scowled, he looked so much like his old, hard self, but I didn't want to upset or confuse him.

"Uh . . . just some repairs that need to get done. We're

taking care of it."

Placated, he nodded. "You're good kids. I don't think I tell you that enough."

My throat was thick. "Thanks, Dad."

"You deserved more. More than the hand you were dealt."

Emotion burned behind my eyelids. I rarely let myself think of the scared little boy I'd been when Mom died. It all hit us differently. Dad focused on me and my potential playing ball. Duke closed himself off. Lee and Katie practically raised themselves in those years, and after he chose the service, she was alone too.

He wasn't wrong. It was a shitty hand, but I could see how it wasn't his fault. He'd been dealt it too, and he'd done what he could before he got sick.

Dad turned, and his eyes moved over me. "The little one, with the freckles on her nose. She's yours, right?"

I swallowed past the lump that had formed in my throat. "Penny. She's my daughter."

He continued to stare at the birds. "Ah, this damn mind." Dad rapped a finger against his temple. "I get mixed up sometimes. She looks like you though. Same goofy grin and wild look in her eyes."

I laughed. "She's a good kid."

"You are too."

"Is she her mother? Not the mean-looking one but the happy one."

I smiled, realizing his very accurate descriptions of Bethany and Lark.

"Lark is special to us, but not Penny's mom. The mean-looking one is actually her mother."

Dad considered that information. "That's too bad. I like the dark-haired one."

I chuckled. "Me too."

I looked out into the courtyard. It hit me that maybe this place wasn't so bad. Dad had some friends, nurses who could manage him on days that were bad, and access to activities that kept his mind active. I'd thrown money at the situation, hoping for the best, and Duke had taken care of the details. I hadn't given him the credit he was due.

"You lose a game?" He shook the small bag, testing out how much seed was left.

I turned to Dad, confused. "What? No."

"You got that pissed-off look on your face like you always do when you lose a game."

He can still read me. That part isn't gone.

I chuckled, then sighed and stretched my arm around the back of the bench. "Nah. Pissed off about a girl."

Dad laughed. "Yeah, they'll do that to you."

I missed this. Talking with Dad and not having every conversation be steeped in disappointment or sadness. I didn't want to push him and ruin it, but I took a chance anyway. "It's Lark, the dark-haired one. I'm in love with her but realized I haven't treated her like she deserves. Plus, she'll be leaving town. It's what she needs to do."

"She break up with you?"

"No. But she might have a new job, and she should take it. Then she'll be gone."

Dad seemed to be thinking about my words. I wasn't sure if he'd registered what I said, but I stayed quiet.

He slapped a hand on my knee. "Then she has to go."

I studied his face. At one time, he knew me and my drive to achieve my dreams better than anyone. "Is this one of those, *If you love them let them go, if they don't come back it wasn't meant to be* kind of things?"

I frowned. That was not the heartwarming encouragement I had been hoping for.

"Hell no—that's horseshit. You let her go so that girl can see what she's missing. Then you do everything you can to convince her to bring her pretty little ass back home."

Home.

I hadn't allowed myself to consider the concept of truly settling in. Sure, the nature of my job meant travel, but if I dug down, leaned on the people who mattered, maybe I could pull it off. *We* could pull it off.

Warm thoughts of sharing a home with Lark filled my mind. I had a lot to think about and even more to do if I was going to step up to be the man she truly deserved.

"I gotta go, Dad. Thanks."

ON SATURDAY AFTERNOON, Penny and I walked through Outtatowner and browsed the shops, looking at blown-glass artwork, trinkets, and an assortment of crap designed to cater to the tourists. For the millionth time, I thought about asking Lark to join us and spend a lazy day in town before getting dinner down at the beachfront restaurant she loved so much.

Meetings and practices kept me busy, and while we still fumbled for stolen moments, we hadn't talked about her audition or what happened when summer inevitably came to an end.

My heart sank every time I thought about it.

"Look at that one, Daddy!" Penny tugged my arm and pointed at a glass suncatcher casting long bands of colored light. It was shaped like a bird with a yellow face and a black mask that stretched across its eyes. It cast sunshine like a prism, and the detailed work was impressive.

"Can we look at it? Pretty please?"

I nodded and followed her into the little shop. "Don't touch it," I warned.

Penny tucked her hands behind her back and gazed at the array of little glass trinkets—birds and fish, a fox.

"What bird is that?" Her nose got closer and closer to bumping the glass shelf.

"I don't know, baby. I'm not really a bird guy. A yellow finch, maybe? Grandpa Red would probably know."

"That would be a horned lark." The shop owner stepped closer as Penny's eyes went wide. "It's a rare and special songbird. They're the only larks native to North America."

"Can we get it for her? Dad, it's the *perfect* present!" Penny was practically vibrating out of her skin with excitement.

I thought back to Lark and our conversations about love languages and all the ways I could show her how I felt. "You know what, Pickle, I think it is."

Later that night I sat on the steps of the porch with a beer and looked up at Lark's apartment. It was dark since she had her book club, and I already missed her. I spent my time thinking about what my dad had said—that Lark needed to see this audition through. It was the only way to be sure I wasn't holding her back, that our relationship had a solid foundation and we both dove in with a clear head.

Dread pooled in my stomach as I thought about her leaving us. We'd miss dinners together. Laughing with Pickle. I wouldn't have her in my bed, warm and pliant. Her laughter wouldn't float through the farmhouse as Penny did her homework and I cooked something on the grill.

Every fiber of my being rioted against the prospect of willingly watching Lark leave us.

32

LARK

Something was definitely up. Wyatt had been acting strange for the past few days, and I couldn't pinpoint what it was. When the Fourth of July came, he invited me to a party where we would watch fireworks on a private lake. It was swoony and magical and exactly what I imagined a small-town Fourth of July to be. When the fireworks were exploding overhead, I sneaked a glance at Wyatt and caught him staring.

I still blushed at his attention. "Everything okay?"

He nodded and rested his chin on top of Penny's head. She oohed and aahed over the fireworks as she sat in his lap.

On Thursday I got his note.

Dinner. Friday night, 8 p.m.

Excitement danced through me, and I pushed away any uneasy feelings that had popped up, regarding them as me just being paranoid. Most nights were spent together after Wyatt arrived home from work. Oftentimes I would excuse myself to the apartment to give Wyatt and Penny some time together, but more and more I would get an invitation for dinner or a walk or to go out for ice cream.

I never said no.

The love between Penny and her dad was so strong, and somehow I'd gotten lucky enough to be a part of it. Things felt easy and natural. The only thing missing was the ability to wake up next to the man I was falling for.

But for now it had to be enough.

I glanced at my phone, and the date staring up at me made me pause. My deadline for the Grinstead Casting Agency was only a few days away. More than once I'd almost deleted the video audition, but then I'd watch it and laugh at how seriously Penny and the boys had taken it, how much fun we'd had, and how they'd defended me when I was teased. After that I always tucked my phone away and tried to put that particular ticking clock out of my mind.

Staying in Outtatowner had never been the plan, but if I was finally casted for a day player part, staying would no longer be an option. I would have to pack everything back into my tiny car and drive the two thousand miles to LA.

My phone buzzed, and a picture of Mom's face lit up the screen. In it she had purple hair, and her bare face was smiling, eyes closed. Affection warmed me as I answered.

"Hi!"

"It's Aubergine, dear."

I chuckled at the way my mother always felt the need to announce herself despite my constant reminders that my phone told me it was her calling. "Yep. Hey, Mom."

I heard muffled talking in the background as she added, "Eagle sends his blessings."

I could hear the low drone of rhythmic, chanting music as she continued. "Lark, I experienced a cosmic shift and needed to call right away."

Oh boy.

"Wow. That sounds important."

Mom's voice was serious. "It is, darling. My spirit guides came to me, and I am supposed to tell you that the winds of change are coming for you."

"Are you into mushrooms again?"

"That is entirely beside the point, Lark."

I stifled a small laugh. It was comforting to know that my mother would never change.

"Well," I offered, "*winds of change* sounds exciting."

"It came with a warning. The guides said, 'Keep the wind at your back and the sun on your face.'"

I scrunched my face as I swapped my phone to the other ear to put in an earring. "Isn't that an Irish prayer?"

"Lark! This is serious. The guides are here to *help* you."

I shook my head and sighed. "Winds of change. Back. Sun. Got it. Thanks, Mom. Did your guides have anything else to share? Because I'm getting ready for a date."

"No, dear. That was the message. I love you. Enjoy your date." Just like that, the line went dead, and she was back to her tantric meditations with Eagle.

I shuddered at the unwelcomed memory of the one and only time I had interrupted them and had gotten an eyeful of naked old-man ass.

AS I MADE my way down the stairs of the apartment, Wyatt was already waiting for me on the steps of his porch. He was ungodly handsome in a white button-down shirt, blue trousers, and a brown belt. His sleeves were rolled up, showing off the veiny forearms I loved so much. I had no idea veins were a turn-on, but holy crap, they were hot.

Wyatt hit me with the full force of his smile, and my chest tightened.

His deep voice rolled over me. "You look amazing."

A giddy zip raced through me, and when I got to the bottom of the stairs, I did a little twirl to show off the coral boho sundress with the lace bodice I had purchased at the women's boutique downtown.

His arms wound around my middle as he pulled me closer. "Better than amazing. You look perfect."

For a moment, my worries of Wyatt and unvoiced fears faded away. He kissed my lips and ran his nose down the length of mine. "Ready?"

My hands played with the short hairs on the back of his head and pulled him down for another long kiss. After we broke apart, Wyatt gazed into my eyes. He took a step toward the yard, and my eyebrows dropped down.

"Come on." His mischievous smile was irresistible. I had speculated we might try the new wine bar downtown or maybe even dinner on the beach, but with my hand in his, Wyatt headed straight for the walking trail.

I clung to his arm and rested my head against his thick biceps as we walked. With Wyatt, the darkness of the trail wasn't nearly as frightening. He clearly knew the way, and in no time we came to the clearing by Wabash Lake.

Arranged in the middle of the shoreline was a thick blanket surrounded by tiki lanterns on long sticks. There was a small cooler and a pile of additional wool blankets. Everything had been arranged perfectly for a romantic, moonlit picnic.

"Oh, Wyatt . . ." My hand went to my throat, where my pulse beat wildly.

"You like it?" He reached into his pocket and pulled out a lighter to ignite the lanterns. They cast a semicircle of warm, glowing light that danced off the water of the lake.

"This is amazing. No one has ever done anything like this for me."

He smiled, satisfied that he'd gotten this right. "I thought a lakeside picnic might be a little more intimate than a dinner on the beach. This late, there will be no one on the trail to bother us. The lake is all ours."

I raised an eyebrow at him. "But, Mr. Sullivan . . . I didn't bring my swimsuit."

He grinned and pulled me closer. "Guess then you'll have to go in *nude*." His playful teasing reminded me of the day we'd seen each other naked. *Best. Day. Ever.*

I tipped my head back to laugh into the starry night sky. His mouth found the column of my neck, and I melted into him.

He caressed my hair, and his mouth slanted over mine. I poured every emotion into that kiss. I never wanted it to end.

Wyatt separated from me and pulled me to the blanket. "Let's eat something. I have plans for you later."

The dark promise in his words had me slipping off my sandals and dropping to my knees before settling into the soft blanket. From the nearby cooler, Wyatt unpacked a roll of sliced salami wrapped in butcher paper, a loaf of crusty bread, and a few different cheeses. He took care to arrange everything on the blanket between us. After he caught me staring, he pulled me in for a quick kiss and continued to arrange our picnic.

How did I get here?

If anyone would have told me that I would have Wyatt Sullivan, former NFL quarterback and head football coach, doting on me and impressing me with a romantic picnic, I would have called them a damn liar.

Yet there we were.

Finally, he stacked two sandwiches, also wrapped delicately in paper, on top of one another and lifted a chilled bottle of white wine from the cooler.

"Did you do all this?"

Wyatt looked offended, his hand spreading wide across his chest. "You doubt me?"

I pinned him with a stare and tried not to laugh.

"Fine." He pulled the cork from the wine and filled two stemless glasses. "I had a little help. But it *was* my idea."

I took the glass he offered and looked out onto the lake. The night was so clear you could see the hundreds of stars reflected on the water's surface. I sipped the wine, and the dry-but-buttery flavors of fruit and tanginess rolled over my tongue.

"Mmm. This is really good!"

Wyatt took his own sip and hummed in agreement. "I caved and paid a visit to Charles Attwater's shop. Just don't tell Lee. He'll be pissed and paint me as a traitor."

"Because Lee's clearly in love with Annie, right?"

Wyatt shrugged. "I think Lee's too stupid to see what's right in front of him, but I'm not going to be the one to tell him that."

We laughed and drank and listened to the sounds of cicadas filling the night air. Wyatt fed me small bites of salami and cheese, peppered with kisses in between our easy conversation. I recognized a glow in his eyes, and it wasn't from the lanterns.

Gently I teased the top edge of my dress with my fingers. "Let's go for a swim."

Wyatt growled as his body covered mine, kissing me as he made quick work of removing my dress.

Stripped down, I stood at the edge of the water with one

hand over my naked breasts. Wyatt stood, gloriously naked and unashamed.

We held hands as we toed closer to the edge of the lake.

"It might still be a little cold," he warned.

I gripped his hand in mine. "Let's do it."

I ran forward, pulling Wyatt with me and splashing the cool water as we ran into the lake. I screamed and laughed. Wyatt lifted me as we got deeper into the water. His mouth found mine, and we tumbled forward, soaking us both. My legs wound around his waist as he supported my weight.

When we broke from our kiss, Wyatt rested his forehead on mine. "Lark."

"Yes?" Our breaths were heavy pants as I clung to him.

He didn't answer but instead moved me lower until he slipped inside me.

I let my desperate cries ring out into the night. Held by him, I had never felt safer or more cherished.

When we came down from the high of our lovemaking, we settled by the outcropping of rocks that I had once used as a hiding place. Wyatt was next to me, chest deep in water, and I rested the side of my face on the arm I had flung across the rock. I openly stared at him. I loved that I could do that now that our feelings were out on the table.

Well, mostly.

Wyatt and I hadn't exactly *openly* discussed our scary, deep-down feelings or what this relationship/arrangement really was, but I didn't care. Things were too good to screw it up with messy talk about labels or the end of summer.

"I think we should talk about the end of summer."

Well, fuck.

Wyatt wasn't looking at me but rather out into the dark woods beyond the far edge of the lake.

His hand was warm on my hip, but a shiver still ran through me.

When I didn't speak up, he continued. "Come August, kids will be returning to school. Practices will start up, and I'll be in full-season football mode—practices, meetings, managing the staff and players. Addressing problems."

I smiled to myself. I had caught only glimpses of Wyatt in coach mode, but I knew that on the field, he was in his element.

"Sounds busy." I mentally started ticking off the tasks I knew I could help him with to make life easier. He'd need to keep his calendar tidy, and I would love the extra time I might have with Penny if her dad had an away game or late night.

"I think you should take the job."

My tongue felt thick, and my heart dropped to my butt like a stone. All I could manage was a confused, "What?"

"The job. In LA. You should take it. There's really no other choice."

I straightened, bracing myself against the rocks and the chill that had settled over me.

This is it. The moment you hand your heart over and he laughs in your face and crushes it in his fist.

"I haven't even submitted my callback. And there's no guarantee that I'd even get the job."

An all-too-familiar line formed on Wyatt's forehead. "Then you should submit it. And of course you'll get the job. I watched you convince an entire town that Bowlegs was having a torrid affair with a knockout like you. Jolly and Ant are still confident that you secretly married him for money."

I laughed at the absurdity of the town rumor mill, but my stomach was tight.

Wyatt wanted me to leave, and this was his out.

"Oh, I . . . um. I guess I hadn't really thought about LA in a while."

Lie.

I had thought about it every single day and almost deleted the video more than once. I should have done it.

"Hey." Wyatt edged closer and moved a wet piece of hair from my forehead before tipping my chin to look at him. "I don't *want* you to go. But you need to see this thing through. Set a goal and go get it. It's what I did with football, and I got to live my dream because of it. Now it's your turn."

Tears swam in my eyes as I fought back a sob. Instead, I buried myself into the warmth of his shoulder so he wouldn't see me fall to pieces.

Could I believe his words? That he didn't really want me to go but thought it was best in the long run? Or were those just nice words so I wouldn't feel the sting of him leaving me once summer was over?

He'd salvaged the rest of the evening by showering me with attention and sweet, reassuring words. The conversation with my mother and her *winds of change*, along with the sinking feeling that, deep down, I might actually wonder how things would have turned out if I did submit my callback tape, nagged me.

I loved Wyatt. If that were real and true and meant to be, I had to believe it would all work out in the end.

So, despite every fiber of my being screaming that it was wrong, that night, while I lay alone in my bed, I pulled up the Grinstead Casting Agency email and finally hit send before I cried myself to sleep.

33

WYATT

"You look like shit, big brother." My little sister, Kate, smiled down at me as her hand slapped on my shoulder.

I scooted out from the booth at the café and rose to wrap her in a bear hug. Her wavy brown hair had gotten longer, and she looked a little too thin, but she was finally home.

"Ol' Catfish Katie is back in Outtatowner!"

She shoved me hard in the shoulder. "Knock it off with that shit!" She looked around the café to see if anyone had heard me. "It's Kate. *Just* Kate."

"Yeah, okay." She knew as well as I did that dumbass nicknames were about the only thing people remembered about you when you left. That and the time you stole your aunt's car to do doughnuts in a parking lot just to accidentally break an axle when you lost control and slammed into the curb.

I grinned at her, remembering how afraid she was to tell Dad, and how I'd taken the heat for it so she could still go to prom.

She looked past me onto the pile of papers on the table. "So what are you frowning over?"

I glanced at my stack of notes and the half-drank, now-cold coffee that the server kept trying to refill. "Not much, paperwork for the season. The less-glamorous side of college ball."

"Where's the little nugget of yours?"

"Pickle's with Tootie, getting supplies for the Little Miss Blueberry Pageant. Apparently she's a *shoo-in* at the Blueberry Festival."

Kate slid into the bench across the booth from me. "Seems like she's settling in then."

"Are you kidding? She's practically the princess of Remington County."

Kate plucked a french fry from my plate, bit it, and then frowned at how cold and mushy it was before dropping it back down and dusting the salt from her fingers. "And how about you?"

Horrible. Miserable. A total fucking moron.

"I'm fine." I shrugged. "Busy."

Kate grinned at me. She always was a shit stirrer. She pointed a long finger at me, swirling it in the air between us, and in her singsong voice she said, "I heard a rumor about you."

I shook my head and pretended to look over the papers in front of me.

Kate sighed and planted her hands on her hips. "Fine. Be annoying. But I want to meet this girl who got *the* Wyatt Sullivan to fall head over heels in loooooove."

Her words sliced through me like a lance, but I schooled my face into bored annoyance. "How long are you staying again?"

She laughed and rolled her eyes. "Oh, whatever, you love me. So tell me about Lark."

Just hearing her name was painful. It was like the single syllable cut off my air supply.

She had been gone for only two weeks, and it felt like I was slowly dying.

Lark got the job because *of course she did*. She'd cried while I'd put on a brave face and told her how proud I was of her.

Though I'd wanted to throw up, I'd held her in my arms and reassured her that we'd be here, in Outtatowner, waiting for her when she wrapped.

I'd wait my entire fucking life if I had to.

I'd offered to buy her a plane ticket, but she'd refused. Lark had said she needed her clothes, and not knowing exactly how long she would have to stay in LA, she'd thought it was best to drive out there. I'd disagreed and told her as much, but once she smiled sweetly and laid out her plan, I'd begrudgingly gone along with it.

It helped her case that she was on her knees when she'd pitched the idea, and that image had run on a loop in my head ever since.

But since she'd left, every time I thought about Lark—which was too damn much—I was convinced I was having a heart attack or a stroke, because there was a splinter lodged in my chest, and the incessant ringing in my ears didn't seem to go away.

"Lark is good," was all I could manage.

Katie squinted at me. She knew I was full of shit. "When will she be home for me to meet her?"

I shrugged. "Dunno."

Lark and I texted every day and tried to connect over Face-

Time, but the three-hour time difference made it difficult. Penny was also miserable without Lark, so anytime we did connect on the phone, Penny would take over and dominate the conversation. I didn't have the heart to take those stolen moments from either of them. We also didn't know when she'd be back, and that was the most torturous part of all.

"Well, you're still a bucket of laughs." Kate slapped her hands on the table and stood. "I'm going to meet Tootie over at the house." She flipped her dark hair over her shoulder. "You boys weren't kidding—that place is a disaster waiting to happen. I guess we're meeting some guy today to go over the work he's going to do. Gotta run interference and make sure she doesn't get hosed by the contractor."

More accurately, it was Tootie running interference to make sure Kate didn't blow a gasket. None of us had the balls to tell her that it was her weasel-nosed ex-boyfriend's brother Beckett contracted for the work. It didn't matter that he was Duke's best friend; she was going to lose it. "Have fun."

She winked and waved goodbye over her shoulder before adding a final little-sister jab. "And hey, Wyatt? Lighten up."

I only shook my head and went back to my work. How could I lighten up when my heart was somewhere in LA?

~

"DO you think she's ever coming back?" Penny's miserable voice cracked, and I clamped my jaw tight to keep it together as I tucked her into bed.

I was tired. So fucking tired of living without Lark.

"I hope so, baby. She's going to try to call tomorrow."

"Why did she have to leave us? Did you make her mad?

Mom says that you made her mad, and that's why she doesn't stay with us."

Fucking Bethany. Irritation rolled through me, but I wasn't about to shit-talk Penny's mother when she was already struggling.

"I didn't make Lark mad. Neither of us did anything to make her leave. It's her job, just like sometimes I have to go away for games." I smoothed her hair as her lip wobbled. She sucked it in and nodded.

My brave little girl.

"I just want her home."

I swallowed hard. This wasn't right. Pickle felt it and so did I. "I do too, baby girl."

I hated seeing Penny as miserable as I felt. I wanted to ram my fist through a wall—make it right for her. For both of us.

I'd picked up my phone to call Lark a thousand times and tell her: *This is a mistake. You didn't need to leave. This is real and I love you and we'll make this work.*

I stopped myself every time. I couldn't be the selfish prick I wanted to be when it came to Lark achieving her dreams. I loved her too damn much. So instead, I let the lies roll off my tongue: *We're managing here. We're so happy for you. Everything is good.*

Heartsick, Penny and I shared the silence while I rubbed her back and shoved down the riot of emotions that were practically killing me. I knew that night, like every other since Lark left, that the low, angry voice would whisper in the dark and remind me I was meant to be alone. Lark was never mine to keep.

"Okay, kiddo, get some rest." I kissed her cheek and tucked her blankets in tight around her, just the way she liked them. "Love you, burrito baby." Halfway across the room I stopped and turned. I infused my voice with false brightness. "One more?"

Only her face didn't brighten. She only shrugged. "No, I'm okay."

My heart broke a little more when I crossed the room anyway.

∼

THE FOLLOWING WEEK, Bethany arranged to take Penny shopping and find a dress for the Little Miss Blueberry Pageant. I was relieved because it was the first real smile I'd gotten out of Pickle in days, and I knew jack shit about small-town pageant dresses—it was squarely in Beth's wheelhouse.

I'd given her a wad of cash and explicit instructions on when I expected Penny to be home. She rolled her eyes and ignored me, of course, and was an hour late, but at least I had gotten a text letting me know they were running late. I'd consider that a small win.

Penny raced from Bethany's car, dragging two new dresses on the ground. "Careful. You don't want to mess those up."

Pickle grinned at her mom and ran right past me. "Hey, Dad!"

I'd wanted a hug, but at least she wasn't moping—or worse, making me feel like the scum of the earth for convincing Lark it was a good idea for her to leave. Not that I needed any help there.

I turned back to Bethany. "Thanks for the heads-up that you were running late."

She smiled primly and batted her lashes. "Didn't want to anger the warden."

"Whatever, I'm not that bad." *Was I?*

"Sure you are."

Bethany always had a way of raising my hackles, getting under my skin, and making me feel like shit. I had turned to leave when she stopped me.

"I'm pregnant."

My muscles stiffened, and a pit opened in my stomach. When Bethany had spoken those same words nearly eight years ago, my entire world had been tipped on its axis. This time, instead of having a meltdown and thinking about all the ways life as I'd known it was over, I'd only thought of Pickle.

"Does she know?"

Bethany stared past me at the front door, barely shaking her head. "Not yet. But I'm going to do it right this time. Really be there for the baby and make up for all my mistakes."

My heart broke for Penny. All she'd ever wanted from her mom was to be loved. The way a mother should love her daughter in the simplest, most natural way in the world.

For Beth, it was easier to start over than to show up and be the dependable mother Penny needed her to be. I was angry for her all over again.

"Goodbye, Bethany." I turned toward the house.

"She loves her like a mom, you know." Beth's words hit me square in the back, and I paused. "The nanny. Penny loves her."

My jaw tightened. "Lark is not the nanny."

Her calculating smirk was back. "I know. Just wanted to see it for myself."

"See what?"

She lifted a finger to point at me. "That. The consti-pated look you get when someone shits all over something you love." She shrugged. "Your fierce loyalty is one of your best qualities."

I wanted to bite back with a petty *clearly not one of yours*, but I shut my mouth. I was too tired to go another round with Bethany when it never mattered in the long run.

When I stared at her, she dropped a hand to her flat stomach. "He offered to marry me, but I don't think I'm going to say yes."

I swallowed, unsure of this new ground we were covering. "Okay."

Tension hung thick in the air.

"You deserve her, you know. Penny." A sad smile crossed her face as she opened the car door. "She worships the ground you walk on. Maybe one of us should show her what a happy, functional relationship should look like."

I waved a weak goodbye and stomped toward the house. I hated to know she was right.

"You're doing great! The director *loved* the direction you took the character." The director of photography was running through the day's notes as someone was touching up my makeup. "Also, when you turn to shoo the cat away, turn your shoulders, not just your neck. Those pesky neck wrinkles are hard to edit out in post."

My hand immediately went to my neck. *Neck wrinkles? Isn't that normal?* "Okay, I got it."

She put a hand on my shoulder and squeezed before turning and calling over her shoulder. "You're doing great!"

I sat back and looked to the ceiling as I let the makeup artist blot fresh powder beneath my eyes.

This is everything I have wanted. Why do I still feel so sad?

So far the shoot for the television series had been a dream. The director was friendly and kind, and the cast and crew were tight and spent lots of time together outside the shooting schedule. Chase Singleton was not at all the self-absorbed playboy he was painted in the media, at least as far as I could tell, and Eliza Stone, one of the principal female actors, was professional, if not a bit frosty. It was a new chapter and a stark difference from my previous experience in LA, when I'd witnessed back-stabbing, snark, and outright lies to get ahead.

It was different and fresh somehow.

Yet my mind and my heart were still stuck in Outta-towner, Michigan, with a particular grouchy single dad and his precocious little girl. I even missed the chaos of organizing the lives of three stinky college boys.

I looked at my phone again and reread our text thread, heightening the ever-present hollow feeling in my chest.

I sighed and slipped my phone back into my bag. I needed to stop comparing LA to Michigan. There were so few similarities, and somehow California always came out lacking.

I just needed to give it time. The gig was the break I had wanted, and filming would wrap in a few weeks, if all continued to go according to plan.

And then I'd be home.

The impact of that thought hit me like a freight train.

Home.

I'd spent so much of my adult life wandering, trying out different cities to see which fit best, to see who I could become. I'd always been searching for a different version of myself.

Turns out the best version of myself was *me*. The some-times impractical, overly sentimental woman who got stuck on the side of a sand dune and secretly high-fived college kids for punching an asshole in the face. I was optimistic and tenderhearted and *real*.

∼

WHEN FILMING FINALLY WRAPPED for the day, the entire cast met for dinner and drinks at an exclusive club I'd only ever seen on my Instagram feed. As soon as we'd arrived, we were ushered into a special roped-off section that overlooked the bar area and had its own hostess. The booth was lush, a large semicircle obscured with dark lighting and a black velvet curtain that could be pulled closed to provide additional privacy.

Ours was tied open in order to see and be seen.

Early in the night I tried to reach Wyatt and Penny, but it was late there, and he hadn't answered. I had missed a text from him—and I assumed Penny, based on the string of emoji and cat GIFs—saying good night. The sinking feeling was back, and I started to type a quick reply.

"Seems like things are going great for you on set." Chase Singleton slid into the large booth next to me.

"Yes! It's been a lot of fun. I feel like I've learned so much already." I slipped the phone back into my purse, and Chase swirled his drink in front of himself.

His lips pursed. "Is this your first day player?"

I nodded and swallowed. I had assumed it was painfully obvious that I had never done anything other than be a background extra for film.

"Well, you're a natural, then." He took a sip of the dark liquid and hissed a breath through his teeth. "I overheard the directors talking. There may be a reunion in the future for Jack and Delilah. I could put in a good word for you."

He winked and my stomach hollowed.

I was the ex-girlfriend Delilah to Chase's hunky leading man Jack. I took a long sip of my pineapple and Malibu through the straw and tried to come up with a response that wouldn't broadcast my sudden reservations.

Eliza slid into the booth with us just as some fans

started not so discreetly snapping selfies with our booth in the background. Eliza posed and pursed her lips and looked flawlessly fabulous. I straightened my shoulders and tried to look interested in the conversation Chase continued to have with me despite the fact I hadn't heard a single word he'd said.

". . . even Eliza thinks Lark is perfect, and she hates everyone."

My head snapped up at my name, and Eliza shot him a prim smile. "I don't hate *everyone*, but yes, Lark, you're doing a great job. It's nice not to have to drag out shooting for missed marks and flubbed lines."

"Thanks, I—"

"Oh!" Eliza cut in, leaning forward. "They're taking more pictures. Quick, pretend I said something funny!"

I tossed my chin up and faked a laugh as Chase's arm slid behind my back. I looked around, and once it seemed like the group of girls had left, my smile slid from my face and I scooted toward the center of the booth.

"See." Eliza winked at me. "What did I say? A natural."

"Is it always like this? People recognizing you and taking pictures wherever you go?"

"If you're lucky." She leaned in and lowered her voice. "I heard Rebecca Tate started paying paparazzi to follow her around. How sad is that?"

Chase and Eliza had a hearty laugh together.

"That seems exhausting," I admitted, "to be *on* all the time." I thought about how many times I'd run to the grocery store in Outtatowner with no makeup on, wearing Wyatt's gray sweatpants. No one ever batted an eyelash, and certainly no one was taking my picture. "I'm not sure I could do it."

Eliza looked at me and smiled sweetly, like we were

having a completely different conversation, and I quietly wondered where the cameras were. "Well, you better get used to it. We all want this series to be the next *Grey's Anatomy*, to be recognized everywhere and not have to worry about auditioning."

Chase stretched in the booth. "Dude, I'd love to coast for a while. That's why I even agreed to a television series in the first place. No more auditions, pick a movie role here and there. It's the dream."

I could feel my eyes widening as what they were saying sank in. If this thing took off, and I was written in as a series regular, that would be it. LA would have to become my home during filming, because there was no way I could ever afford to fly back and forth from California to Michigan often enough to make it work.

"Don't look so scared. Everybody wants this." Eliza clinked her champagne flute to my now-empty glass. "Welcome to the big leagues."

The drinks kept coming, the food was divine, and we didn't pay for a single bite of it. Our entire group was dancing and laughing and having fun, while a single thought ran on a loop in my head: *I was finally enough—this should have been perfect.*

THIS HOUSE IS TOO DAMN QUIET.

Sprawled on the couch, I stared at the white ceiling of the living room and mentally noted the spots we had missed when painting. I needed something, anything, to keep me from thinking about Lark and how I'd pushed her to go for this job in the first place.

Summer break was coming to a close, and everything should have been clicking into place. I loved the thrill of a new football season. Everything was new and hopeful as the team had a fresh start with a new season. There was a buzz in the atmosphere—charged.

I felt none of it.

To make matters worse, campus reopened and Michael, Kevin, and Joey loaded up the car and moved back into an off-campus house. They would spend their last couple of weeks with the team, and I could only hope they didn't get hurt or into trouble. I did my best to give a stern-but-supportive pep talk before they drove back to the city.

Watching them drive away was nothing like when Lark

waved her arm out the window and disappeared around the bend in the road.

It was like the life had been sucked out of me when I watched her little gray car drive away. Plus, I refused to let her in on how things were really going here. What was the point? It would only make her feel terrible and second-guess her decision to take the job in the first place.

Her texts were brief but upbeat. I wondered if she was doing the same things as me—putting on a brave face and barely making it through the day.

I sighed again and was contemplating going for a run when a text came through on my phone. Hope leaped in my chest as I snatched the phone off the coffee table. Disappointment flooded me when I saw it wasn't a message from Lark.

DUKE

> Heard Kate and Tootie stole Pickle for a girls' night sleepover. Let me guess, you're sitting alone and miserable? Crying yourself to sleep?

He wasn't too far off, but I wasn't about to tell him that.

> Yes. Doing whatever the hell I want is really an inconvenience.

DUKE

> Meet Beckett and me at the Grudge. Have a beer.

I didn't have a reason not to go, other than to sit in the dark and feel sorry for myself, so I sent him a quick reply and changed my clothes.

Tourist season had been in full swing for a while now, so the divide between the Sullivans and Kings was less apparent inside the bar. I scanned the unofficial Sullivan side and raised my chin after I spotted Duke leaned against the back bar with his friend Beckett. When I walked up, he slid a beer bottle in my direction.

"Thanks."

"Hey, Beckett." I shook his hand. "Good to see you again."

Duke took a pull of his beer and rested his forearms on the bar. "Kate's gonna be a problem."

My brows knitted together. "Problem?"

Duke shook his head and sighed. "Surprised you haven't already heard about the one-sided shouting match that happened over at the house. Our sister is less than thrilled with our choice in contractors." He tipped his beer toward Beckett.

He wasn't stupid enough to talk shit about our little sister, but I didn't miss the way he tensed at her being the topic of conversation.

I still decided to poke the bear. "Think you can take her on? She's a pistol, that one."

Beckett's throat bobbed and he nodded. "Yeah, it'll be fine."

I eyed him a second longer. He was quiet, but there was something about him that exuded confidence. Duke said he was the best, and if he was willing to help us out, despite our sister's temper and foot stomping, then so be it.

We needed his help. We needed Katie to get Aunt Tootie on board to take care of the house before it collapsed around her, and there was no way we were hiring the Kings' construction company and willingly welcoming them into her home.

Beckett was our guy, and she'd just have to deal with it.

I scowled at my beer and took another long pull. The

bar felt crowded and too loud, and I just wanted to be home and miserable. I swallowed another gulp.

"You trying to get drunk or bail already?" Duke raised one eyebrow at me and made me feel fifteen again, the way only an older brother could.

I shook my head, unable to lie to my brother, and took another drink. "Hell if I know."

Beckett stayed quiet in the background while Duke's eyes scanned the crowd. They seemed to snag on someone before flitting away, and I couldn't seem to figure out who he kept looking at. I tensed, hoping it wasn't a King looking for trouble.

Duke shook his head. "Yeah, women will do that for you."

I shoved one hand in my pocket. "It was stupid. I pushed her to go for the job, and now I'm not sure if she's ever coming back."

"So things are going well for her, then?"

"Sounds like it. She says there's even talk about extending her part—writing her in as a more long-term cast member."

Duke shook his head. "Shit."

"Yeah." I tried to ease the tension in my neck, but it was useless. The knot seemed to be a permanent part of me now. "The worst part is, she deserves this. What kind of asshole would take that away from her as soon as she got it? Mostly I just keep my mouth shut and tell her how happy I am for her."

Beckett seemed to ease away, giving us space to talk privately. Duke turned his shoulders to face me. "You told her, though, right? How you feel?"

"I don't want to hold her back. But I'll be here if she ever does make it back to Michigan."

"You know who's great for advice?"

I groaned and rolled my eyes. I had been getting enough advice to make me sick.

"Dad."

I huffed a humorless laugh. "I did talk to him."

"And?"

"He said I let her go, but then"—I used air quotes to help illustrate how ridiculous Dad's advice had been—"'bring her pretty little ass back home.'"

Duke tipped his beer and nodded as if to say, *See? There's your game plan right there.*

I sighed. "I don't know, man. I have the season coming up, Penny's going to start school in the fall . . . everything is just so *much* right now."

Duke's gaze fell over the growing crowd inside the bar. "You know, you're a fucking moron. If I had the chance to be with the woman I loved, I sure as hell wouldn't be sitting here crying about it. I'd be coming up with a way to make it happen."

The woman he loved? What the hell does Duke Sullivan know about love and heartache?

Annoyed, I finished my beer and planted it on the wooden bar top with a clank. "Thanks for the advice, big brother, but I'm good."

Duke laughed, and my molars ground together. "You are so far from good, it's not even funny. Have you even seen yourself this summer? You laughed. You got to know your family again. Penny has a *home* here, and Lark was a big part of that. Are you really willing to risk that because you can't muster the balls to tell her how you feel?"

I was beyond frustrated with my brother, but mostly because I didn't appreciate him calling me out like that in the middle of a crowded bar.

"I gotta go."

Duke scoffed and signaled the bartender for another round as I stormed out.

~

I COULDN'T STAND the thought of spending the rest of the night alone in the house. Staring up at the dark windows of Lark's apartment every night was torture enough. Instead of going home, I headed toward the black waters of Lake Michigan. Most of the little shops that dotted the marina were closed for the night, and only a few people walked down the pier or along the quiet beach.

I slipped off my shoes and let my toes sink into the wet sand. Lark and Penny had practically lived on the beach this summer, and I couldn't think of it without it mingling in my mind with her warm cinnamon-and-citrus scent. Even my hometown had become a place where I couldn't escape her.

I didn't want to.

Somewhere along the way I'd shed little bits of my controlling nature in order to let Lark in. She took the little slivers I'd offered and wedged herself so deeply into my core that I couldn't imagine myself without her. Her smiles, her laugh, the way she loved life and everyone in it.

Lark had willingly given herself, and I had slowly, reluctantly done the same. I shared more with her than anyone before, and while it was vulnerable and frightening in a way I didn't like, it was also safe. Comforting.

After I'd walked a long length of beach, I looked up to realize I was near the dune on which Lark had gotten herself stranded. When it happened, I had hid my attraction to her with a gruff indifference. Even then I knew getting close to Lark had the potential to change everything.

I thought back to her offhand comments about love languages and realized exactly what I needed to do.

MY FIST POUNDED on Tootie's front door twice before I turned the handle and let myself in. "Hello?"

"Back here!" Tootie's voice was filled with laughter as it floated down the hallway.

My boots stomped on the creaking wooden floors as I made my way through her house. In the large living room, Tootie, Penny, and Katie were sitting on blankets and pillows with something that looked like green mud smeared all over their faces.

"Hey, Daddy!" Penny's crooked white teeth were stark against the mask. "We're beautifying."

I smiled. "I can see that. I didn't mean to interrupt girls' night, but I needed to talk with Tootie."

My aunt unfolded herself and groaned as she rose from the floor. I motioned toward the kitchen, and she followed.

As soon as we were out of earshot, I turned. "Can you look after Penny for a few days?"

Worry crossed her face. "Of course. Is everything okay?"

I sighed and ran my hand across my face. "No. But it will be. I need to go to LA."

A huge grin spread across her face when she realized what I was implying. Her hands planted on her hips. "Well, it's about time. Don't worry about us. We'll be just fine. You bring our girl home."

Affection for my aunt filled my chest. I hugged her and

stomped toward the living room. Penny was delighted to hear she would get a few extra days of girl time, and I assured her that I would head home as soon as I could.

"Will Lark come home with you?"

Unease rippled through me. "I'm not sure, sweetie." My plan was only half-formed, and I hoped to work out the details on the red-eye to LA.

"Okay, well, don't screw it up."

I laughed and tension eased from my shoulders. "Thanks, Pickle. I'll do my best."

36

WYATT

THE SUMMER SUN FELT DIFFERENT IN CALIFORNIA. Sure, I'd been to LA before for games or the odd trip, but viewing it in the context of Lark's home, it all felt wrong. LA was too loud. Too busy. It lacked the quaint, slow pace of a place like Outtatowner.

I had subtly been keeping tabs on Lark via text. The night before she was her typical chatty self, and I knew work for the week was wrapping today.

It was early, but at 7:00 a.m. West Coast time, I'd already sent a *good morning* text. I followed it up quickly as I hauled my backpack over my shoulder and exited the plane.

> I have a surprise for you.

LARK

> You're so sweet! I have a surprise for you too.

I smiled to myself as I arranged for an Uber. *Not as good as mine.*

> Okay, you first.

The incoming picture made my heart sink to the floor. It was a selfie of Lark, smiling and lovely as ever . . . in a fucking airport. The large windows in the background provided a clear view of airplanes and a tower behind her.

No. No no no no no. This can't be happening.

> Please tell me you're still in LA.

I watched as three bubbles appeared and disappeared four times. Then . . . nothing.

> Lark, are you in LA?

Finally, a text came through.

> LARK
>
> I wanted to surprise you and Penny. I thought you'd be happy.

I immediately dialed her number. When it connected, I didn't even let her get a word in. "Are you in LA?"

"Wyatt. Hey. Yes, look . . . if you don't want me to make the trip, just say so. I—"

"Where are you?" The words rushed out harsher than I'd intended, but I *had* to see her. Immediately. Relief that she hadn't left the city flooded over me.

Emotion filled her voice. "LAX. My plane is boarding in five minutes."

Five fucking minutes.

"Do *not* get on that plane." My eyes scanned the screens as I searched for outgoing flights from LA to Chicago. One of them had to be hers.

Gate 28. Five minutes.

I took off like it was fourth and goal in the fourth quarter and hauled ass toward the gate. Ignited by excitement and my love for Lark, I wove around luggage carts and families with slow-ass children. I was sure I looked crazed, but I couldn't fuck this up. She deserved the big act of service, the words of affirmation—all of it. I needed to show her in every way how much she meant to me.

As I approached the gate, the flight attendants were scanning the boarding passes of the last remaining passengers. Lark wasn't among them.

"Hold up! Wait!" I called between sucking in breaths of air.

One flight attendant looked at me, startled. "Are you on this flight, sir?"

"No, I—" I bent over, sucking wind, and was convinced I was going to puke all over the startled flight attendant.

"I'm sorry, sir. Boarding is over. If you're not a ticketed passenger, I am going to have to ask you to leave."

Damn it! Why did I hang up? I should have told her I was here so she'd stay.

"Are you Wyatt Sullivan?" A young kid wearing my old NFL jersey walked up to me, looking hopeful and a little stunned at my erratic behavior.

I straightened and exhaled. "Yeah."

He held out a piece of paper and a pen. "Do you think . . . ?"

Anger burned in my throat. I'd fucked it up. I bit back my annoyance and tried to focus on the young fan in front of me. I hastily scrawled my name across the paper and offered it back with a thin smile.

"Thanks, man. I'm excited to see what you do with the Midwest Michigan team."

I nodded woodenly as my hands dropped. A small crowd had gathered once people started to realize I wasn't just some late passenger, but someone worth getting an autograph from. Murmurs and whispers surrounded me, and I felt like an asshole.

I was sure by later that afternoon there'd be some splashy news report printed about the scene I made in LAX.

I'm sure the board of directors will love to see that one.

Defeated, I turned.

Standing in front of me, with her hands on her hips and a smile on her face, was Lark.

My woman. My whole heart.

"Wyatt." Her warm hazel eyes gleamed with unshed tears.

Cell phones were raised in our direction, no doubt filming my epic fuckup. I took two long, determined strides toward Lark.

"You're here," she said softly.

My heart still hammered in my chest. "I didn't think I'd be chasing down an airplane, but yeah. I'm here."

Lark's arms wound around my neck, but I stepped back.

"I'm sorry, Lark. I lied to you." Her sweet face scrunched as I put my hands on her hips to steady myself.

I have to get this right.

"I've *been* lying to you. I'm happy for you and so damn proud that you landed this role—that part is true. But I'm fucking *miserable*. I know I'm supposed to smile at you and tell you everything is peachy, but I can't do it. I won't. I know I'm demanding. My schedule sucks. My hometown is ridiculous, and my family is a *lot* to handle sometimes. You have this whole bright future ahead of you and—" I waved my hand around us as my heart pounded. "If this job and LA are what you want, we'll make it work. But I can't go weeks without seeing you. I won't. Being apart from you hurts. *Physically hurts.* I love you too much."

A startled little gasp escaped from Lark's lips. Her chin was wobbling, and worry flickered over me. *Maybe I was too late.*

When a tear spilled over her dark lashes, I swiped it away with my thumb, and her face leaned into my palm.

"Wyatt." She sighed. "How are we going to make this work?"

I wanted to reassure her, tell her I have everything figured out, but that would be another lie. So instead, I gave her more truth. "I will love you. Every second of every day. You will never have to wonder if I'm thinking about you or missing you. If we're apart, you're with me. Here."

I planted her hand over my heart and covered it with mine. It beat against my chest, and I only hoped she understood. "You're it for me. Forever."

"I was coming home, Wyatt."

I pulled Lark closer and rested my chin on her head. "I know, baby."

She stepped back and shook her head. "No. Home. Like, *home* home."

I looked at her, trying to figure out exactly what she was implying.

Her watery smile brightened. "We wrapped today. The directors pulled me into an office and offered me a job as a series regular. They want Delilah back and are working with the writers to make that happen for the next season."

My heart ached, knowing that it meant a more substantial long-distance relationship. But I had meant what I said. I would always support Lark, and if this was what she wanted, I would make it work. There was no option to live in a world where Lark wasn't mine.

"They told me how they plan to spin the relationship and make it a running story line. It's the break every actor hopes for."

My throat filled with sandpaper, and I tried to swallow past it. "I understand, and I'm so proud of you. I know—"

"I turned them down, Wyatt."

My heart stopped. My mind went blank.

Lark's tinkling laugh and the brush of her fingertips across my furrowed brow had me pulling her in closer.

"But this is everything you've wanted. What you've hoped for."

She smiled. "I thought it was. I've been searching for a long time, and I realized that moving all the time? Even acting? Being someone else? It was a way for me to hide." Lark's voice wobbled. "But I don't want to hide anymore. I want to be seen."

Her eyes closed as fat tears tumbled down her cheeks. I brought her close and kissed the tears away. "I see you. Baby, I see you."

I SMILED at Lark over the top of her small gray car as I shoved the last duffel bag in the back. After my near miss at the airport and several autographs later, we had decided to go back to the apartment Lark was staying at. One look around the dingy apartment and it was settled.

Lark was coming home.

I held her hand in mine as we piled her stuff into the car and headed east. Lark held her phone and smiled at the screen. Someone had filmed the whole scene at the airport and offered to send it to Lark.

She had already watched it four times but still wore a goofy grin when she did.

I snagged the phone from her hands and frowned at her. "I think you like watching me look like an idiot."

Her hand fluttered to her chest as she blinked. "Me? Enjoy watching grouchy, always-in-control Wyatt pour his heart out? Never."

I tossed the phone into her lap. "You're a shit."

Her easy laugh filled the car, and I grinned beside her as I pointed the vehicle toward home.

37

LARK

"FIVE MINUTES! I SWEAR I'LL BE READY!" I swiped a light coat of tinted lip gloss across my lips and fluffed my hair in the bathroom mirror.

Wyatt's chuckle sounded behind me as he leaned on the doorframe. "I don't believe you."

I shot him an annoyed look in the mirror and fixed the edge of my lip gloss with my finger.

Penny popped her head into his bedroom. "Dad, can Cheeto come with us?"

Wyatt sighed before looking over his shoulder. "Absolutely not."

She grumbled and sulked away with her little hamster tucked into her hands. Wyatt crossed his arms and frowned.

I moved into his space and wrapped my arms around his middle. I leaned into the hard plane of muscle and listened to his heart thump against my ear. "Everything okay?"

His arms tightened around my shoulders. "Fine."

I smiled against his chest. For all his bravado on the field and outward appearances, there were still parts of him that felt alone. For so long, it was easier for him to white-knuckle it through life. It was still new for him to be surrounded by people who loved him.

"You know, we don't have to go if you're not feeling up to it," I offered.

His lips gently kissed my hair. "No, we should go. But let's stop at the Sugar Bowl and pick something up before we head over."

My heart soared for him. The Sullivans and all their heartache were slowly healing. Together.

"DID YOU SEE THIS?" I slanted my phone toward Wyatt as he pulled out of the driveway.

"Hmm?" he hummed.

"I texted the group to let them know we would be a few minutes late because we were stopping by the Sugar Bowl to grab a dessert . . . Duke said he already stopped there."

Wyatt looked over, brows pinched. "Duke hates that place. He never goes unless he's dropping off berries for Huck."

I lifted my shoulders.

"Well, all right." Wyatt made a turn and headed toward Aunt Tootie's house. Cars were lining the gravel driveway, and Three-Legged Ed ran beside us when we pulled up. I leaned out of the car, trying to shoo him away, but he kept pace with us, his tongue lolled out to the side in a goofy grin.

I spotted Beckett Miller's work truck off to the side and lifted a finger. My brows shot up.

Wyatt's lips formed a thin line. "Yep. He's sticking it out."

Penny leaned forward from the back seat. "Aunt Katie said that Beckett is an 'intolerable, pigheaded asshole.'"

A shotgun burst of laughter erupted from me as Wyatt looked at his precocious little girl. "Penny . . ."

She shrugged. "What? She said it, not me."

"We don't talk like that. Beckett is Uncle Duke's friend, and he's doing us all a big favor by working on the house." Wyatt narrowed his eyes at me while I struggled to get my fit of giggles under control.

He shook his head. "All right, you two, let's go."

The weather was still warm, so we gathered in Tootie's huge yard to dine outside. Penny took off like a shot toward Lee, Ed yipping and bounding after her. Wyatt rounded the car to meet me and immediately tossed his arm across my shoulders and pulled me in close.

I sighed and melted into him as we walked. "Intolerable, pigheaded asshole." I laughed again.

Wyatt let his lips brush across my hair. "Those two are going to kill each other before the renovation even starts."

I laughed again, knowing full well that Katie had every intention of making Beckett's life miserable. "Most likely."

As we walked up, the conversation flowed over itself, everyone talking and laughing and picking at the small appetizers Tootie had placed on the table. The afternoon sun was warm, and puffy clouds made sure it wasn't too hot.

The whole scene was picturesque and perfect. If only you could ignore Kate shooting daggers across the guacamole and Beckett completely ignoring her to talk with Tootie about where he'd start working.

Football season was right around the corner. Penny would be starting school, and for the first time, it felt like all the pieces of this broken family were falling into place.

The Sullivans still had some healing to do, but for now

they were together. Wyatt had let me into the darkest, loneliest parts of himself, and bit by bit he was letting the rest of them in too.

I looked around at their smiling faces. Katie's eyes brightened when we walked up, and my heart pinched in my chest. They may be a little lost, a little broken, but they'd welcomed me with open arms. They'd chosen me, accepted and loved me, and claimed me as one of their own.

Three Months Later

We were down twenty-four to twenty as the final quarter was coming to a close. My palms were sweaty and I felt sick. MMU really needed the win.

"He's definitely getting fired after this one." Penny shrugged and shook her head.

"Penny! C'mon. Positive thoughts!" I clamped my teeth together. *Positive thoughts. Positive thoughts.*

I looked out onto the field from the family-box suite and into the packed stadium that held dueling fans in their schools' colors. It was Saturday, and just like the ones that came before it, we were here and ready to cheer for our team.

Once the season had started, I'd learned pretty quickly that the most valuable commodity was time. It felt like Wyatt was always being pulled in a thousand different directions, but not once did he ever make our time feel less important. In fact, he'd set some boundaries with the board of directors, and when Wyatt said it was "family time," he meant it.

Sure, our definition of family had also expanded.

There was a gravitational pull to being part of a community, part of a family. We'd emptied ourselves into being a part of the team and the players' lives.

Joey, Kevin, and Michael would always be a little more special. I watched with pride as the hulking frame of number twenty-three turned toward the box and thumped on his chest.

Kevin.

Penny and I stood and screamed for him. It was something he'd started at the first game—a show of love and appreciation—and it nearly made me cry every single time.

The team taught me that I needed them as much as they needed me, maybe even more. The players knew that Wyatt's door was always open, and we would be there for them if they ever needed anything. Attending a university in rural Michigan meant that many were away from home, missing holidays and birthdays with their families. We did what we could to fill in the gaps.

Being a part of a huge extended family also meant you shared their burdens. When you won, you rode that high together, but if we lost, that shame and burden followed us.

My hands clamped together. The nerves were something that never seemed to get any easier.

When a player on the opposing team got past one of our linemen, Penny stood from her seat and cupped her hands like a megaphone. "Come on, Fitzy! Get the molasses out of your cleats!"

I threw my head back and laughed. Penny loved the game and was nearly as passionate about it as her dad.

My eyes found Wyatt. He was standing on the sidelines, his arms crossed over his chest and a deep line in his brow.

God, my boyfriend is hot.

A sexy little thrill raced through me as I recalled all the dirty, delicious things we'd done the night before. I'd teased him and called it his *pregame ritual* and loved that only I was privy to the unleashed and thoroughly masculine side of Wyatt Sullivan.

My teeth sank into my lip. My stare flickered between the game and the timer.

My eyes clamped closed as I threw up a silent prayer to the universe.

Penny launched herself into the chair with a huff and tugged my shirt. We hadn't done it. With only seconds to go, our quarterback had been sacked, and with it our chances of pulling off a win had been sacked too.

I swallowed hard. A loss was difficult for all of us, and I was sure I'd hear rumblings around town about how Wyatt and the team sucked. Petty words most likely drummed up by the Kings and the stupid town rivalry.

I looked down onto the field with pride. Win or lose, we were still in it together.

Wyatt searched for me, as he always did, pulling the headphones off and lifting his chin. The subtle, silent action always sent melty warmth spreading through me.

No matter what happened on the field, Wyatt always searched for me.

After the game and press conference, we made our way back to Outtatowner.

Penny had fallen asleep in the back seat, and I hummed along to the radio while Wyatt fielded calls and recounted the game to a few reporters.

Once we got home, however, work was done. It was one

of the many things Wyatt did to ensure our time together was sacred. He worked hard to leave the game on the field and his home focused on his family. On us.

Wyatt caught me staring. "What?"

I smiled at him. "You love me?"

A smile crossed his face as he continued down the dark country roads toward our small town. "Of course I love you." He lifted my hand to kiss my knuckles. "I've been working my ass off to show you in every love language possible."

An album of memories flipped through my mind. The wildflowers, time with his friends and family, the picnic, sweet daily texts, his words, his touch. Wyatt had found a way to show me his feelings in every single love language.

Turns out quality time was the love language we both craved. That and the filthy words of affirmation he came up with when I was pinned beneath him weren't bad either.

After Wyatt carried the snoring Penny to her room, he walked into the kitchen. I turned and smiled at him. So much had fallen into place in the last few months that it was hard to believe sometimes. I still technically had the apartment above the barn, but I hadn't used it at all in months.

In the soft glow of the kitchen light, Wyatt's gaze darkened on me, and my pulse ratcheted higher. He reached behind him and pulled at the collar of his polo to bring it over his head.

"What do you think?" I asked. "Have I earned a nickname?"

Wyatt's grin widened as he stepped closer. "I'm sure eventually something will stick, but I don't care what it is as long as I can call you *mine*. Now, let's shower."

I sucked my lower lip into my mouth. I loved those little moments when he transitioned from coach to lover but forgot to drop the hard edge from his voice. "Oh . . . Coach Wyatt," I teased. "Postgame shower? I think I know that story line."

Wyatt reached forward and hooked a finger into the belt loop in my jeans. "Oh yeah? How does that one go?"

I batted my lashes at him. "I think it's the one where the coach needs some cheering up and ends with me on my knees." My hand trailed down the hard lines of his abdomen and lower, until I palmed him through his pants.

Wyatt growled. "You are devious."

When the gap between us closed, Wyatt released a breath and planted his forehead on mine.

"The only thing I need right now is you, under a hot shower, with your hands in my hair and screaming my name."

My heart squeezed, and I climbed him like a tree. "You're on, Coach."

EPILOGUE

Wyatt

Two Years later

I SWALLOWED A GROAN AS I WATCHED A PRETEEN TAP-dance through a painfully awkward rendition of "My Heart Will Go On."

Talk about a downer of a song choice.

It was the third Little Miss Blueberry Pageant I'd had to endure, and time wasn't making it any less painful to watch. Next to me, Michael's knee bounced, and I glanced at him.

"Relax, it'll be fine."

He clenched his jaw and shook his head. "I know, but this is her year. I can feel it. She deserves this."

I smiled to myself. Michael was a good kid. He was twenty-three now, and though we'd all hoped his dreams of the NFL would pan out, it wasn't in the cards. He had, however, become one of the best offensive graduate assistants I could ask for. When he was not working with quarterbacks and receivers, he substitute taught at a local high school.

He had also become an extended part of the Sullivan family.

I slapped my hand on his shoulder, hoping to distract him. "Did you see the fancy footwork Joey pulled off on Sunday?"

Michael's narrowed eyes sliced in my direction. "I taught him that move."

An easy laugh erupted from my chest. After he'd graduated, Joey had been a second-round draft pick, and his career had shot off like a rocket. Same with Kevin. Both were integral players on their pro ball teams, and I felt nothing but sheer pride anytime I saw them play.

Of all my players, those three boys and the summer I'd spent keeping them out of trouble had bonded us for life. Lark still called them "our boys" despite the fact they towered over her and outweighed her by a hundred pounds.

I scanned the crowd for my wife and frowned.

The talent portion of Pickle's pageant showcase was scheduled to begin, and I hadn't seen Lark since she'd waddled off toward the Gyro Man's food truck. My chest ached when I caught a glimpse of her long brown hair lifting in the breeze. Her smile was wide, and she held up the small white Styrofoam container like it was baby Simba on Pride Rock.

I shook my head and laughed. When she approached, I stood from the seat and pointed. "Sit down."

She frowned at me and ran a gentle hand down her large pregnant belly. "Daddy's so grouchy."

Lark groaned softly as she maneuvered into the small chair beside Michael. She was weeks away from giving birth to our first child together, and though she liked to grumble about it, she loved how protective I had become of her.

Still a bit out of breath, Lark lifted her hair from her shoulders and sighed. "I just saw Pen. She's ready."

I moved to stand behind her, swooping her hair to the side and gently rubbing her tired shoulders. My eyes searched the edge of the stage, hoping to catch a glimpse of Pickle and discreetly throw her a thumbs-up or something.

When the music shifted from one performer's modern interpretive ribbon dance to Metallica, I paused.

Lark's shoulders bounced under my hands, as she could barely contain her giggles.

"What did you do?" I growled.

She snort-laughed. "I have no idea what you're talking about." Then she proceeded to stuff a mouthful of gyro into her face and smile up at me with chipmunk cheeks.

What a shit.

With the darkening sky, my beautiful, sweet nine-year-old confidently pranced up the stage, wearing a black leotard with fringe and rhinestone sparkles all over it. She was wearing heavy makeup I didn't love and was holding a long black baton.

I pinched the bridge of my nose. On the beat drop, Penny lit the ends of the baton on *actual fire*, and I nearly had a stroke.

Michael shot to his feet, both fists in the air, and shouted, "Hell yeah!"

The crowd followed suit and was enamored with how graceful and lively she was as she twirled her flaming death stick and leaped across the stage.

Lark clapped and cheered while I was freaking the fuck out.

Finally, the song came to a close, and the entire crowd

was on their feet and screaming for my little girl. Her smile was a mile wide, and she extinguished her baton with a sassy hand on her hip and a wink.

She's grounded for a year.

I glared down at my beautiful wife, and she scrunched her nose at me and laughed. Michael cheered beside me.

"Did you know about this?" I asked him.

He laughed. "No way, but that was *awesome!*"

"Don't worry." Lark swatted the air between us. "Lee was right there the whole time with a fire extinguisher. It was the only way the stick-in-the-mud pageant director would allow it. If you ask me, the only issue was that the director knew his niece wouldn't win anyway. Penny nailed it!"

I couldn't deny the love and pride Lark held for Penny. They were inseparable, and despite the fact she was her stepmother, Penny loved her fiercely.

"Is that supposed to make me feel *better?*" I rolled my eyes. Apparently I was the only one who didn't believe the Little Miss Blueberry title was worth lighting oneself on fire for.

I looked down at my gorgeous wife and sighed. I could never manage to stay annoyed with her for long, especially when she saw the good in just about everything around us.

LATER THAT NIGHT, we celebrated Pickle's *epic win* with pizza and ice cream at home. Aunt Tootie and my brothers were there to celebrate with us. We'd moved out of Highfield House and into a sprawling ranch of our own. It was on the outskirts of Outtatowner and was what Lark had called a "cozy little coastal ranch." At more than three thousand square feet, she and I had very different definitions of *cozy*, but I'd learned long ago that Lark's sunshine and optimism were qualities I could never snuff out. Not that I wanted to—my wife brought happiness to every corner of my life.

If anyone had told me a wanderer would become Outta-towner's golden girl, I could have guessed that would be Lark. After I fired her as my assistant and promoted her to wife, I told her she didn't have to work if she didn't want to. I'd always take care of her.

She'd laughed in my face.

Turned out Lark had a knack for organizing chaos, so while she may be a terrible waitress, she was a damn good teacher. She started taking classes at MMU and has been working on her teaching degree while still fielding the occasional call from LA. Her contacts there assured her if she ever thought about returning to acting, they'd answer her call. I'd mentioned it once, wanting to make sure that Lark knew I'd support her in whatever direction she wanted to go in life. If that meant LA, we'd figure it out. She assured me, however, that once she experienced it for herself, she knew that life wasn't truly what she wanted.

Lark had the heart of a teacher.

"You give that thing an eviction notice yet?" Duke passed Lark with Three-Legged Ed sniffing at his feet.

Lark sighed and rubbed her belly. "Oh yeah. We're ready. Wyatt's planning his football training already."

I walked past and dropped a kiss on the top of her head, and she closed her eyes to hum at me. "Never too early."

Lark made a firm line with her mouth, and her voice dropped low to mock me. "Get those kids good and ready for a tough season."

After all this time, her ribbing still made me laugh. I shot her a halfhearted scowl, followed by a wink.

Lee cleared his throat from the doorway to the living room. "Excuse me, may I have your attention?" He swooped his arm wide. "May I present Little Miss Blueberry herself, Penny 'Rat Face' Sullivan!"

We burst out laughing as Penny leaped into the kitchen with her arms spread wide. We all clapped and hollered. After a graceful bow, she slapped Lee in the arm. "You're the worst."

He stuck his tongue out at her and chased her around the room as he tried to tickle her. "My name is Pickle!" she squealed at a decibel not meant for human ears.

As the chaos swirled around us, I looked across the room at Lark. *I love you,* I mouthed.

She grinned, her hazel eyes dancing with affection. *I love you more.*

Coming home to Michigan was the best decision I had ever made. Everything in my world had clicked into place the moment I'd locked eyes with Lark Butler. She'd tipped my whole world, somehow set it right side up, and all it had taken was *one look.*

Need more Wyatt & Lark? Check out their exclusive BONUS SCENE at https://geni.us/onelookbonus

SNEAK PEEK OF ONE TOUCH

Falling hard for my ex-boyfriend's rugged older brother was *never* in the plan.

Beckett Miller may be my brother's best friend, but he's also the last person on earth I want to ask for help. He's stubborn, demanding, and doesn't care at all what people think of him—everything his little brother wasn't, and definitely **everything I should *not* want.**

Thanks to my own stubbornness and my three infuriating siblings, he is the only one who can help me renovate my beloved aunt's farmhouse.

Beckett thinks I'm a doormat and I *know* he's an arrogant prick, but toss in one late night game of tipsy strip poker and before long, endless summer days turn into scorching hot nights.

Listen.

I can fix everything around me: my friends' problems, my brothers' love lives, maybe even the decades-old rivalry that divides our cozy, coastal town. Beckett's snarl and heavy sighs are no match for me.

The only thing I can't seem to fix is the way my body reacts when he swings a hammer. I built walls to protect my heart after what his brother did to me, but I'm finding it could all come crumbling down with just ***one touch.***

Find ONE TOUCH on Amazon!

ACKNOWLEDGMENTS

First (and always) to my dear sweet husband who never reads my books but also never questions me when I demand we try something out "for research." Sometimes it's sexy and sometimes it's seeing how long it would take a seven-year-old to dig a hole in the backyard. Dang, our kid was fast . . . I'm calling her if we ever "get into trouble."

Dear sweet small town romance reader - you are the reason I do what I do. Thank you for taking time away from school drop off, dirty dishes, late night TV, and the million other responsibilities to escape into my stories. I don't care that your houses might be messy or that you're a little tired. I only care that my stories can bring you happiness. Your comments, posts, reels, TikToks, reviews, and DMs fill my cup! Thank you for letting me know the ways my characters have touched your life.

A HUGE thank you to my friend and assistant Steph. You stepped into the middle of my mess with a smile and have worked so hard to jump right in! It was exactly what I needed, exactly when I needed it and I am so grateful for you. Plus, I have the added bonus of having someone who truly understands my hatred for that freaking YouTube channel.

To the incredible author friends I have made...Laura, Ana, Melanie, Catherine, Harloe, and SO many others that provide encouragement, laughs, and company in what can sometimes feel like a really lonely job! While we may be scattered around the country, when we're together, watch out! I can't wait for us all to be together again.

Hey, Elsie! Jake kind of annoyed me right before I wrote this, so if you still want to run away together, I'm in.

What would this world be without Kandi Steiner? Pretty damn sad, if you ask me. I don't know what I ever did to deserve your love and friendship, but I will protect it fiercely. You are the sweetest soul and if anyone ever looks up "pure goodness" in the dictionary, they're going to see your hot ass right there. I would say I want to be you when I grow up, but we all know I'm the old lady of the group so . . . cool. ILYSM!

To my friends Nicole and Jenn - thank you for understanding that sometimes I can't escape my books and I forget to talk about anything else.

Trinity - are you stalking me? Honestly, I think you're right...maybe it was me who slid into your DMs. Either way, I'm SO happy we connected. Your enthusiasm, laugh, and general positivity is food for my soul. Your commitment to make "Eggburt" a thing has brought me so much joy.

To my very, very patient editors James, Becca, and Laeticia - I would be lost without you. Thank you for being flexible with your time, especially when I tell you I am nearly a month early on my deadline and then come back and tell you I changed a third of the book. You all push me to be better and I am forever grateful.

To the incredible group of women behind the scenes, the Vixens! You are the most incredible, enthusiastic, and loving street team I could ever ask for. My goal was to create a group where people would be welcomed, excited, and have a good time. YOU did that. Thank you for helping to get the word out about daddy Wyatt.

Finally, to Eggburt - May you rest in peace.

HENDRIX HEARTTHROBS

Want to connect? Come hang out with the Hendrix Heartthrobs on Facebook to laugh & chat with Lena! Special sneak peeks, announcements, exclusive content, & general shenanigans all happen there.

Come join us!

ALSO BY LENA HENDRIX

Chikalu Falls

Finding You

Keeping You

Protecting You

Choosing You (origin novella)

Redemption Ranch

The Badge

The Alias

The Rebel

The Target

The Sullivans

One Look

One Touch (summer 2023!)

One Taste (charity novella)

ABOUT THE AUTHOR

Lena Hendrix is an Amazon Top 20 bestselling contemporary romance author living in the Midwest. Her love for romance stared with sneaking racy Harlequin paperbacks and now she writes her own hot-as-sin small town romance novels. Lena has a soft spot for strong alphas with marshmallow insides, heroines who clap back, and sizzling tension. Her novels pack in small town heart with a whole lotta heat.

When she's not writing or devouring new novels, you can find her hiking, camping, fishing, and sipping a spicy margarita!

Want to hang out? Find Lena on Tiktok or IG!

Manufactured by Amazon.ca
Bolton, ON

34603777R10238